SHATTERED JUSTICE

SUSAN FURLONG

KENSINGTON BOOKS
www.kensingtonbooks.com

KENSINGTON BOOKS are published by

Kensington Publishing Corp.
119 West 40th Street
New York, NY 10018

All Kensington titles, imprints, and distributed lines are available at special quantity discounts for bulk purchases for sales promotion, premiums, fund-raising, educational, or institutional use. Special book excerpts or customized printings can also be created to fit specific needs. For details, write or phone the office of the Kensington Special Sales Manager: Attn. Special Sales Department. Kensington Publishing Corp, 119 West 40th Street, New York, NY 10018. Phone: 1-800-221-2647.

Kensington and the K logo Reg. U.S. Pat. & TM Off.

Library of Congress Card Catalogue Number: 2019950845

ISBN-13: 978-1-4967-1172-4
ISBN-10: 1-4967-1172-6
First Kensington Hardcover Edition: January 2020

ISBN-13: 978-1-4967-1174-8 (e-book)
ISBN-10: 1-4967-1174-2 (e-book)

10 9 8 7 6 5 4 3 2 1

Printed in the United States of America

Patrick: It's been two years and three more books, yet in my heart, time stands still.

Author's Note

It's estimated that almost thirty thousand Irish Travellers reside throughout the United States. Descendants of nomadic Irish peoples who immigrated to the United States during the Great Famine, the Travellers settled throughout the country in extended family groups or clans, with the largest concentrations living in South Carolina, Georgia, Texas, and Tennessee. As itinerant workers who speak distinct dialects of Irish Cant known as Gammon or Shelta, they are often marginalized for their unique lifestyles and esoteric customs.

I am not an Irish Traveller. I'm a story writer, and while I have tried to portray Irish Travellers as accurately as possible, they are a secret, closed sect of our American society. Endogamous, they prefer to live quietly, frequently going to great extents to protect their privacy. Travellers are often stereotyped as immoral and lawless, yet these characterizations overshadow what I have come to know as a culture filled with decency and built on strong family bonds and unbreakable fortitude. Through my writing, I hope readers will come to have a greater understanding and appreciation for the Irish Travellers' unique way of life.

The source of justice is not vengeance but charity.
—Saint Bridget of Sweden

CHAPTER 1

Shot glasses were raised, a toast was made, and a buck-naked man galloped by on a stick horse.

I hovered, dark and low, in the corner seat, cowboy music thumping through my veins, my heartbeat taking up rhythm with the pounding bass. Strobing lights, clinking glasses, the smell of stale beer, bad breath, and chintzy perfume. And the man—one hand clutching yellow plastic straps attached to a crazy, smiling horsey head, the other waving through the air, in time with his thrusting hips . . . *Yeehaw! Ride 'em, cowboy.* Bucking bronco . . . sex on a stick.

Never seen anything like it. Couldn't hardly believe I was seeing it now.

The barmaid returned with another half-dozen drinks, which would, in times past, have been the only excuse I needed to stay. Now I eyed the drinks and squirmed, wishing I had an excuse to leave. Maureen (Mo) Black, a distant cousin on Gran's side, I think—hard to tell when you have as many kin as we do—passed a glass my way and, after a quick *clink, clink,* downed her drink. I watched her, then set my own glass down, untouched.

"Lighten up, Brynn. It's a hen party. Have some fun." To prove the point, she trained heavily lined eyes on the cowboy and waved a wad of dollar bills in the air, thick gloss glistening on the edges of her lips.

Cowboy spied green and rode our way. I sank farther back in my seat, a mere shadow lurking in the corner, as my table-mates clamored to shove dollar bills in his G-string: Nina, Mo, Queenie, Dee Doherty (the bride-to-be), and Meg, too. Mo, the wildest one of the bunch, went for gold: she flashed a fifty and strategically placed it in her cleavage. Cowboy leaned down and, the horseshoe stud in his earlobe catching the light, dove into her breast. Gasps and giggles from the girls, and a few seconds later, he came up for air, with the fifty between his teeth. The ladies let out a whoop, all the encouragement Mo needed. She stood and mounted the stick horse and shimmied in close to Cowboy, her tangerine nails gripping his muscular flanks as she whispered in his ear. He grinned, and off they rode.

I wanted to leave, too, but not on a stick. Just to go home, see my dog, and go to bed. Not that I didn't want to be with my friends. I did. It'd just be easier if Jack Daniel's hadn't been in-vited to the party.

But I stayed. Mostly out of support for Dee. And as the gals enjoyed their next few rounds, dress sizes, menu choices, and flower colors dominated the table talk.

"Stockings or bare legged?"

"Hair up or down?"

"And that crazy Elva O'Neil had better not show her face at the wedding. Bitch." Giggle, giggle.

More drinks, a wink, and a sly grin, and the conversation took a different turn.

"Can you believe that Mo Black?" As if we didn't all know her last name. "Riding off with that cowboy like that. And she's married. What a slut." This from sweet Nina Gorman, the blond, doe-eyed backstabber sitting next to Meg.

A tsk-tsk, a lopsided pout and slurred words from Dee. "She's r-r-ruining my party!"

Sympathetic nods, more drinks and a darting glance . . .

"Haven't y'all heard?"

"No. What?"

"Her husband can't anymore?"

"He can't?"

"No, not since that bad fall. You know, last summer, the roofing job?"

"Really? You mean . . . ?"

"Yeah."

"Aw . . . no wonder."

And just like that, sympathies changed. "Poor Mo. And so young to go without . . ."

Nods of agreement all around. Glasses up, a toast to Dee and, what the heck, a toast to Mo and her cowboy, too.

Heads tipped back; liquid disappeared; eyes glazed over.

My eyes glazed over, too, but not from booze; I wasn't drinking any. Hen parties weren't my thing anymore. Neither was ladies' night at the local bar. Which I hated. Not the bar or ladies' nights, but I hated that I'd lost those fun times. The smoky haze, the clinks of glasses, the screeching of chairs across the scarred wood floor, and the incessant music on some mind-numbing loop . . . I'd loved it all, but the hardest part was the pervasive smell of whiskey mingled with beer and sweet libations. I couldn't deal with it now. I'd spent a fair amount of time at this very pub, escaping into a bottle, downing a few pills on the side. That was the old me. The new me was sober.

Most of the time.

Another drink came my way. I scanned the bar, stacked three deep with men buying drinks for ladies. They cast hopeful looks our way, wanting to cash in on the cowboy's spoils. One of the guys raised his glass in my direction. Blue jeans and flannel, well built and a youngish thirty-something, a great prospect by any girl's standards, just not this girl's. Not tonight, anyway. I broke eye contact and pushed the drink aside. Girls like us came with a certain stigma, an assumption that we were easy. Truth was, we were not so easy, less than others, really, but that never stopped us from enjoying a few free drinks. We were Travellers; or gypsies, as most called us; Pavees, as we called ourselves; nomads by nature but rooted now in this tiny corner of Appalachia. We'd settled in a place called Bone Gap, a remote and densely wooded holler about ten miles outside McCreary, Tennessee. Mostly we kept to ourselves, choosing to stick to the confines of the clan. But some, like me, straddled both worlds, ours and that of those we called "settled" people. Non-Pavees. Outsiders.

A knobby elbow jutted in front of me. I flinched and scooted over a bit. Regina McGill, Queenie, as we called her, was next to me, nervously working a strand of reddish-blond hair around her finger. *Twirl, twirl, twirl . . .* Itching for a cig, probably. A nasty habit, she'd be the first to say, and then she'd excuse it by saying something about how even the most fickle were faithful to a few bad habits (one of her favorite sayings), and I'd laugh at that, because there is nothing fickle about Queenie. She's the most loyal friend a girl could hope to have.

"Not drinking tonight, Brynn?" she asked.

I eyed one of the still-full shot glasses. "Don't know yet."

Meg shot me a nasty look. Queenie chuckled, then winced, grabbing her cheek. Bluish-purple marks haloed her left eye. Her carefully applied makeup had faded, along with her inhibitions. Her husband had been beating her again. Mean-ass drunk. 'Course, I was a drunk, too, or so they've told me, but never a mean one.

"What set him off this time, Queenie?" I asked.

She lowered her eyes. "You know how he is. Doesn't take

much to upset him. Don't worry. It's not that big of a deal. I'm fine."

I hated what he did to her. She deserved so much better. But it probably wasn't a big deal to Queenie. Nothing her husband dished out could come close to what she'd endured in her childhood. She kept them covered, but I'd seen the little dark circles tracking up and down the white flesh of her legs. Burn scars. I hated that, too. Poor Queenie. I craned my neck, my own scar stretching and puckering like an accordion. At least my scar, acquired when my third Marine tour ended with a bang, was from the enemy, not the lit end of my mama's cigarette.

Nina let out a sigh, plucked an olive from her drink—*what I wouldn't do for a single drop of gin from that olive, and I'm not even a martini girl*—mouthed it with her pouty lips, and sucked the pimiento from the middle. The guy at the table next to us groaned and shifted in his seat. She didn't notice. Her focus was elsewhere, her eyes flitting over the items strewn across the tabletop: Queenie's sunglasses, Mo's scarf, change from my earlier soda water, an empty shot glass or two . . . Nothing was off-limits. Nina had sticky fingers. Something I'd figured out back in high school, when I saw her pilfer a push-up bra from the back aisle of Logan's Department Store. I'd kept it from the other gals, then and now. Covered for her, actually. Any one of us would do as much. That's the thing about Pavees—we take care of our own.

The music changed from country to rock, intermission until the next strip act. I slid my stray bills into my pocket—*no need to tempt Nina*—and scanned the room for Mo. She was nowhere to be seen. Still off with the cowboy, I guessed.

Dee tossed back yet another drink before pushing back from the table. The bride-to-be abandoned us for the dance floor, where she moved to her own beat, arms outstretched, head bent upward as she spun on her tiptoes, spun and spun until she tripped and fell.

"Poor Dee Dee," someone said. Queenie or Meg or maybe Nina. I'd lost track of the conversation, all my energy spent on not drinking, my self-control waning. Sobriety was overrated.

I looked around the table. Heads were bent forward; hands cupped over painted mouths.

"Do you know why Dee's getting so scuttered?"

"No. Why?"

I stifled a moan. More gossip, a staple of any girls' night. I leaned a bit closer and listened, against my better judgment.

"Because she doesn't really want to go through with it, you know."

Heads bobbed in agreement.

"Riley's no catch, after all, but she's not getting any younger. Better to marry someone, anyone, than to get put up on the shelf." That was Traveller speak for *old maid*. Which in our clan meant any girl who made it into her twenties without being married and spawning a brood of kiddos.

Like me.

All eyes looked my way.

Now might be a good time to leave.

Instead, I traced the rim of one of my lined-up glasses, round and round, and then dipped. In went my finger; out it came again, dripping with gold. Liquid gold. I caste a quick glance in Meg's direction. She was busy typing on her phone. A social media post probably: Hen party with the girls. #funtimes.

Yeah, right.

One drop. One drop, that's all. . . . I touched my finger to my tongue, then hungrily wrapped my lips around it and sucked like a starving baby at its mama's tits. I went back for another dip. . . .

"No you don't." Meg snatched the glass, tipped it back, and

drained my fun in two quick gulps. "You've worked too hard to give up this easily."

The girls looked my way, then quickly pretended not to have noticed. But Meg was still in my face, glaring, daring, or maybe hoping. I couldn't tell for sure. But she was right. I'd worked too hard to give up this easily.

I pushed away from the table, made my excuses, and headed for the door.

CHAPTER 2

The next morning's sun broke hot and angry through the cracks in my pink lace curtains. I slept in my childhood room, in the only home I've ever known—my grandmother's thirty-year-old mobile home. Larger than most of our neighbors' trailers and campers, and still movable—something that was important in our nomadic culture—yet aesthetically rooted in the late 1980s. Gran never was one for change.

I pulled Wilco close, his muscles rippling against my body, pulsating and twitching, and accompanied by little whimpers. A dream. A good one, I hoped. Like me, my sixty-pound former combat partner, and once the best damn HRD (human remains detection) dog in the entire Middle Eastern conflict, suffered from flashbacks and reoccurring nightmares. Getting blown up by an IED tends to do that to a girl. And her dog.

I sat up and brushed the back of my hand against his dark snout. He was a Belgian Malinois, and so his coat was darker than a German shepherd's, his face sleeker, and eyes more alert. Though smaller than the shepherds, which were so often used in military and law enforcement work, the Malinois were more aggressive, more energetic, and faster, too. Not fast enough to avoid an IED, however. No one was.

A twitch of a whisker, a slight curl of his lip, and a cock of his ears. His ears, two black triangles, erect and ready, yet useless. The explosion had robbed Wilco of his hearing, and more. So much more. I moved my hand along the ridge of his spine, from neck to withers, then down to the rounded nub of his back leg. It was gone, too. Bone and bloody flesh alike, blown off his body in one searing instant, practically disintegrating midair. Gone forever. I knew the feeling. I ran my hand under my sweat-soaked T-shirt. My breasts, two mounds, but one soft and plump, alive; the other a hard bulge, dead and useless, like my dog's nubby leg. Wilco and I were alike in that way. We'd both lost part of ourselves out there in the desert.

But we had each other. It had been a struggle to get the Marines to turn him over to me, but maybe that was the one blessing from the injuries we shared: Neither of us was deemed fit for further service. So we were released as a team. Always would be.

My cell rang. It was my boss, Sheriff Frank Pusser.

"You home?" he asked.

"Yeah."

"Sober?"

Every damn time I talk to him . . . "It's six o'clock in the morning. What do you think?"

"I've seen you high out of your mind this early in the morning. Have you forgotten?"

"No."

"Good. Don't. We need you at McCreary Elementary. A piece of a body was found."

My fingertips fell from my breast to my bare leg. "Which part?"

"Come see for yourself. And bring the dog."

*   *   *

My throat constricted with anxiety as I drove by a line of cop cars blocking off access to the playground area. *Not a kid. Please, God, not a kid.* I continued two blocks down and slipped my crappy station wagon between two economy-sized cars and headed the rest of the way on foot, keeping a tight grip on Wilco's lead. About fifty yards out, the scent hit his nose, his over two hundred olfactory cells kicking into action. He pulled against my hold, tail rigid, ears twitching, his head bobbing as he scooped up scents, anxious to move us toward the decay. Displaying clear signs of his alert, trained into him as his singular task, was something he still did well, even deaf and three legged.

"Good boy, good boy." I yanked him to a stop, and followed this with a generous belly rub. He'd detected the partial. No surprise about that, as we knew it was there, but he'd still done his job and earned his reward.

Not wanting him too close to the scene, I secured him to a basketball post and headed solo to where Pusser stood with a group of people—some uniformed city cops; a couple of my colleagues, Deputies Parks and Harris; and a few civilians I didn't recognize. School workers, probably. A perimeter around nearby monkey bars had been cordoned off. A department photographer was already snapping shots, while a group of forensics specialists stood off to the side, ready and waiting. One hell of a turnout for so early in the day.

Pusser spied me and broke from the group. "Come look at this."

I followed him, my feet crunching into the graveled ground, my eyes already trained on the crudely scrawled words spray-painted on the concrete pad in front of the jungle gym. I turned to Pusser. "Hear no evil?"

He bit down hard on a toothpick between his teeth and motioned for the photographer to move out of the way. He did. And I saw it. A pair of severed ears hanging from a low bar, blood-stained, blue-tinged flesh, strung up to dry like anemic chili peppers.

The sun glinted off an all too familiar earring piercing one of the lobes—a silver horseshoe stud.

So much for good-luck symbols.

CHAPTER 3

Drops of sweat formed above Pusser's lip. Mid-June, not even 7:00 A.M., and already too damned hot. But that wasn't why he was sweating.

"I've seen this before," he said. "Back in Nam. A paratrooper, crazy-ass mother shit, went frickin' nuts, took out a bunch of Cong and cut off their ears. Wore them around his neck like a damn souvenir."

I raised a brow Pusser's way. The blue vein on his temple pulsated above his sweat-sheened, pockmarked skin. My boss, early sixties, with an extra twenty pounds plus around the beltline, looked ready to pop an artery.

I understood. I'd seen this type of thing, too. Different era, different war, same perversion. My second tour, a recovery mission, netted Wilco and me an overnighter in a border encampment. I was taking Wilco for a walk when he went nuts, all crazy-like and on scent outside one of the housing compartments. Sarge opened the place, and we found a dozen strings of ears hanging to dry: trophies, souvenirs, zombie parts, whatever. Turned out they were from dead insurgents and were intended to be sold to eager bidders on the black market. Mutilation and desecration turned a pretty penny. A tribunal would have condemned the soldier's actions as dishonorable and morally repugnant. *Well, no shit.* Thing was, they deep-sixed the story and kept it out of the press. Rumor had it that the trophy collector, in turn, deep-sixed himself while in custody. Handy. A bit too handy. No need for his commanders to do more than mark down the bastard's death as another nonhostile casualty and bury the case of defilement, along with dozens of ears.

Haunted warriors and untold truths.

"What are you thinking, Callahan?"

"I recognize these ears."

Pusser's head swiveled.

"The earring, anyway. I saw it last night on a stripper."

His well-chewed toothpick dipped down. He snatched at it.

Harris had meandered over and loomed next to me now, but I kept my focus on Pusser. "A male stripper," I added. "Dressed in cowboy boots and a hat. Not much else. It's the same earring, I'm pretty sure. I saw it up close. He left with my friend Mo." Visions of those ears half sunken in Mo's bosom gave me shivers. If the perp would cut off a man's ears, what would he do to . . . ? "I need to go check on her."

"I need you here." Pusser got the location of her trailer from me and radioed in for a deputy to head out to her place. They'd get to her place sooner than I could from here, but Mo was my friend. I wanted to be there. Then again, by saying that she'd left with this pair of ears, I'd set her up as a main suspect. And acknowledged her as a friend. Not a good combination for an investigating officer. Pusser wanted to send a unit out there before I got to her. *Obviously.*

Harris mumbled something about whoring gypsies and strippers. The guy hated me. Hated all Pavees, like many I worked with. But Harris especially hated me. The feeling was mutual.

Pusser turned to him. "What is it you want, Harris?"

"Parks and me, we're wonderin' about protocol."

"Protocol? You do what I say. That's it."

Harris sneered. "Yeah, but what about the city cops?"

Off a ways, a dozen or so uniformed officers huddled together, Deputy Nan Parks's county-issued brown khakis standing out among the group of blue. Short and round bodied, with her arms crossed, she looked like a middle-aged prison matron holding off a riot.

Pusser squinted at them, then back to Harris. "I don't get what you're saying. We cooperate with the municipal cops all the time. We're all in it together."

"Tell that to Johnson." He crooked a thumb to point, his lips curling in contempt.

"That's *Lieutenant* Johnson to you."

"Whatever. He's acting like he's boss."

"Tell me, boy. You got a problem with the fact that his uniform's blue or that his skin's black?"

Harris picked a piece of lint off his shirt and flicked it off the tip of his finger.

Pusser's jaw tightened. "Look, Harris. All you need to know is that I'm your boss and you do what I say. Got that?" He mumbled something about stupidity and walked over to talk to the photographer.

Harris narrowed his eyes on the flapping ears. "Serial killer."

"We don't know that yet."

"Come on, Callahan. *Hear no evil?* You know what's next, right? See no evil. Speak no—"

"I know how it goes, Harris." I pivoted away and sucked in a deep breath, inhaling an undercut of onion and bacon on the warm summer breeze. My stomach roiled; I gagged back a wave of empty-stomach nausea. My morning coffee wasn't cutting it. I needed solid food. The McCreary Diner was just a block away. Meg would be working the morning shift, dishing out a smile with the daily breakfast special: biscuits and gravy, two eggs, juice and coffee. I wondered how bright her smile would be after last night's late party, considering she had handled her drinks and a couple of mine as well. Yet the diner always offered a homey atmosphere . . . chitter-chatter, newspapers rustling, the smell of burned coffee, farmers spouting the weather forecast, which would be "sunny and hotter than Hades" today.

Hot enough to hang out a pair of ears to dry.

"So, you know the vic?" Harris asked.

"I didn't say that."

"Oh, that's right. You don't know *him*, just his ear. And probably another part of him."

"I didn't know him at all, Harris. Not even his name."

"Yeah, I believe that. I mean, why ask names, right? It only complicates things." He winked and laughed, an arrogant laugh that made me want to pistol-whip him. Thankfully, Pusser called me over to where he stood with Johnson. He told Harris to stay put.

Johnson gave me a once-over and extended his hand. A large hand, strong, with a calloused palm. "Tell me what you know about our victim."

"I saw him perform last night. He's a stripper. Ladies' night at the McCreary Pub. It was my friend's bachelorette party." I told him about the guy's act, stick horse and all.

"Think he's still alive?"

"People can lose their ears and still live." *I've lost part of my skin and an entire boob, and yet here I am.*

Johnson extracted a notebook and pen from his back pocket. "I need the friend's name."

"Mo. Mo Black."

"Mo is"—his eyes scanned my black hair and fair Irish skin—"one of you all?"

You all. As if we were not a part of "real" society. Surprising. Thought he'd know better, considering he'd probably spent his fair share of time on the receiving end of that type of ignorance.

"You mean a *woman* or . . . ?"

Pusser jumped in. "Just give him the names of everyone who was with you last night at the bar, Callahan." He turned to Johnson. "I've got someone on the way to check on the Pavee woman now. I've told the officer to keep her sequestered until Callahan can get there. She knows these people. They'll open up to her." Pusser's gaze swept the nearby lot. "But I want the dog to search the field first. If this is murder, the body might be nearby."

The school was in a residential area, mostly older ranch homes just off McCreary's Main Street. The playground backed up to a vacant lot, overgrown with heavy thatch, nettle, and trash-snagged thistle.

"That's probably a waste of time," I said.

"Why's that?"

"The field's overgrown. It'd be difficult to penetrate those weeds and dump the body without clear signs. There's no disturbance in the vegetation. No signs of penetration, trampling, bent stalks, nothing. If there's a body, it's not here."

Pusser zeroed in on me. "Search it, anyway."

Wilco stood by my side at the edge of the field as I pulled out my water bottle. The ears were newly severed, so the body would be fresh, but that wouldn't make a difference to Wilco's nose. The moment the heart stops beating, the soul lifts away, and what's left ferments to an after-death cologne unique to the individual, a chemical bouquet gathered and composed and arranged throughout our lives: fluoride and antibiotics, food dye and corn syrup, plastic residue, toxic cleaners, tar and nicotine, alcohol and alcohol and . . . *I could use a drink.*

I squatted next to my dog, unscrewed the water bottle's lid. Not exactly what I had in mind, but I took a long swig, anyway, and then doused Wilco's muzzle. He pranced paw to paw, head bobbing, tongue lapping, as he slurped up the sloshing liquid. I laughed, placed my cheek on his wet snout, and inhaled the smell of his fur. Wetness intensified his doggy smell, and I could inhale it forever. "Okay, let's do this, boy." My dog was deaf, but that never stopped me from talking to him. Everyone needs someone to talk to, and sometimes the best listeners are those who don't hear your actual words.

I stood and surveyed the field. Killers are lazy. They'll carry or drag a dead body only so far. And people tend to move toward their dominant hand, so a right-handed killer would enter the field and move right. Since 90 percent of the population is right-handed, I'd hedge my bet in favor of searching the right side of the field first. I unclipped Wilco's lead and gave the signal.

Off he went. Zigzagging at first, nose pressed to the ground, then lifted high into the air, back and forth along the edge of the field, stopping here and there to sniff a piece of thistle-snagged trash. I motioned for him to go deeper into the brush. Confused, he trotted back to me, more interested in the empty water bottle than in doing his job.

"Anything from the dog?" Pusser joined me, sweat rolling down his forehead, pooling in the deep pockmarks on either side of his nose.

"Look for yourself."

Wilco made a shallow foray into the weeds, playful and excited, popped back out, lifted his back nub and shot a stream of doggy urine into the grass.

I shuffled my feet. "A waste of time, just like I thought. There's nothing out here, boss." I needed to check on Mo, didn't have time for this wasted effort. If someone had overtaken that stripper, and Mo had been with him . . . I had to know she was okay.

"Oh yeah? How's that?"

"Slicing off ears would take time, and if the vic was alive, someone would have heard him screaming. The perp did his dirty work someplace else. We'd be better off looking for abandoned buildings. Maybe something nearby, where . . ." Wilco's tail went rigid. I gave him my full attention. "Wait. He's onto something."

Pusser stood still next to me, my dog worked, the world seemed to slow—quiet and hot, the sun burning off the morning dew, gnats and other bugs buzzing—and my heart soared. Wilco was on scent. *Good boy, good boy.* Rapid pacing now, back and forth, with exaggerated movements, deep draws of air, snorting and more snorting, a sneeze, rapid ear twitching, and blazing eyes. I lived for this. So did Wilco.

Wilco pounced into the thicket, spun around, stopped. He nudged a foam take-out container, sat abruptly, and focused on me.

A hit.

"What's this?" Pusser pulled gloves from his utility belt and headed over.

I followed, clipped Wilco's lead, and pulled him out of the thicket and away from the evidence. I knelt down, placed my nose to his snout, looked him in the eye, smiled, and ran my hands over the soft fur on his head. Back and forth, faster and faster, down his back. He lifted his nose, closed his eyes, rocked back and over, legs splayed. Belly rub. The ultimate reward.

"You done yet?"

My head snapped up. "Yeah. Why?"

Pusser held up the Styrofoam container in his gloved hands. Dark stains covered the inside. "Blood."

I stood, looked closer at the container, and nodded. "One pair of ears," I said. "To go."

CHAPTER 4

The bar owner had verified the identity of the stripper from last night, based on when he disappeared and his signature earring, and had given us the man's address. Chance Walker was his name, and he lived in a one-bedroom ground-floor unit just a few blocks from where we'd found the ears. Pusser had also gotten the call that his officers had found Mo at home. He had told the officers to stay put until I could get there. But first, he wanted Wilco and me to help look over Walker's place.

The landlord keyed us into Walker's apartment, and a cat darted between our legs. Wilco barked as it scurried into a clump of scraggly evergreens just outside the door. I reined in Wilco's lead and kept him close to my legs as I entered, my shoe sinking into a soggy patch of carpet, diffusing the smell of cat piss. Pusser gagged and coughed. Cat urine and burned popcorn and sickly-sweet pot—a fetid aroma that hung in the air, thick and acrid. Wilco shook his head, waving it back and forth, letting out a series of short snorts. Poor dog. Talk about overload.

Pusser looked at him. "Is he onto something?"

"Just stench. No dead humans. There's nothing here." The

place wasn't much bigger than a hotel room. If someone was decaying within these walls, Wilco would have hit on it. Hell, we'd smell it and see it ourselves.

Parks came up behind us, gave an uneasy look around the mess, gloved up, and got busy. I guided Wilco to the front-room window, parted the curtains, and took note of Walker's view. Not pretty. His apartment overlooked a frontage road and the back side of a megastore's loading dock, flanked by stacked wood pallets and industrial-sized dumpsters. Something else, too—a white minivan parked in the front and facing the apartment. Strange. I'd seen the same type of van a couple times in the past few days.

Parks yelled from the bathroom, "One toothbrush, one razor. No sign of anyone else living here. No prescriptions."

An officer came in behind us. "Bartender says Walker works days at the plastic plant. We checked with them. He didn't show up for work today. Didn't call in, neither."

Parks stepped out of the bathroom and into the narrow kitchen. Food-crusted dishes and empty beer bottles littered the counters; black flies swarmed the cheese droppings that had hardened on the cardboard round from a bake-it-yourself pizza. She opened the cabinet doors and the fridge, then slammed the fridge door shut and gagged. She leaned over the sink, her stomach contracting with a dry wrenching.

Pusser looked her way. "You okay, Parks?"

"Fine." She took a deep breath and glanced over with watery eyes. "Nothing useful in the fridge. Just stinks worse than the rest of this place."

Pusser turned back to the officer. "Anything from the hospital?"

"Nothing."

"What about family?"

"His father is listed as the emergency contact in his personnel file. We haven't been able to reach him."

"Vehicle?"

"The landlord hasn't seen his car since yesterday. But we've got the make and model."

"Good. Put out a BOLO on him and the vehicle. Get a press release out to local media. Let's get the public on this. See if we can turn up something."

I tucked my chin and grinned. I could just see that BOLO. *Be on the lookout for a white male, midthirties, average build, last seen wearing a cowboy hat, boots, and a thong. Approach with caution. Easily provoked due to missing ears. May be armed with a stick horse . . .*

"Something funny, Callahan?"

"No, boss. Nothing." I turned to a small table crammed in one of the main room's corners. It was strewn with junk: stained food wrappers and beer bottles, an ashtray with cigarette butts and the clipped end of a joint, bills and more bills. I used a pencil to push around the papers. Cable and Internet invoices, sewer and water bills, car payment, credit cards . . . The guy had racked up a pile of debt. *Deep-bosom diving must not be lucrative enough to pay the bills.*

I dropped Wilco's lead, told him to stay, put on gloves, and moved to the dresser in the bedroom. All the typical stuff I'd expect to find in a single guy's drawers: crumpled jeans, concert T-shirts, socks, boxers, condoms, an empty cologne bottle, a cigar box, loose change . . . Some weird things, too: bow ties and cuffs, silk masks, a leather tool belt, and wicked-looking steel-studded thongs. Costumes, tools of his trade. Mr. Walker was a versatile performer. I set the cigar box on the dresser top for a close look. Baseball cards, a broken watch, a rusty pocketknife, a braided leather bracelet—secreted treasures and stashed mementos.

Wilco whimpered from the other room, agitated, his nose twitching in my direction. I signaled, and he shot into the bedroom, dug his paws into the carpet by the dresser, his head twisting and nostrils flaring like those of an angry bull. He turned a couple times, backed up, then came forward again with a deep *sniff . . . sniff*—and *zing!*—a rigid tail with a slight hitch at the end.

"He's onto something," I called out. Pusser came over. Parks too. I squinted at the stuff in the drawers. "Trace amount of blood, probably. He can sniff any decay."

Pusser bent in closer. "Can't you pinpoint it?"

I pulled Wilco's lead, guiding him closer. He ran his nose along the edges of the open drawers, dipped into the clothing, paused a bit on the thongs, went on to the next drawer, pulling in air, searching, searching, then went up on his haunch, wobbly with just one back leg. His front claws etched white grooves in the dresser's well-worn finish as he stretched out and pushed his snout against the cigar box. *Got it!*

I pulled him back, squatted down to his level, while Pusser looked at the contents of the cigar box. "Could he be wrong? I don't see anything here. Just a bunch of crappy old stuff."

"He's not wrong. He's picked up on something." We'd had false alerts before. In Iraq. A dead contractor crushed under piles of rubble. Wilco alerted right away, and I rewarded him, but we dug and dug, and there was no body. We searched again. He alerted again. Certainly we'd missed something. But after hours of digging, we found nothing. Eventually, another team member found the dead contractor some fifty yards away. Wilco had been eager to please me and even more eager for the reward, so he'd given a false alert. He'd lied. It took hours of retraining, but I eventually broke him of it.

The lab would find something in this cigar box. I was sure of it. Related to the case? Who knew? But Wilco didn't lie anymore.

CHAPTER 5

A group of guys huddled outside Mo's home, an old green and white school bus parked in a back lot of our trailer park and half hidden in the trees. One of them was her husband, Hughie Black, a big guy, bald, with bushy eyebrows and a square beard. Rumor was that he'd turned mean since his accident. He looked mean now. I kept an eye on him as I approached.

"*Gralta*, Hughie." Our Shelta word for *hello*.

The officers Pusser had sent out here to check on Mo had gotten nowhere with her. She'd refused to talk to them, and they'd left. So, after Pusser and I had finished at Walker's place, Parks and I headed this way. Mo was one of the last people to see Walker. We needed to talk to her. And I still needed to see for myself that she was okay.

Hughie stepped forward. "Leave us alone, Callahan. All of you."

"We're here to see Mo, that's all. Won't take but a second."

"She doesn't want to talk to you."

"She doesn't have a choice." I tugged Wilco's lead and headed for the door.

Hughie blocked my way, arms crossed.

"Don't be difficult, Hughie."

"This is family business." He unfolded his arms, let them drop to his hips.

I stood firm. "Come on, Hughie. You know me. I'll make sure you all get a fair shake here." Empty words. Pavees never got a fair shake. I knew it. So did he, and he looked unconvinced, so I leaned in close and whispered in his ear, "It's either me dealing with your wife, or some *graansha*." A stranger, an outsider. "Which do you want?"

He cast a grim look at Parks, who stood off to the side, eyeing the men, hands resting on her utility belt, in quick reach of her weapon. Hughie half growled under his breath, stepped aside, and allowed me to pass. My knock rattled the door, which was split in the middle so that it folded back for long-gone schoolchildren.

Queenie answered. Reddish-blond hair hung over her face, obscuring the still bluish tinge along her jawline. Her eyes darted between Parks and me, then settled on me. "She's in the back."

Our footsteps echoed on the metal floor as we passed by the small cooktop range, the microwave, and a hinged tabletop that folded up and latched against the wall to allow for extra room. Mo and Hughie had repurposed the school bus, gutting it and converting it with bunks and a small kitchen, just big enough for them and their two kids. No indoor bathroom, but Hughie had rigged a shanty with a latrine and a cistern for collecting shower water. Innovative, if you asked me. But clan folks here didn't like it. As if Bone Gap was subject to some sort of neighborhood covenant system. Rusty RVs, crappy mobile homes, thirty-year-old pop-up campers—none of those get a second glance, but use some resourcefulness, buck the norm, and it's instant hate. Guess there's always someone shoved to the bottom rung, no matter how short the ladder.

Wilco leaned against me as we pushed through a curtain of

beaded strings dividing the kitchen from the sleeping area. *Click-clack, click-clack*, and we were in the kids' room. Colorful pictures dotted the walls: rainbows and droopy flowers, a smiling purple horse, and stick figures with hats. Blond-curled twins with pink, dirt-smudged faces sat next to each other on a flowered bedspread. One of the girls, wide eyed, and clutching a stuffed animal, sucked her thumb. I dipped my chin, tried to catch their gazes. They wouldn't engage. Wouldn't even look at Wilco.

A few more steps and we were in the back of the bus. I stopped short. Mo was on the rumpled bed, pale and trembling, holding a dish towel packed with ice to her mouth. At the sight of us, she tensed.

I turned to my partner. "Parks, why don't you check on the kids. Make sure they're okay."

"Sure thing."

I leaned down, tugged gently on Mo's hand. She lowered the towel. Her mouth was swollen; dried blood had crusted over a split in her bottom lip. "Did Hughie do this?"

Queenie spoke up from behind me. "I asked her that. She won't say nothin' about it."

Mo touched the ice-packed towel to her lip again and pointed a shaky finger at a pack of cigarettes on a nearby dresser.

Queenie reached over, mouthed a cig, and flicked a flame over the end. She took a few quick puffs, getting it going, before handing it to Mo, who could barely purse her swollen lips to suck on it. "It's my fault. I shouldn't have . . ." She caught a drag, inhaled, her eyes closing into tiny slits.

"Shouldn't have what, Mo? Tell me."

"Hughie didn't want me going last night. Told me nothin' good would come of it, but Dee . . . she's one of my best friends. How could I not go to her hen? I have no self-control. That's all. I deserved this."

The air in the room hung with moisture from too little ventilation and too many bodies, and her smoke clung to me like an extra layer of stinky, wet skin. Wilco shook his head, waggling it back and forth, the tobacco irritating his nostrils.

"No. No one deserves a beating, Mo. What Hughie did to you is wrong. It's illegal. I can arrest—"

"No." She withdrew, sinking farther back into the pillows, arms stretched across her chest, cig between her fingers, ash dangling.

I took the cigarette and passed it back to Queenie. She flicked it, took a couple drags, and stubbed it out.

Parks ducked back in. "They're fine."

I kept my focus on Mo. "What time did you leave the cowboy last—"

"His name was Chance. Honest to God, Brynn. His name was Chance. I thought . . . Well, I thought maybe it was karma. Outta all those women last night, he took me. Like maybe this was *my* chance."

Yeah. Amazing he chose you. The one with the nifty fifty between your breasts.

"Your chance for what, Mo?" I asked.

"My chance to get out of this hellhole."

My back straightened. "Away from Hughie? Because he beats you?"

"No. You don't understand."

Parks spoke up. "Understand what? That he's a stinkin' wife beater? And your children? Does he beat them, too?"

Mo's eyes went wild. "No!" She cringed, and her finger flew to the wound on her lip. It'd reopened. A tiny stream of blood dribbled onto her chin. She dabbed at it with the towel. "Hughie's a good father. He'd never do something like that."

Parks frowned. "Yeah. A good father who lets his girls see him beat on their mother."

She glared at Parks. "You don't know nothing about us, knacker."

Parks shook her head. A bleeding woman huddled in a rusting school bus, scared kids, and a gaggle of violent men milling around outside, looking for more trouble . . . What was she supposed to think?

Mo shifted and groaned, still dabbing at her bleeding lip. Queenie took a bottle of vodka from the top dresser drawer and unscrewed it. "Here, Mo. Drink some. It'll help calm you."

Instant brain zap, like a thousand pinpoints thrust into my gray matter, lighting up the receptors, desire screaming through my skull . . . My muscles balled in anticipation of the liquid salvation. I thought I'd made it through last night's temptations unscathed, but my body knew better. I glanced at Mo, watched her drink from the bottle, like I'd seen her do so many times, and my mind flashed back to before: Before the explosion. Before the Marines. Before, before . . . the time of befores.

Me and Mo, two young Pavee girls, wild and crazy, different, but the same. We're at the top of the lookout tower, legs dangling, bare feet, tank tops, browned skin, clear, crisp mountain air, blue hills stretched out before us like a rumpled quilt, whiskey and vodka.

A clink of bottles, a mischievous grin from Mo and she raises her bottle of vodka. "Vodka drinkers mix well with others. Whiskey drinkers do well on their own."

It's a challenge. I clink my bottle with hers. I drink. She drinks. We laugh and then it's my turn. I raise my whiskey. "Vodka drinkers start fights. Whiskey drinkers end fights."

We slam it back. Our own special philosophy, born of drink, rationalized in the immortality of youth. I wipe my lips and laugh.

Her own laugh is light and airy; then her expression flattens, and she raises her bottle again. "Vodka drinkers believe in the afterlife. Whiskey drinkers know there is only death before us." She tips her bottle and takes a long drink, her gaze never leaving mine, taking in my reaction, gauging my emotions.

I don't lift my bottle. I can't.

Her words had settled in my gut, dark and sullen, black and greasy. They were meant to cut, to hurt. And I'd deserved it. Earlier that year, Mo had lost her mother to cancer. She'd taken it hard, and her mother's death had rocked the clan. A young, vibrant woman, so unfair, so young, so . . . so . . . blah, blah, blah . . . I should have felt bad for Mo, but I hadn't. My mother was dead, too. She'd abandoned me as a baby, turned to drugs, and then did the unthinkable: killed herself. Or so I'd been told. No wakes and no keening.

Suicide was the ultimate sin in our clan, a desecration that marked the family, and the stain of my mother's sin had marred my soul, making me not worthy of the sympathy of others. And I resented it. And in a moment of desperate bitterness, I'd struck out at Mo, telling her that there was no God, no afterlife, that she'd never see her mother again. There was nothing but darkness and emptiness and death, eternal death, all those things the desperate young girl in me had felt. Later, I'd apologized. But it was too late. My hate and anger had come between us.

"Brynn? You okay?" Queenie held the bottle out. "Want some?"

I stared at the bottle. *Death. Death. Whiskey and death.* A childhood game of words and drunken wit had become a reality: I'd come to know both whiskey and death intimately. Mo's comment way back then wasn't just a verbal retaliation, but a moment of ominous clarity in the fuzzy drunkenness of youth. A mystic prediction. And it'd come true.

"Brynn?"

I blinked.

Queenie waved the bottle in front of me. "A drink? Do you want a drink?"

Do I? One sip. An orgasmic release, tension gone. I needed . . . no, wanted that sip. *Get ahold of yourself, Brynn.* I laughed it off. "I'm not a vodka girl."

A slight grin from Mo. The first since I'd arrived. "I remember." She reached for the bottle. Another swig and a pass back to Queenie. Eyes sparkled, more sips, another pass and another, like keep-away, and I was the kid in the middle.

"What time did you get home last night, Mo?" I asked.

Liquid dribbled from her swollen lips. "Late. Maybe three."

"I saw you and Chance Walker ride off on his, uh . . . horse at about midnight. Where'd you two go?"

Parks made a noise and covered it by clearing her throat. I shot a look her way, then turned back to Mo. "Where'd you two go?"

She became still, her eyes blank and her bloody lip raw against pale skin.

"Mo?"

"Out to the parking lot. To his car. That's all."

"What did you do?"

Regret filled her eyes. "You know. Messed around for a while."

"Then what?"

"I left."

"Did you come straight home?"

"Yeah."

"What was Chance doing when you left?"

"Don't know."

"Come on, Mo. What was he doing?"

She shrank back, pulling her arms in close and lowering her gaze.

Parks spoke up. "Was your husband waiting up for you when you got home? Is that when he beat you?"

Mo fingered the threads on her comforter.

Queenie spoke for her. "I came over about an hour ago. I couldn't find my glasses from last night and thought maybe Mo had picked them up by mistake . . . And, anyway, I came by to check, and I heard Hughie. He was so angry, yelling and cussing. Guess some officers had been over. And then I heard the girls crying. I was worried . . . so I just came in and . . . I found her like this."

Mo kept her gaze down, her hand trembling. Wilco nudged

it with his nose. She touched his head, tentative at first, then braver, and stroked him between the ears. No one spoke as we watched Wilco work his magic on Mo, sensing her pain and calming her in the only way he knew, by opening himself up to her, allowing her touch.

Queenie broke the silence. "There's more." Her gaze travelled between Parks and me. "You should know what he did." She pulled the back of Mo's shirt away from her neck. Parks and I leaned in to see. Strangulation marks, angry red patches, circled her neck, and fingertip contusions tracked a distinctly deadly pattern behind the ears. I knew what I was looking at, because I'd seen these types of markings before. On corpses.

I turned and stormed through the bus, Wilco on my heels, sensing my anger and dragging his lead behind him. I burst out the door and went for Hughie. "You damn son of a bitch. You could have killed her." I was two inches from Hughie's face, and his breath smelled like a booze-soaked rag. My own mouth watered. Every one of my nerves screamed for a swig of liquid balm.

Wilco stood by, lips curled back, canines gleaming white and sharp as his growls rumbled from deep inside. The others backed up. Hughie backed up, too, one eye on my dog.

"Call him off. I didn't do nothin'."

"Nothing?" I stepped in even closer. "Is that what you call it? Nothing?"

His face hardened; hate swirled in his eyes. "Back off, Callahan."

The bus door clanked open. Parks stormed toward us. "Callahan. He didn't—"

"Didn't mean to let her live?" Blood whooshed around my eardrums. Fury blurred my vision. "You ever touch her again, I'll . . ." I pushed him back.

He stumbled, recovered, and shoved back. Not hard. Not violent. But enough to get me out of his space.

Wilco reacted, ears back and snarling as his powerful jaw clamped onto Hughie's jeans, claws digging into the ground, head whipping side to side, muscles contracting. Fabric tore as frothing slobber sprayed the air, along with anguished, panic-filled screams of "Get him off me!"

Parks jumped in, snatched the dangling leash, and yanked. I pulled from the collar, digging in my feet and leaning my weight back.

Wilco released, and I fell back, pulling him with me, and we landed in a tangled pile on the ground. Hughie scooted across the dirt, hands out, shielding his face.

"I didn't touch my wife. She came home like that. Won't tell me nothin', either."

Parks pulled me aside and whispered in my ear, "He's telling the truth, Brynn. It wasn't him. She told me herself, right after you stormed out."

"Then who . . . ?"

"Walker did it. Walker beat her."

CHAPTER 6

Thirteen folding metal chairs were arranged in a circle amid stacked cases of mac 'n' cheese and toilet paper. One chair had a black jacket slung over the back and a worn Bible on the seat. I chose a chair on the opposite side of the circle, as far away from the Bible as possible.

The addiction counseling group met every Tuesday evening in St. Brigid's basement. Tuesdays, because on Monday and Wednesday and Saturday, the room served as our local food pantry. This was my first meeting. I'd arrived early, full of skepticism and pissed off. "Mandatory," Pusser had said. Attend this group or lose my job. *So stupid.* My time would be better off allocated to working the Walker case, not spent in a cold church basement that smelled like Goodman's Grocery Store, surrounded by a bunch of addicts and a do-gooder priest.

I stretched and rubbed the balled muscles of my neck. It'd been a crappy day: a trip to the ER to check Mo's injury—she was okay—formal questioning, paperwork, checking in with the crime-scene techs and the county medical officer who'd examined the ears. Nothing conclusive yet. A lot of investigation work was a waiting game.

Waiting, waiting . . . Where was everyone? Wilco lay at my feet, muzzle resting on his outstretched legs. He looked bored. *Get used to it, buddy. This is our new Tuesday night routine.* I looked up at the sound of a steel door thumping open. *Finally.* Footsteps echoed on the back stairs, and people filed in one by one: rumpled clothing, stale nicotine, grease-stained fingers, business wear, a college sweatshirt, cologne. . . . A diverse group, and each surveyed me with overt curiosity. A newbie. Fresh fodder. I slid my hands under my legs, glad that I'd taken time after work to change out of my uniform into jeans and a tank. The presence of a deputy sheriff probably wouldn't do much to encourage honest discussion among people who had done who knows what to facilitate their addictions.

The chair next to me squeaked. I turned to see someone familiar. "Jake?"

He bent and rubbed his fingers between Wilco's ears. "You brought our K-nine hero. What's his name again?"

"Wilco."

"That's right. Will comply. Military dog."

"Yup." I looked at Jake's profile. Dark hair, thinning, but not bad. Still dressed from work in chinos and a button-down. He was fit. Actually, in great shape for a guy in his . . . How old was he? Early forties?

He turned and faced me. I looked away—never did like full-on stares—and adjusted my dog's collar. A dozen or so others shuffled into the room. Wilco's attention followed his nose, and he gathered scents from the clouds of unseen odors only he could pick up from the eclectic attendees as they settled in for the hour.

"What are you here for, Brynn?"

"A little bit of everything. You?" I tried to meet his gaze.

Jake Sheehan was our assistant DA, a tough prosecutor and well respected in police circles. Who knew he had a problem?

"Booze. Lots of it for a long time. It ruined my relationships, lost me a wife, almost lost me my job at the DA's office."

"You been coming to these meeting for a while?"

"A year or so."

"This is my first meeting."

"I know."

"Not sure I belong here."

His eyes narrowed. "What? You're better than the rest of us?"

I tensed. "No, that's not—"

"Good evening, everyone. Welcome." A middle-aged woman in polyester slacks, orange-framed glasses, and sensible black shoes spoke. "I'm Margaret, this evening's chairperson. This is a closed meeting. All of us are here because we have a problem. Everything you say is completely confidential." She swiped at her bangs, thick, straight, and gray, and shifted toward the chair next to her. "Father?"

Colm, Father Colm to most, but I knew him before the "Father" bit, held out his hands to the people on either side of him. They all did the same. Reluctantly, I did as well. *Get used to it, Brynn.* Jake's hand grabbed mine. The lady on my other side reached out. Their palms were cool, dry; mine were slick with sweat. I wanted to pull back, wipe them on my jeans, but Colm started reciting, clearly and deliberately, a prayer. But not the "Hail Mary" or "Our Father" or any prayer from my youth. This prayer spoke of serenity and peace, of surrendering and accepting help. . . . *Surrender? A good soldier doesn't surrender.*

Colm finished, and everyone's hands slid free. Mine felt empty and awkward and out of place. Hell, I felt out of place. I dropped my hand to Wilco, my comfort zone, but he had already surfed the smells and had tucked his head to his paws to wait out the meeting. I slid my hands back under my legs.

"My name is Mitch." My gaze darted to the guy next to Colm. Dark hair, fuzzy beard, big hands, he ran his finger along the collar of his stained T-shirt. "I'm an alcoholic." He turned his head to the gal next to him.

"Lily. Booze and pain meds." Asian, thin, with thick glasses. Stylish clothes. She didn't look like an addict. Probably wasn't. I mean, pain meds, I get that. I used to take them by the handful. My fingers grazed over my scar. I'd needed them.

"Ashley. Wine." I looked at the next person in the circle. Wine. Yeah, I'd believe that. Cute sundress, sandals, salon-kissed highlights. *Another glass of merlot, please.* Big deal.

"Juan. Whatever I can get my hands on, man."

Chuckles all around.

Except from me. Two more people to go. Sweat pooled in my armpits. I lifted my elbows. A quick glance. No stains, but my ears whooshed, my head pounded, and my lips felt cold.

Jake leaned in and whispered in my ear, "You don't have to say anything."

"Josh. Everything, including heroin. I'm in deep." *Yes, yes, you are, Josh.*

"Jake. Alcohol."

"Brynn." My voice caught. I licked my dry lips, swallowed. Nothing more came out.

"What's your demon, Brynn?" Lily pressed.

I shot Margaret, the chairperson, a quizzical look. She gave me one back.

So much for not having to say anything.

"My . . . my demon?" My gaze swiveled to Colm, settled on the collar around his neck. Clean. White. Pure. My fingers grazed the dirty red, puckered flesh of my own neck. A dozen or more doctors, and not one had been able to erase my scars.

"Your demon, lady. What are you here for?" It was crazy-eyed Mitch. That dude was doing more than just booze, I'd bet on it.

"I'm here for . . . It's mandatory. For work. My boss—"

"You don't really have a problem, do you?" It was Lily again. I looked her way. "Excuse me?"

She pushed her frames up her nose. "I'm hearing you say that you don't have an issue. Or it's not your fault."

What's your problem, lady? Can't you see the scar on my neck? "I'm a vet." I brushed my hair aside. "I've got injuries and—"

"Suit up and shut up, lady. Like you're the only vet in here? The only one injured?" Mitch glared my way.

I glared back. *Asshole.*

"Ashley. Booze."

My head whipped to the left. *Hey. What the hell?* It was still my turn. My skin prickled.

"Toby, meth." Skinny, acne, bad teeth. One nervous cat.

"Alan, booze."

And back to Margaret, our leader. She read some rules, and everyone recited a creed like a bunch of robotic idiots. Brainwashed. That's what these people were. This was one weird deal.

The wall clock said 6:15 P.M. Forty-five minutes to go.

Lily straightened in her chair. "I'd like to announce that today marks my third month sober."

The room filled with the click-clacking noise of snapping fingers, like a thousand crickets all at once. Wilco cocked his head, not at the sound but at the sudden movements; lifted his snout; took a deep, long sniff; put his head back down.

What . . . ? This is crazy.

Jake leaned over. "We snap instead of clapping."

"I'm happy for you, Lil. But I'm struggling." Silence. Heads pivoted to Juan. He leaned forward, elbows on his knees, head shaking back and forth. "My woman, she's fed up. Said I'm no fun no more. We had a fight this weekend. She wanted to score some. I said no way . . ." *Snap, snap, snap.* He held up his hand.

"But I messed up. Couldn't say no to her for long. Just some weed, man. And beer, but it set me back. The craving's bad now, know what I mean?"

"Why didn't you call your sponsor?" It was Jake.

Sponsor?

Juan grimaced. "Weak. I'm weak. I can't do this."

Jake shook his head. "Yes, you can, Juan. It's a daily choice. Today is a new day. You're sober today, right?"

"Yeah. Yeah, I am. Nothing today. I'm clean today."

Colm pressed his fingertips together. "Thanks be to God."

Snapping, sharp and loud. Juan brightened and sat a little straighter.

Jake spoke up again. "You're with the program now, Juan, and no one expects you to go it alone. That's why we have sponsors, right?" Nods all around. "Call next time. Call."

I pressed my lips together. Didn't need any damned sponsor, thank you very much. It'd been over a month since I'd had a drink. A real drink, that is. Those two little finger dips at the party didn't count. What would these people think of that? "I haven't had a drink for over a month."

Heads snapped my way. But no fingers.

The Asian woman perked up. "So you're a drunk."

"No. Didn't you hear me? I haven't had a drink for over a month."

Mitch scowled. "What else besides the booze? A little weed?"

"No. Of course not. I used to take painkillers, but they were prescribed. I was in—"

"Did you take them as prescribed?" Back to the Asian woman again, her tone clinical and condescending. What, did she think she was some sort of expert?

"No. But my doctors didn't understand my pain. I have an inj—"

"Right. Injury. You were in pain. Got it." Asshole Mitch rolled his eyes.

I turned back to the Asian woman. "You don't understand." I avoided looking at the others, focused on this gal. Ms. Booze and Pain Meds, she might get it. "I'm a vet. I served three tours, barely lived through an IED, and saw things. Death. A lot of death."

"Really? Me too." She didn't look like a soldier.

"Where'd you serve?"

"On the children's ward. I'm a pediatric nurse. I watch kids die every day."

Mitch waved his hand. "Don't bother with her, Lily. She's too far from acceptance. Give her time. At least she's here." He looked at me and shrugged. "That's the first step."

The snapping started now. *Click, click, click.* Being sober a month didn't count, it seemed, but being here, on their sacred turf, now that was praised. Smiles all around, the sort of sweet, patronizing smiles that made my stomach turn. I glanced at Jake. He stared straight ahead, finger snapping with the others, but the edge of his lips curled. He was laughing at me. They were all laughing at me.

Screw them! Time to leave. I jerked forward.

Jake's hand shot out and clasped my forearm. "Don't leave. Give it a chance."

I sank back in the chair and clenched my teeth. Like I had a choice. Put up with this crap or lose my job.

Toby's voice cut through the clatter and my anger. "I went out last week."

The room grew silent.

Jake bent close to my ear. "*Going out* means 'falling off the wagon.'"

Toby scratched his forearm, self-baiting, vicious. The skin turned an angry red. "It was horrible. Worst fall yet, a frickin' two-day binge, man. Ended up in the ER."

Colm leaned forward. "It's over, Toby. You're back on track now. What you do from here on out is your choice."

"That's right. Leave the past in the past," someone said.

Then someone else added, "One day at a time."

From the other side of the circle came, "Learn from your mistakes, Toby."

Advice resounded from around the circle until I thought I'd puke. As if addiction could be cured by a few words of encouragement. *Just show up here, week after week, and it's all good. Right.*

Toby stopped scratching and looked at Colm. "Thanks for being there at the hospital, Father. It meant a lot."

Lots of snaps this time.

And on and on it went. Confessions. Encouragement. Snapping. Another prayer. One of the guys got up and read a poem he wrote about sobriety. Yes, a poem. *Poets and addicts.* I didn't belong here. I'd been sober on my own for a non-snap-worthy month, and I had no love for evocative words spliced together into some free-form nonsense that passed for poetry. I wasn't at all like these people, thank God.

And then the meeting was over.

Jake touched my elbow. "I'll walk you out."

"Brynn." Colm approached. He held his hand out. "Hello, Jake."

"Father." They shook hands.

Colm turned to me. "Can I talk to you for a minute, Brynn?"

"Sure."

Colm stared at Jake, his gaze friendly but direct.

Jake took the hint, told me he'd be outside, and clomped up the stairs with the last of the attendees. The steel door thumped shut. Awkwardness, thick and suffocating, settled around Colm and me. He meant well, sure. Now. But we had a history before his priesthood. Nothing about our past relationship, or maybe I should say the lack of a current one, ever settled right when we faced each other alone.

I cleared my throat. "What's up?"

"I'm glad you're here."

"I have to be. Pusser told me it was this or lose my job."

"He's right. You need the support."

"From these people? Weren't you listening? They were all against me."

"That's not what I heard." His expression shifted. Subtle but less priestly now, more personal, slightly . . . awkward? "I take it that you know Jake from work."

"He's the assistant DA. A good guy. I didn't expect to see him here. Didn't know he had a problem."

"Everyone has a problem of some sort. Yours just happens to be addiction."

"I'm not an addict."

He lowered his chin, eyebrows raised.

"Okay, I *had* a problem, but I haven't done anything for over a month. No pills, no booze, nothing. And without meetings or a sponsor."

"One month doesn't erase addiction. Have you already forgotten?"

I blew out a long breath and reached for my dog's leash. "Forgotten what, Colm?"

"That I found you. Half dead. Strung out on pain meds and booze."

Shame burned through me. *Naked. You didn't add "naked." Or "intentionally overdosed."* He'd seen me, the worst of me, all of me. I looked down. Couldn't, wouldn't look at his face. I didn't want to see what was there. Pity? I didn't need it. Didn't want it. Especially not from Colm. He'd left me without a word years ago, confessing only after I returned, maimed for life, that he'd been too cowardly to admit back then that he'd turned to God and the priesthood. Fine for him. Just one more abandonment in my life. And now he was offering his counsel and pity to me, the broken addict?

I jerked Wilco forward, pushed past Colm, and headed for the door. "I've got to go."

"Brynn, wait. Wait a minute. I didn't mean to—"

I kept going and didn't look back. Couldn't.

CHAPTER 7

Zombieland, the locals called McCreary County Nursing Home. Home of the living dead. In a way, they were right. It felt postapocalyptic here. Moaning, hissing oxygen machines, drooling mouths, liver-spotted skin, the sharp sting of urine and antiseptic, and gray everywhere. Gray walls, gray furniture, gray hair, grayish skin . . . gray, that undefined color in between black and white, the color of limbo, the zone between life and death. Some, a lucky few, might recover enough to go home. But for many, it was the last stop before dying.

I'd been in the gray zone before myself. A trauma unit back in Afghanistan, a brief stop along my way to a German hospital. It was a lot like this place, hard and sterile, the constant drone of hissing voices pierced by the intermittent *beep, beep, beep* of machines. Dozens of soldiers on gurneys, bloodied and mangled, most writhing in pain, but some motionless, barely breathing, hooked up to machines that kept them alive while, I imagined, their spirits hovered overhead, waiting to see if the surgeon could make their bodies inhabitable again. Souls in abeyance.

Purgatory with nurses.

Gran's nurse aide was in her room. Sandie or Sadie . . . I could never keep it straight. She was a small thing, late thirties probably, but worn and rough, with sunbaked, pebbly skin and tight lines radiating from black-rimmed eyes. She was feeding Gran, who sat slumped like a rag doll, propped up with pillows, her gaze locked on the television screen. The local newscaster was reporting on today's crime. The camera panned the crime scene and showed Wilco and me in action. The aide did a double take.

Gran let out a low, crude grunt. Wilco went straight to her, sniffed, and nudged her hand, but she didn't notice.

"Hey, Gran. How are you today?" I stepped in front of her and turned off the TV.

Her head bobbed; eyes rolled my way. The nurse shoved another spoonful of mush through Gran's flaccid lips, scraped the top of the spoon on her upper teeth, and then wiped the excess. Gran gummed the food, her eyes fixed on me. A blob popped back through her lips. The nurse caught it with a napkin and smeared it sideways before it dribbled down Gran's chin. A couple more swipes and it was gone, cleaned away, and she was ready for another bite. Just like feeding a baby.

"She's doing great. Aren't you, Mrs. Callahan?"

No response, just tired eyes that looked at me. She recognized me, yes, but from a struggling, debilitated body.

"She had a little setback yesterday, or so the staff thought, but it was just a little stomach issue, wasn't it, Mrs. Callahan? Got it all cleared up, and she's eatin' good now, aren't you?"

As if Gran could answer.

I looked for the woman's name tag, but she wasn't wearing one. I mustered a fake smile for Gran. "Glad to hear it." My voice sounded chipper, although I felt anything but happy. *Keep it positive, Brynn.* How many times had Meg told me that very thing? *Stay positive. Don't say anything to upset Gran. She needs to heal.*

Just eighteen months ago, Gran was a sharp, vibrant woman. A series of small strokes, then one large stroke had landed her in this situation. My fault. I'd come back to Bone Gap to help care for Gramps before he died, but instead, I'd brought nothing but misery. I'd betrayed our clan by working with settled law, and both sides had doubted my loyalties. Much worse, my presence had triggered memories in Gramps's decaying mind of the day I'd left Bone Gap, the day another clan member, Dublin Costello, had raped me. Gramps had blamed me, had kicked me out, and had never told Gran. Until he spit out the truth in his dying delirium.

And then that sharp, vibrant woman, the one person in the world who loved me more than life itself, had taken action. What happened then had changed everything for us both. But I loved her all the more for it.

I had hid the truth of Gran's actions from the very law I had sworn to uphold, watching Gran, who was already imprisoned in a living hell from the stress of what she had done, from the guilt for killing the man who'd destroyed my life.

The aide spooned another mouthful into Gran. Shove, scrape, wipe, and repeat, her skinny arms a well-tuned machine, sinew and muscle contracting in even cadence.

"Is she swallowing any better?"

"We're working on it, aren't we, Mrs. C?"

Gran's eyes blinked, blue and watery, and her mouth opened again like that of a jittery baby bird waiting for a piece of worm. In went another spoonful, something orange this time, pureed sweet potatoes or maybe carrots. Gran gagged, then coughed, orange spittle spurting from her mouth.

The aide jumped up and wiped her face. I took her place next to Gran. "You okay, Gran?" I bent closer, straining to hear her. "What is it, Gran?"

Her wordless breath came out as hot, fruity little puffs laced with a stale mucus.

I covered her trembling hand with mine and traced my thumb along her raised blue veins. "I'm sorry, Gran. I wish I knew what you—"

Another grunt, this one louder and settling into a low growling sound. She was shaking now.

The aide appeared and stroked Gran's arm. "Calm down, sweetie. It's okay."

The attention agitated Gran more. Her good hand shot up to her face, and her nails dug into her skin, tearing the flesh, dark red blood seeping through the scrapes.

"Gran!"

The aide hit the call button with one hand and grabbed Gran's hand from her face with the other. "This is Sadie in room one-oh-nine. Assistance needed." She clasped Gran's hands, held them firm to her sides. "Easy, Mrs. Callahan. It's okay. It's okay."

I backed up, helpless and confused. "What's going on? What's wrong with her?"

"She's frustrated. It's normal when they can't communicate. Don't worry. But I'm going to have to ask you to leave so I can get her calmed down."

"Isn't there something I—"

"No. Please just leave."

That night, I slept with gritted teeth, tossing and turning, my mind racing—shriveled ears, Gran's blood-streaked face, stupid Lily's self-righteousness . . . *snap, snap, snap*—until the sun broke through the slats in my window blind. And then my cell phone rang. It was Parks. There'd been another crime.

A tongue this time.

Thirty minutes later I was staring at it, strung up and swaying in the morning breeze. A dark stripe against the fresh cerulean-blue sky, coated with feasting black flies, buzzing, swarming, legs rubbing together . . . *a fleshy fly strip*.

My roiling stomach surprised me. I'd seen plenty of body parts before, but that was war and the grotesque was expected. But not here. Not hanging from a rafter in a pristine park pavilion.

I looked to where Parks stood with a couple other officers. "Where's the message?"

She pointed a shaky finger inside the pavilion. "Look up."

Leaning forward, I shielded my eyes and raised my chin. There, in the shadows of the underside of the pavilion, the message was scrawled in black spray paint: SPEAK NO EVIL.

"Where's Pusser?" I asked.

"On his way. I was in the area when I got the call. The other guys got here about the same time." Two town cops were working to cordon off the scene, unraveling a spool of yellow crime tape around the entrance of the pavilion.

We were at Southside Park, its name a misnomer. The park ran along the northwest side of town, a green space wedged between a residential area and the plastic plant. Employees spent their lunch hours here, smoking and eating sacked lunches. Across the main road was a small strip mall with a dollar store, a Mexican restaurant, and a video-gaming place. On the adjacent corner, an old Victorian served as the McCreary Funeral Home. Budget shopping, gambling, greasy-spoon eating, and eternal rest—a natural succession of human services.

I had tied Wilco to one of the nearby picnic tables. Enticed by the smell of decomposition, he whined and pawed the ground. *Let me work. Let me work*, he seemed to say. A dark sedan pulled up, followed by the local television van. A white van—I'd seen one like it outside Walker's apartment and other times. Out of the van climbed reporters and cameramen. *Great. Has the press been following me?* Another county cruiser pulled behind them. Pusser this time. And with him, someone I hadn't seen for a while—Agent Grabowski.

They headed our way. Tall and spindly, with a brown freckled scalp, narrow, slanted eyes, and a hawkish nose, Agent Grabowski reminded me of a praying mantis, and Pusser looked like a squat dark beetle waddling next to him. Grabowski's hand reached out for mine and was dry and firm. There were the usual greetings and small talk, a few curt questions, with even curter answers.

Pusser glanced at the press van and grunted. "Damn press. Ears, now a tongue. Mark my word, this'll go national by to-morrow." Severed body parts made for titillating headlines. His eyes darted toward the pavilion. "Figured we'd see another body part soon. That's why I called you, Joe." Pusser and Agent Grabowski were on a first-name basis. Old friends and confi-dants, they went way back to their rookie days but had parted when Grabowski left local law to pursue a criminal-profiling ca-reer with the Feds.

Parks filled Grabowski in on the ears. "We didn't find the victim's body at the previous scene, and it doesn't seem to be around here, either. Not nearby, anyway. And no extraneous blood easily detectable. Same method as before. Looks like the same twine was used, and there's another message."

Grabowski's lips pressed thin as he surveyed the scene. "Speak no evil?"

Parks pointed up and nodded.

"The ears were identified to be from . . . ?"

"Chance Walker," Parks said. "A stripper. Callahan recog-nized his earring."

Grabowski raised a brow my way. I didn't react. He moved on with, "What else do we know about the kid, other than he took his clothes off for money?"

"Stripping was Walker's side job," Pusser said. "He worked the day shift at the plastic plant over there."

Grabowski squinted at the plant, then at the strip mall across the street. "Which might point to this being Walker's tongue, too. Or the perp just likes to use public spaces to display the trophies. This could be a second victim." Grabowski glanced around again at the storefronts. "He would have waited until the stores were closed before setting this up."

Parks stared at the plant, little lines of sweat dripping from her hairline. She looked shaky. The tongue must have gotten to her. It had gotten to me, and I had seen plenty of fermenting body parts.

"Didn't your husband used to work at the plastic plant, Parks?" I asked.

She looked my way. "Huh?"

"Your husband. Did he used to work here?"

"Yeah. Third shift. Hated it. Said it was like working in a prison. Bells for everything. Even breaks. And there was no smoking inside the break room. Smokers used the loading dock out there." The dock was visible from where we stood.

Pusser crushed a fresh toothpick between his teeth. "The entrance to the plant is gated, with security cameras, so maybe we'll be lucky and he parked along this road." He turned to Parks. "Check in with the general manager. See if the parameters of their outside security cameras reach this far. If so, maybe the perp is recorded. See if anyone saw anything that night, and get me a list of Walker's work buddies. We'll start there." He swiped his brow. "Techs are on their way. We'll get the scene processed and then see if the ME can tell us if this tongue and the ears belong to the same person."

The image of Chance Walker being slowly dismembered settled on my brain and soured my gut. "We need to get a lead on Walker."

Grabowski's eyes narrowed. "I doubt we'll find him. The nature of these messages indicates revenge, meaning the victim or victims are chosen for a reason. That means they have a history with the perpetrator. A connection. He doesn't want us to figure out that connection until he's done with the third and final act."

Pusser picked up on what he was saying. "But Callahan recognized that earring, and we released Walker's name to the press . . ."

"Exactly. He knows you've identified the victim. He'll be more careful from here on out. And more desperate to execute his plan."

CHAPTER 8

I drove, with Grabowski folded into the passenger seat, his cowboy hat skimming my cruiser's roof as he messed with the radio, trying to tune in his favorite bluegrass station. We'd interviewed the shift supervisor at the plant. He had said Walker and a guy named Randy Silvas were good buddies. We were on our way to Silvas's place.

Grabowski landed on a song and sat back. "I heard about your grandmother. I'm sorry."

"Thanks." I kept my eyes on the road. The sun burned hot through the windshield. I turned up the air and adjusted the stream to hit my face.

Grabowski's knee bounced in beat with the music. "You doing okay?"

"Yeah, fine."

"You sure?"

"I'm sober, Grabowski. Over a month."

His knee stopped bouncing. He looked my way.

"What?" I asked. "You don't believe me?"

"It's not that. Just . . . well, it can't be easy."

"Withdrawals were hard, but I'm fine now."

"I see."

"No, really. I mean, it's hard, but I've handled a lot worse."

"True."

Finally, someone who gets me. "You should see these meetings Pusser has me going to. They're stupid. The people are . . . they're . . ."

"They're what? Addicts?"

"Come on. Not you, too."

"You don't think you have an addiction problem?"

"Give me some credit. I haven't had anything for over a month now, and I'm handling it fine. That's without the meetings, the sponsors, the, well, crap they hand out like sugar pills."

"That's great, Callahan."

"What do you mean by that?"

"Just what I said. That's great."

Like he knows anything about it. I turned down the next block. Slashes of black and red graffiti marked the concrete pillars of the underpass: a crudely drawn pitchfork, exaggerated letters morphing into reptile heads, a swastika. *Welcome to the neighborhood.*

A pothole rattled the car, and Wilco woofed from the cage in the back, then settled again. I continued another two blocks, Grabowski staring out the window, his mouth clamped shut, fingers tapping to the banjos and fiddles of his life-is-so-happy music. I brought things back to the reason we were sitting together, listening to this garbage.

"Any other takes on the case?" I asked.

"Not much. Hoping Silvas can give us some insight." His cell rang; he turned down the radio, stretched out his legs, and pulled it from his pocket. "Grabowski. Yeah, Frank, what's up? Really? Okay. We're on it." He pointed a couple blocks down to a fast-food place. "Turn around in that lot up there. A call came in to dispatch. Someone saw a car matching the description of Walker's vehicle. We're not far from its location."

Fifteen minutes later, we pulled in front of an old textile mill by the river and got out of the cruiser. A crippling union dispute back in the 1960s had shut it down for good. The fixtures and machinery had been stripped and sold to China; the workers, left jobless. The mill was abandoned and derelict now, and all that remained were bitter memories and two stories of crumbling brick and shattered windows, smothered by chest-high weeds and overgrown brush.

Walker's car was the only vehicle parked out front. It was empty and the doors unlocked. Grabowski slipped on gloves, and opened the passenger door, then stooped low to peer inside. "Keys are still in the ignition."

I snapped on gloves and opened the driver's-side door. A travel mug, loose change, a fast-food container, gum wrappers, and a few CDs were scattered on the passenger seat. Even more junk in the backseat. What would the techs find under the surface? Blood? Semen? Something linking Mo to this vehicle?

Grabowski straightened up. "Pop the trunk for me."

I did, then crouched and ran a gloved hand under the seat. Nothing. I lifted the edges of the floor mat. Small pebbles and dirt and a crushed cigarette butt, nothing else. I stood. "No obvious blood."

"Nothing's obvious here, either, except the guy was a pig. Techs will have their work cut out for them." I heard Grabowski rifling through the trunk. It was probably full of trash, too.

Wilco would detect blood if it was there. I started toward the back of my cruiser. "Yeah, too dirty to be certain, but—" I whipped around at the sound of squealing tires. A flash of chrome, a gunning engine . . . a white van speeding toward me . . . I stood rooted and confused. *What the . . . ?*

Arms grasped me from behind, Grabowski's arms, and pulled me up and back. The van crashed into Walker's car, the air exploding with the sound of metal on metal and shattered glass. We hit the ground, skidded against the hot pavement, skin peeling from my right arm. Grabowski cried out in anguish.

I pushed off him, dazed and confused, hot blood dripping from the gash in my arm. Grabowski was quiet now. Motionless. I rolled over, touched his face. "Grabowski, Grabowski . . ."

The van's gears popped. It was moving again, shimmying backward, tires spinning; the putrid smell of hot rubber stung my nostrils. It screeched to a halt. Silence. Silence.

I reached for my gun, my fingers rubbery. The perp was still here, trying to run us down now. He'd come back, covering his tracks. Or maybe the body was still nearby, and we'd interrupted him from harvesting yet another—

A sharp clank of the gears.

I rose up, made it to my knees. *It's coming back! It's coming back!*

"Grabowski. Get up. Get up!"

I lifted my weapon and fired as the van barreled toward us. *Bam, bam, bam!*

The windshield shattered. The van veered to the left, ran up on the curb, and smashed into a guardrail separating the parking lot from the river.

I pulled myself upright and kept my weapon trained on the van as I advanced toward the driver's side. "Get out of the car. Out! Put your hands—"

The door popped open. I stared down my sites, finger on the trigger.

Nothing.

Then a rustling sound; a flash of color, blue, dark blue; the weeds around the door bending and parting . . .

Where is he? Where is he? "Police. Come out now!"

Nothing.

Behind me, a moan. Grabowski! I turned and yelled into my

shoulder radio. "Officer down. Officer down! Medical transport needed. Saunders Road. Old textile mill."

He clenched his lower torso and rocked in pain. "I'm good. Go after him. Go!"

I hesitated.

"Go!"

I sprinted to my cruiser and released Wilco. He bounded out of his cage and sat rigid, ready for my command. I scanned the area again and saw a disturbance in the tall weeds near the walls of the plant, a flash of flesh, an arm, he was moving fast now. I raised my gun. "Stop!"

He vanished.

I broke into a run, Wilco beside me, not trained for chase and apprehension, but in the game. There was a loud scraping sound, then a thud, and behind me, Grabowski's voice, hoarse and strained, "He's inside the building. Wait for backup."

Backup, like hell.

I burst through the overgrowth, treading weeds; bending thistles snapping back, hitting my face, stinging my skin; sucking in pollen, nostrils clogged, my chest on fire. Faster. Faster. Despite only three legs, Wilco shot through the tall weeds like a flying arrow. I reached the side of the building, turned sideways, and shimmied between some thorny branches, my cheek brushing against the rough brick wall, my feet snagging on fallen bricks and clumps of broken-off mortar. The door was ahead. Almost there. I pulled it open. Wilco darted around my legs and entered the building. I followed, weapon raised, my eyes blinking against the darkness.

I cupped my flashlight under my gun and progressed into the factory, dank and damp, my heart pounding in my ears, my eyes bulging against the darkness. *Where are you? Where are you?*

Light streamed through slats in a boarded-up overhead window, luminous stripes playing across pulleys affixed to a long beam running the length of what once was the looming room.

CHAPTER 9

A couple of hours later, I parked my cruiser a few blocks from Silvas's place and slumped back in my seat, shaky and alone, except for my dog. At least I always had my dog.

Grabowski had been transported to McCreary County Hospital with a probable hip fracture. The scene was still being processed, but Pusser wanted Silvas questioned now more than ever, so Parks was en route to meet me.

It was Wednesday, a regular shift day, and Walker's "good buddy" Silvas hadn't been at work and hadn't come forward about his missing friend. Sometimes best friends become best enemies. Or both fall victim to the same crime.

Wilco and I had scoured the area around the mill, and just like inside the building, Wilco had given no alerts, nothing that related to human decay. Forensics would tell us more, but I knew either Walker had been taken alive from that scene or someone else had driven his car and left it there.

I knew something else, as well: the hit-and-run incident at the mill had nothing to do with this case.

I sat in my cruiser, my right knee bouncing against the keys

Rows of rusting axels and remnants of disintegrated belts dangled like, like . . . I cringed. *Like hanging ears and tongues.*

A shadow swooped overhead. I ducked, traced it with my gun and light, and flinched as a startled bird streaked from one ceiling beam to another. I took a breath.

Plink. Plink. I tensed, swung left, right, back to the left. Someone was there. I pulled in, chin low, moved forward slowly and silently. Wilco worked around me, nose to the ground, moving in and out of the shadows, his breathing magnified by the stillness and heaviness that surrounded us. The wail of a siren broke through, distant but growing closer. My own dust-filled breath echoed around me, ragged and labored.

Footsteps sounded behind me. I swung around, and my light caught the back side of a blue shirt and a black baseball cap. Wilco's sharp bark pierced the air as the perp ran off. I took off in pursuit, running blind, my feet pounding the concrete floor. My elbow struck something; my kneecap slammed into hard metal. . . . *Crap!* Piercing pain radiated through my leg and hip. I stumbled forward, caught myself, pushed upright, and kept moving. Ahead, a crack of light, the sound of a heavy door sliding, and a figure outlined against the brightness. I gained ground, moving closer. . . .

I raised my gun. "Police. Stop!"

He stopped, turned, and I saw familiar features. Not a man but a woman. Strands of long hair fell loose from under th baseball hat and framed her face: elegant bone structure, hi cheekbones, and golden-hazel eyes that were wild and full rage.

A face from the past. Katie Doogan.

I lowered my gun.

She turned and vanished through the door.

dangling from the ignition. *Jingle, jingle, jingle . . .* My encounter with Katie Doogan at the mill had amped up my adrenaline. She knew the truth, held the key, well, the gun actually, the weapon that Gran had used to kill Dublin Costello. Evidence that could destroy what little was left of Gran's life. What was Katie doing here now? And why had she been stalking me? My brain was on fire, neurotransmitters inflamed, endorphins coursing through my blood, sharp and hot, encircling my nerves and shattering my resolve. I shoved my hand into my pocket. Empty. *Oh yeah. I don't do pills anymore. Damn.*

Bounce, bounce, jingle, jingle . . .

Get a grip, Brynn. You don't need them.

Wilco nudged me, his piercing eyes imploring attention.

"What?"

He nudged again, forcing a smile from me. I reached across the seat, pulled him close, and inhaled his doggy smell. His coat was peppered with prickly seedpods from the thicket at the mill and the sticky residue of stinkbugs. It would take time to brush him out, but the very thought of time spent with my best friend relaxed me. My muscles loosened; my body quieted.

Wilco, my fix.

I surveyed Silvas's neighborhood: slummy tract houses with patchy roofs, crumpled gutters, mildewed siding . . . homes originally built to accommodate the middle-class sprawl of the early fifties but left behind in the fat eighties, when residents traded up for brick McMansions and cul-de-sac neighborhoods.

Parks pulled up next to me.

I took a deep breath and rolled down my window. "Silvas lives a couple blocks down."

She nodded. "Let's do it."

We progressed down the potholed street, passing chrome-wheeled lowriders, Caddies, and a souped-up Camry or two, and pulled in front of Silvas's place. I clipped Wilco's lead and waded through shin-deep weeds toward Silvas's front door, Parks at my side. Bugs bit along the edges of my socks like a dozen sharp needle pricks. A mosquito buzzed my ear, and my shoe sank into something soft.

"Crap." I lifted my shoe.

Parks smirked. "Looks that way. Smells that way, too."

I swiped the bottom of my shoe across the weeds, the pungent poo odor stinging my nostrils. Brown goop clung inside the treads of my sole. Wilco perked up and dug his nose in for a deep sniff. The shiternet, I called it. A doggy search engine. Given Wilco's olfactory cells, a pile of poop served him better than any Google search. One or two sniffs and he'd acquire a database of info on the defecator: When was he here? What had he eaten? Healthy or tasty . . . He strained his neck.

"No!" I yanked back, but with one chomp, he'd devoured the pile.

Parks scowled. "Gross."

I smirked back. "Just a snack."

Parks rolled her eyes.

Wilco licked his chops: *Yummy. More please.* He began sniffing around. Then he stopped, tensed, with ears back and tail rigid. His head jerked toward the right. I turned. A dash of movement and low, throaty snarls—another dog, big, dark, fierce, and on the attack. The air exploded with growls like thunder and clashing teeth like lightning; a storm of slobber hit my shirt and made wet-khaki polka dots.

The damn dog lunged for Wilco's throat!

I leaned back, the lead rope taut, and pulled, putting my weight into it, but I was powerless against the fierceness of the fight. Parks pulled her Taser, aimed at the wiry flanks of a part Doberman. A sharp yowl pierced the air, and the dog dropped, bounced back up, and ran off howling, his stub of a tail tucked.

The sleek black of his coat gave a final glint as he rounded a hedge.

Wilco. Wilco. I knelt and ran my hands over his fur, slobbery wet and matted, but no blood. *Thank God.* His muscles twitched with the aftereffects of the fight; his nostrils flared and pulsated. I pulled him close, nudged his head with my forehead. His eyes shifted, briefly focused on me, and seemed to say, "What?" I laid my head alongside his, breathed into him, and felt his breath, short spurts, hot and wet, against my own skin. Deep breath in and exhale, warmth and strength . . . comfort for us both.

A door banged open. My head snapped toward the house as a man ran out, then a woman, who sprinted right behind him.

"Hey! Stop! Police!" I jumped up, took off in pursuit, Parks behind me, barking into her radio for backup.

The two darted around overgrown shrubs and out of sight.

"Left, left," Parks yelled. "Between the houses."

I veered left. Then came a staccato *click, click, click* from the right, heels on asphalt—it was the woman, short skirt, blond hair and moving fast. "Parks, the woman. Over there!"

"I got her." Then Parks disappeared.

I continued running, getting closer and closer. Wilco bounded beside me, his leash trailing. The guy hopped a short, wide hedge, misjudged, and went down, screaming with pain, rolled out of it, and clamored back up. I gained a little. Ten yards, seven yards . . . My utility belt jingled, sweat-soaked fabric bound my knees as I cleared the hedge. Behind me Wilco yelped in frustration as he made a three-legged clamber over the bushy barrier. I plunged forward. Five yards, three . . . I pushed off, arms out, and was airborne for a brief second before slamming into his back. *Thud.* Air expelled from my lungs; rocks and gravel and pieces of asphalt scraped my skin. My jaw whipped back, causing hot, searing pain, and blood filled my mouth, oozed around my teeth and under my tongue, and trickled down my throat. I held on; his sour stench burned the lining of my nostrils. We rolled, me on top, him on top, me on top. An elbow hit my nose, tears sprung, and my eyes and nose dripped. Wilco's jaws snapped the air as he raced to catch up. Closer and closer. *Snap, snap.* He connected; the guy screamed out in agony.

"Aah!"

"Down! Down, boy!" Mute commands to his ears.

His lips curled, and blood-soaked canines sank into the guy's flesh.

"Call him off! Call him off!"

Wilco's head jerked up and back, and his claws gripped the pavement, screeching like nails on a chalkboard, as I dragged him off by his collar.

The man was under me, stomach down and trembling, with blood gushing from his shoulder. I cuffed him, anyway, and flipped him over. He was a little guy, maybe five feet six and skinny, his gaze hard and cold under stringy strands of black hair.

Parks returned, sweat soaked and sucking air. "I lost her." She looked down at the man. "Randy Silvas?"

He turned his head.

I slipped on gloves, ran my fingers through his pockets, and found his wallet and ID. It was Silvas. We double-teamed him, flanking each side, lifted him to his feet, and led him back toward the house.

He cried out in pain. "Your friggin' dog bit me."

I could not have cared less. "Where's Walker?"

"I don't know him. And I ain't seen him."

"Right. So how do you know you haven't seen him if you don't know him? What about the woman? Who's she?"

"Just some whore Walker picked up. Been hanging around

him some time now. Lot lizard. She works at Lucky's. I don't know her name."

"If she's Walker's friend, then why's she at your house?"

He clamped his mouth shut and looked away. Anger pinged my brain, engulfed me. I clenched his injured arm and pushed it upward, hard. He screamed out in agony.

"I asked you a question. Getting a little extra benefit from your friendship with Walker? Or taking over after you killed him?"

Parks tensed. "Easy. We don't need trouble." She nodded toward an approaching officer.

Reinforcements had arrived. One of the officers was coming our way, gripping a large trash bag. It clinked with each step. "Look what I found out back." He opened the bag for us.

I looked inside: a spent can of lighter fluid, an empty jug of antifreeze. "Cookin' a little meth, Silvas?"

He rolled his head, whimpered a little. "I gotta see a doctor, man. I'm in pain. Your dog bit me."

"That's what happens when you run from the cops." I shook him. He winced and let out a low, guttural moan.

Parks pulled me back. "That's enough, Brynn." She turned to the officer. "Call for a med transport." Then she got in my face. "I mean it. Ease up."

I let go. "Fine. You handle it. I've got to take care of my dog."

"Stop it, Brynn. We need to get you and Wilco both checked out, too. Here." The proverbial mom, always prepared, she dug in a pocket for a tissue and handed it to me. I swiped at my lips. It came back with a blood smear. Just a loosened tooth from the grounder. My hip barked louder. And, oh yeah, there was the shredded skin on my arm from the mill.

I watched an officer on the radio as another read Silvas his rights. Parks watched, as well.

"Silvas is our guy, Brynn," Parks said. "Meth head on the

run. Walker likely threatened to tattle on the guy. The messages fit." She looked relieved as she said it. Like she really believed it. And maybe she was right. Maybe this would close the case of the dismembered stripper. But it didn't do a thing for my problem about Katie Doogan.

CHAPTER 10

Black clouds eclipsed the sky as I pulled into Bone Gap that evening. Color faded from the landscape, replaced by an ominous shadow scudding over the eclectic collection of trailer homes, RVs, and campers. Wind gusted from the west, rocking our mobile dwellings on their axles, the creaking of swaying metal hauntingly eerie in the silent pre-storm stillness.

I let Wilco out of the cruiser. He stiffened, raised his snout, and inhaled the low-hanging ozone, his deaf ears erect and alert. "Come on, boy." I wanted to get inside our trailer before the rain hit, but Wilco spread his paws wide and lowered his head to the ground. Hunkered in that quivering way that he felt, that I also felt, when the demons called.

Distant thunder rumbled.

I jumped and grabbed for Wilco's collar. Lightning flashes messed with his mind, remnants from the IED explosion. And I didn't need flashbacks crippling my dog. Not now. The day had already been brutal: Silvas and the meth lab piling loads of paperwork on me. Images of Grabowski writhing in pain. Gran's incoherent struggle, which tore at my brain—today worse than ever. And Katie Doogan's sneering desire to kill me. Why?

I squatted, ran my fingers over Wilco's back, and then tugged his collar. "Come on, boy. Come on, please."

Clouds closed in on us, and the first heavy drops of rain began, like the pelting of shrapnel. He clung to the earth with extended claws and quivered. I was losing hope of getting my dog's mind back to a safe place.

Distraction. I needed to distract him.

I popped the back of my cruiser and pulled out my stash box. Water- and air-proof, my dog scent kit resembled a fishing tackle box, but inside layers of protective foam nestled plastic containers of nose-work scents: blood, bone fragments, bits of tissue and placenta. I picked placenta. It excited Wilco like nothing else.

A flash of lightning and more thunder. The storm was closer now. Wilco trembled at my feet. I unscrewed the lid, and his demeanor flipped like a switch, from panicked and useless to alert and on task. His will to work and please me trumped everything else, even his war-sickened mind.

His eyes locked in on the container, his nostrils flaring. I crossed the yard and entered my trailer, leaving the door open behind me. Inside, I turned. Wilco had followed me. He was sitting, stock-still, eyes intense, alerting.

I shut the door and recapped the scent sample, then dropped to my knees to pet him, long, soothing strokes, nape . . . withers . . . rump. "Good boy!" He rolled onto his back for a belly rub, and I was more than happy to give it. After a minute or two of full-out fun, I sprawled next to him, pulled his back to my stomach, and dug my hands into the warm skin of his underbelly.

We stayed like that, spooned together, human to dog, friend to friend, until the first wave of storms passed.

Later that night, rain lashed against the windowpane above my bed, and thunder rumbled and roared around me. Wilco, deaf to the sounds, was better. I'd spent almost an hour brushing his coat, nabbing the stickers, coaxing out the twigs, and using dog-friendly cleaner to dissolve the gooey and sticky remains of our day in the field.

He could use a bath, but that could wait. I could, too, but again, it could wait. The medics had cleaned my arm and slapped a patch on it after I refused any further treatment at the hospital. With no more than a sore mouth and hip, all I needed was some time with my dog. Wilco's grooming time had been cleansing for us both. He slept tangled in the sheets next to me, his breathing an even cadence. His nightmares had settled, and I was grateful.

But sleep didn't come easy for me. My body was exhausted, but my mind animated by rumination. I knew what was coming that night. Nightmares. With the stress, the weather, it was inevitable, especially without my meds or a drink. . . . I *craved* a drink. But the booze and the pills, they only eased the pain; nothing eradicated it. I'd seen too much darkness, too much death, the integrity of my own consciousness burned out by the enemy's fire. Nothing could make me unsee the evil. It was ingrained in my gray matter, loomed in the recesses of my mind, always waiting, waiting to overtake me. . . . *Boom, boom, boom* . . . Thunder crashed like outlying mortars.

I can outlast the storm. I can.

I clenched Wilco tighter and waited it out, fifteen minutes, twenty, an hour. . . . *I'm so tired.* . . . And finally the rain slowed to a pitter-patter, and the thunder receded to a low, distant roll. The storm had receded; I was left sweat drenched and exhausted. I rose and opened the window and settled back into bed, praying for peaceful sleep. The humidity had broken, and a light breeze whispered through the curtains above me, carrying the sound of rustling leaves and a passing car's tires slapping on wet pavement. As I drifted, the sounds faded away. . . .

Traffic sound from a nearby city, Habbaniyah or Ramadi, or where the hell are we . . . ? Searching for survivors, searching for bodies . . . a burned-out Humvee, skeletal metal, unbearable heat, my dog panting, sweat, blood, a leg, a finger, a tongue and an ear, part of a vertebra, dripping meat, human meat, a charred rib bone flaked with ash . . . All around, blood and flesh are fermenting together in a chalice of courage—human tincture poured out over desert sands as a freedom offering, a broken sacrifice. My gut churns; my throat is slimy with bile. . . . Voices and laughter, the guys huddled together, smoking, yakking it up . . . a rumbling sound. Thunder?

I turn, a blue Caddie hauling ass right for . . . "Run, guys. Run!" An explosion, death vapor raining down. Sand and toxic fumes, black and sooty. Sarge! He's on fire, stumbling about, anguished screams, burning, burning. He turns, lifts his arms, begging me . . . I shoulder my gun, aim, hesitate. "I'm sorry, Sarge. I'm sorry . . ." My finger hard on the trigger . . . Crack, crack, crack. Is that thunder? A high-pitched eeh pierces my eardrums, my teeth rattle, hot brass pelts my face, and the monkey-piss stench of propellant stings my nostrils. . . . "I'm sorry. I'm sorry . . ."

I jolted from my nightmare. More thunder. It was another wave of storms, not just outside, but also in my mind. I reached for Wilco; he was still, deaf ears oblivious to the onslaught. A small blessing for him. Yet God left every sound and sight and smell of the past vivid in my brain.

It wasn't fair. I didn't deserve this.

Endorphins surged through me, hot and euphoric, hitting my heart and spreading, encircling my nerves. Shaky, cold, dizzy, desperate . . . a drink. I couldn't do this anymore. I needed a drink. Just a little to get me through.

My sweat-soaked skin shivered as I padded toward the kitchen on autopilot, past Meg's room. I paused, listened to her soft snoring sounds, a rustling of bedsheets, and then went on to the kitchen. I opened the cabinet under the sink. I had seen it a few days ago, had meant to dump it, but hadn't. I pulled it from behind the drain cleaner, around the dish soap, the cleanser, and out of the cabinet, uncapped it, and brought it to my lips.

Don't do it. Don't drink it.

But I did. I swallowed. Instant balm, a release. My muscles smoothed, and my body warmed. I tucked it close and carried it back to bed with me.

This I deserved.

CHAPTER 11

I woke up late Thursday morning, clutching an empty bottle, my tongue like sandpaper, my pores oozing liquor-infused sweat, my gut bloated and roiling. I made it to the shower. Hot water pelted my back as I bent over and puked into the drain. I pressed my naked toes against the bile and food chunks, squished them into the drain's grate. *Stupid, worthless drunk. Stupid, stupid . . .*

Heaved dry and shaky, I stood up straight and raised my face, closed my eyes, and turned into the shower stream, determined to sober up and straighten up. The water washed over my face, my neck, my scarred skin, sweeping away my resolve, just like it had all those years ago, on that day out at the falls. Colm and I, we had been alone below the rocky cliffs, and I had stood in the water stream, afraid, unable to swim, knowing I could never navigate the waters below—so dark, like death. And he had been relentless, calling to me from the deep, and I . . . scared, because the deep had seemed too immense, too powerful, and I had stood, rooted in my fear and unable to answer his call.

Just like now. Weak, fearful, stuck . . .

That day, I had overcome my fear and jumped. He had caught me, and it should have been a triumph, an accomplishment, to help me face life's later fears and uncertainties. Instead, not long after that, he'd left. And with him, any sense of safety. Not in his arms or with anybody.

Everyone leaves me. I'm all alone. Then and now.

Voices from last Tuesday usurped my own inner voice. *Leave the past in the past . . . Think forward. Learn from your mistakes . . . one day at a time . . .*

Right! I snorted, and water sputtered from my cracked lips. *Like yesterday, which sucked. Today probably will, too.*

I turned off the water, stepped out, and groped for a towel. A noise stopped me in my tracks—a shuffling noise beyond the bathroom door. *Crap!* I should have let Wilco out first thing, especially since it was already later than normal. *Damn hangover is no excuse.* At least Meg had likely already left for her early shift and wouldn't find her cousin off the wagon and reeling from the fall. I wrapped the towel around my body and stepped into the hall. If Wilco had an accident, I could take care of it before—

"Hey, Brynn. It's me."

My back hit the wall at the sound of a male voice. "Doogan?"

He stepped from the blackened living room into the dimly lit hall, dark hair partially covering his angled face, his lean frame relaxed. Too relaxed. Wilco hadn't even barked. He wouldn't; he knew Kevin Doogan and trusted him. "Yeah, it's me. It's been a while. How've you been?"

"How'd you get in here?"

"Door was unlocked."

Meg. She'd gone to work this morning and left . . .

"I knocked, but—"

"You need to leave." Wet hair stuck to my face. I clutched the towel to my bosom, aware that it barely covered my buttocks.

He approached. I stood like a deer mesmerized by oncoming headlights, soon to be a red smear on the pavement.

"We need to talk, Brynn." The light from the bathroom landed on his features as he approached. His eyes were glazed and dilated. Booze? Dope?

"I'm clean, Doogan. Sober." My first lie.

He stopped, blinked. "Okay."

"Are you?"

"Am I what?"

"Clean."

He shrugged. "Just a little weed. To take the edge off. Things have been—"

"Your wife tried to kill me yesterday."

"What?" He ran shaky fingers through his hair. "She's crazy."

"She tried to run me over. She hit another cop. He's in the hospital."

His eyes snapped to mine. "Is she in jail?"

"No. Ran off before I could get her."

We stood silent a moment. I heard his ragged breath, or maybe it was mine. He reached out. "Listen, there's—"

I slapped his hand away, a silly womanly slap, not what I had intended. What *had* I intended? "I don't care. Leave, Doogan. I don't want you here."

His usual brooding hazel eyes turned dark. Cold. I ran my tongue over my dry lips. My gun was in my dresser drawer. Ten seconds, maybe fifteen, and I could have it in hand.

"You're scared. Why? I'd never hurt you, Brynn."

No, you pretended you cared for me, used me like a play-thing, abandoned me for your wife, who I didn't know existed, then suggested that I service you on the side. I ought to put a bullet in your head just for that reason. "Depends on your definition of *hurt*, I guess."

His eyes softened. He reached out, rested his hands on my shoulders. "Brynn."

"Don't." But his hands felt good. Part of me wanted to give in to him, strictly to honor the sacrifice he'd made for Gran, for me. He'd been on the run for months now, all to cover an act that settled law would call a crime, but clan law would deem justified. Another part of me knew the real reason I wanted to give in to him: I wanted him.

His gaze skimmed my scar, angry red from the heat of the water, and rested on the roundness of my breasts. He stepped closer, calloused hands moving down my shoulders. The roughness prickled my skin; my chest rose and fell. I clenched the towel tighter against my body, aware that under my towel, my one nipple stood erect and ready, while the other, the nerveless one, the one that had been blown off and rebuilt, remained flat, limp, nothing more than a blob of grafted skin and silicone. Half numb. Half woman. Half Pavee. Only half sane.

He looked up, held my gaze. "I love you, Brynn. And I told Katie how I feel. That's why—"

Love. He loves me?

He leaned in closer, the tiny scar below his jawline, the curve of his lips . . .

"No." I turned away, couldn't look at him. How could he lie about being married?

His hands fell. Confusion played across his features. "Katie and I stopped loving each other a long time ago. It's you that I—"

"Leave, Doogan. I want you to leave." Another lie. Every part of me wanted him to stay. But my voice held firm even as I trembled and ached for him.

"Okay. I won't touch you. Won't . . ." He stepped back,

took a breath. "Katie's out to kill you. She still has the gun. Let me stay, in case she comes after you again."

He'd sacrificed everything to protect my grandmother. But he had abandoned me once already. I couldn't face it yet again.

"I can take care of myself, Doogan. Get out."

CHAPTER 12

It was another hour before I made it into work. As soon as I cracked the door to Pusser's office, Wilco shot inside and went straight to his desk. Pusser bent to pet him, jerked his head back, and glared at me. "You haven't been late like this since you were drinking."

My heart jackhammered.

"Why are you late, Callahan?"

I held my gaze steady. "Dog ran off this morning. Took me a while to find him. That's why I missed roll call. Sorry." *Practiced lies. Drunks do that well.* "How's Grabowski?"

"Pissed off. Doesn't take well to being laid up. He could use some good cheer."

Yeah, well, couldn't we all. "I'll try to pay him a visit." I slid into one of the chairs across from his desk and took out my notebook while Wilco sniffed his way around the room: Pusser's shoes, the garbage can, a half-dead houseplant tucked next to the dented metal file cabinet, and back to me, where he finally settled at my feet.

Pusser leaned back in his chair, its black vinyl cushion sighing under his weight. "We didn't get much from the van. You don't recall anything on the driver? No hair color? Nothing?"

"Little guy. That's about it. Wore a hat." Another lie. They were coming easily these days . . . but no way could I tell Pusser it was Katie in that warehouse. "What about Silvas?"

"He's not talking, but we've got enough to put him away for meth manufacturing. He's got himself some slick lawyer. It's wait and see at this point. A connection to the van would help seal the deal. Give us some leverage to maybe get him to talk. But . . ." Pusser leaned back and pulled a plastic cylinder from his front pocket, tapped out a toothpick, and crammed it between his lips. "But no identifiable skid marks, no brake marks we can use for identification. Nothing. Someone was trying to run you down."

"Silvas? An accomplice?" I let it hang. My hand dropped to my dog. I rubbed his fur between my fingers over and over. Soft. Soothing.

"Not Silvas. We know where he was at that time." Pusser's stare settled on my hand for a second; he chomped down hard on his toothpick and switched directions. "The stuff from Walker's apartment's at the lab. Looks like there's blood on the bracelet."

"That could be from anything."

"Yup. Probably take a couple days to get more information. But we do have something. The blood in the container your dog sniffed out is from the ears. I had Parks check into the container. Nothing much there. It's standard and could be from any restaurant in the county or anyplace that uses foam take-out containers."

"Okay. Anything on Walker's family?"

Pusser shook his head. "Nope. Parents moved away years ago to Nebraska, father has dementia and is in a home, and the mother says she hasn't heard from her 'wayward son' in years. We did get the preliminaries back from the medical examiner.

He ran blood-type tests on the ears and tongue. That blood doesn't match."

"Two different victims." *That's not good.* "Someone else connected to Silvas?"

He shrugged. "We don't have enough to figure that out yet." He shuffled a pile of papers. "There's something else I need to discuss with you."

I froze. Wilco nosed my hand, begging for more petting.

Pusser pulled out a photograph Parks had taken of Mo's bruises. "She claims that Walker did this."

"That's what she said."

"You people are known for taking matters into your own hands."

"Nothing that extreme." *Liar, liar . . .* An image popped into mind: young Joey Ward running down the street, trailing blood, squealing like a wounded animal, and carrying three of his severed fingers in his hand. He'd got scuttered and touched Barny Gorman's wife. Retribution came swiftly and without mercy in the clan. To this day, Barny said Joey was lucky it was his fingers and not his pecker. We all agreed. Especially Joey.

"How do you think Hughie Black would take to some guy sleeping with his wife and then roughing her up?"

"It wasn't Hughie. He isn't capable. He was in an accident and got hurt bad. The guy can't even work now. He's no match for Walker."

"Maybe he had help. Parks said there were a lot of men hanging at his trailer."

His cronies. The guys at the trailer with him. "True. Bad bunch. Lazy. They run backroom gambling parties and bare-knuckle fights instead of working. But killers? I don't know. It doesn't fit. Why two victims, then? And why the messages?" We weren't the message-leaving type. We dealt with these things inside the clan, quietly, swiftly, and mercilessly. Just ask Joey Ward.

Pusser sighed. "Only other thing we got is the blond woman. The one at Silvas's place."

"A prostitute. Silvas said that Walker picked her up at Lucky's, the truck stop down at the east end, where the highway cuts off. Said they'd been seeing each other for a while."

"You get a look at her?"

"Briefly. Parks got a better look."

"Good. Take Parks and go to Lucky's. See if you two can spot her. See if you can catch her in the act and make an arrest. It'll give us leverage."

Lucky's wasn't actually a truck stop, but a former car dealership gone bust and turned into a diner, with the added bonus of a huge parking lot. It was one of the few places for rigs to pull off the winding highway between Johnson City up north and Sams Gap down by the state line.

I rarely ate here. Didn't have the stomach for it. As far as diners went, Lucky's was pretty much a greasy-spoon establishment.

It got even greasier when Harris slid into the booth across from me.

"Where's Parks?" I asked.

"Some sort of emergency at home. Pusser sent me." He held up his hands. "Hand sanitizer?"

"Don't have any."

"Can't believe I'm here. I've got better things to do than chase after some prostitute." He soaked a napkin in his ice water and wiped his palms. "You been in that bathroom back there? It's gross."

Didn't know Harris was so obsessive. Or clean.

"Clogged toilet," he explained. "Crap's floating everywhere in there."

I pushed aside my slice of chocolate pie, brown and gooey, and squirmed, my bare legs sticking to the vinyl seat. We were dressed to blend into our surroundings. Harris wore jeans and a concert T-shirt; I was in cutoffs and a tank, my idea of casual. And I'd left Wilco at home. A dog sniffing around the rigs might put drivers on edge.

The waitress popped by, set a piece of pecan pie down for Harris (must have ordered on his way in), plopped down our ticket, topped off our coffee, and sashayed back to the counter.

"Waitin' on that burger, Charlie."

Charlie, the cook, looked up, swiped his brow, squinted at the metal spindle of tickets, and sighed. Then his head went back down again, and a silver-edged spatula flashed over the grill.

Greasy food, greasy hair, the smell of burned coffee and onions, the clattering of silverware, and some guy with circles of sweat radiating from the pits of his Iowa 80 T-shirt ogling me from two booths over. He caught my gaze, raised his brows, and licked his lips.

Ick.

Across from me, Harris continued to whine between bites of pecan pie. "Damned people working this place don't take care of nothin' . . ." He picked a nut from a tooth, swished coffee around his mouth, and swallowed.

"We need to stay focused, Harris." I turned and looked out the window. "Check it out. Things are picking up out there."

Outside, heat radiated off cracked asphalt as a couple rigs pulled in, one after another, chrome sparkling in the midday sun. A dark-haired woman—not blond, like the one we were looking for—trolled the rigs, wobbling on spiked heels, rig to rig, door to door, with no takers, until she hit on a big black outfit with naked woman mud flaps. The window rolled down; she went up on tiptoes, leaned forward, all smiles and chatting, chatting. . . . The door popped open, and up she climbed. Down the line, another woman—this one much younger—jumped out of a cab and adjusted her skirt before moving to the next rig. But no sign yet of Walker's friend, the prostitute, or as he put it, the lot lizard. I sighed. Lot lizards, mattress maidens, sleeper leapers, pavement princesses . . . whatever name people gave truck-stop prostitutes, they never called them what they really were.

Humans. Women. Someone's daughter, someone's mother.

"Is that her?" My gaze swiveled to where Harris pointed at a blond head weaving in and out of the line of trucks.

I snatched up our ticket and stood, looked back at Harris. "Yup. Let's go."

The woman was elusive. By the time we got outside to the trucks, she was nowhere to be found. Harris and I split up. I started in the back with the owner-operated rigs, customized with sleek chrome accents, double-stacked exhaust pipes, oversize sleeper cabs, and catchy logos, like "Get Carried Away" and "Miles and Smiles" and "We're Trucking Awesome." *Clever.*

It was hot and miserable. My head still hurt from falling off the wagon, and now, just twenty minutes into my search, I was high on diesel fumes. Sweat trickled down my back; my too-short shorts crawled up my crack; my thighs were chafed raw from rubbing together. And I'd gotten nothing. She'd simply vanished. I was about to give up when my cell vibrated.

A text from Harris. **Row 2. Black, Covenant Hauling.**

I spun and headed that way, spotted Harris, and caught up to him. "What's up?"

"I saw the girl. She just boarded that truck over there."

I followed his gaze. A black rig with an oversize sleeper compartment, a cross affixed to the front grill, and TRUCKING FOR JESUS painted on the side. "*That* truck?"

"Yeah."

Figures. "Okay. How do you want to handle this? Should we wait or—"

"Are you kidding? It's too damn hot out here." Harris headed for the truck. I followed and positioned myself on the passenger side, just in case our girl made a run for it.

Harris banged on the driver's-side door. Movement, muffled words, and then loud and clear, "Go away. I'm busy."

Harris banged again. "Open up. Police."

More noises, a man's low rumbling interspersed with the high-pitched sound of a woman's voice. I mounted the running board, cupped my hands against the glass, and peered inside. I looked past the trashy cab littered with rumpled cigarette packs and empty energy drink cans to the sleeper, where our love-birds scrambled to get dressed: a shirt, a knee, a naked butt, more than I wanted to see. . . . I shook my head, stepped down, pressed my body back into position, and waited.

Harris knocked again. "Open up, now!"

Around us, elbows jutted out of open windows as onlookers stared and CBs crackled. A couple rigs fired up and pulled out.

I could hear our guy finally open his door and step out on Harris's side. His voice was dry as he spoke. "Is there a problem?"

"I need to talk to the woman," Harris said.

"There's no wom—"

"Hey, now, I see you got a cross on the front of your truck. Don't you know that Jesus don't like it when you lie?"

Or fornicate, I'm pretty sure.

"Look, mister . . ."

"That's Deputy Harris to you."

"Whatever. Is this really necessary?"

"I just saw a prostitute climb into your cab."

"A what . . . ? No . . . I don't do that type of thing." I imagined him raising a hand to his chest, as if swearing on his holier-than-though heart.

I rolled my eyes. *At least I'm an honest sinner.*

Harris laughed, deep and raucous; then I heard the sound of metal clinking. He'd pulled his cuffs. "Okay, buddy. Turn around. Hands behind your back."

"Shit, man. What the hell's your problem?"

And bad language, too. My, my . . .

The door by me cracked open, and out slid a leg and then an arm, followed by the rest of the woman, bony, blond, and heavily inked. The same woman I'd seen running from Silvas's place.

I snatched her arm; she startled, twisted, but I planted her against the side of the truck. "Not so fast, lady. We need to talk."

A couple of hours later, back at the department, her neon-blue fingernails percussed on top of the interview-room table. *Tap, tap, tap* . . . "I do what I got to do, that's all. And I make good money. Supply and demand. I learned that early on."

Nikki Russo was her name. I placed her in her early thirties, but it was hard to tell. She was hollowed out, skeleton thin; her face was covered with raw sores; she had cracked lips; and her teeth were a slimy brown. What type of "good money" could someone in her shape get?

"You learned early on, huh? How early, Nikki?" I was trying for an understanding approach. Worked better with dopers than going hard core with the questions.

"I was 'bout eight when they took me from my mama." Hot, sour breath wafted my way as she spoke. Wilco was with me again. He lifted his head and took a deep, long sniff.

"Was your mother a prostitute, too?"

"An entertainer."

"Okay, an entertainer. Did she entertain men?"

"Yeah. They came to the house."

I can only imagine.

"Then I went to a foster home. They's the ones that turned me on to drugs."

This woman had never stood a chance. I shook it off. *Stay focused, Brynn. You're a cop, not a social worker.*

Harris ran his finger under his collar and rolled his neck. "Enough with the sob story, lady. Chance Walker. Do you know him?"

Nikki looked down. Her lips tightened; nails worked the table again. *Tap, tap, tap . . .*

My hair dripped sweat. It felt like a damn sauna in here. "He's missing, Nikki. Maybe dead."

She didn't react. Either didn't hear, didn't care, or already knew. "I need a smoke." She ran trembling fingers through her brittle hair, and tiny flecks rained down on the table, like a shower of bleached whiskers.

Harris shot me a look.

"Not now, Nikki." I shifted tactics. "It must be hard working Lucky's lot."

"It's not bad. Like I said—"

"Supply and demand. I remember."

We fell silent. She picked at her skin. Then scratched. Then picked again. She was coming down hard.

"Tell me, Nikki. What's your demon?" *Damn. I sound like those freaks at my addiction recovery meeting.*

Harris eyed me weirdly.

But Nikki didn't miss a beat. "Meth. I got it bad."

"Silvas get you hooked?"

"Silvas?"

"Randy. You were running from his house. Remember?"

"Oh, him. Randy's his name?"

"What do you know him as?"

"I don't know nothin' 'bout him. He's a friend of a friend, that's all."

"Walker's friend?"

Her eyes darted about. Scratch, pick, scratch, pick . . . red streaks pricked with blood. She was practically crawling out of her skin.

Wilco whined.

She started crying.

I pressed her, anyway. "When did you see Chance Walker last?"

Her voice turned high and tight. "Can I go? I need to get out of here."

Harris smirked.

We got her where we want her now. "You can go just as soon as you tell us about Walker. I promise."

"Don't . . . don't do this to me." A string of snot leaked from her nose; she sniffed it up like a spaghetti noodle. Her eyes darted now, glazed. Was she talking to me or remembering something?

"Do what?" I thought of the bruises on Mo. "Was Walker hurting you? Or did he make you do something you didn't want to do?" Had Nikki been part of Walker's murder? Meth users were liable to do anything for their next fix. But one look at this scrawny, whimpering mess and I doubted she'd have the stomach for anything. Yet she knew something. She had to.

I leaned in. "Look at me. What is it, Nikki? What are you afraid of?"

Her head swiveled; she jerked upright and thrust a finger toward the corner of the room. "You see that?" Her eyes were wide with fear.

I looked at the corner, then back at her.

Harris looked, too. He whipped his head back around, his eyes bulging. "What the hell? What's she seein' over there?" He looked again. "I don't see nothin', do you?"

No, stupid. I don't. "She's hallucinating, Harris."

Withdrawal clawed at Nikki's brain. Things would go only downhill from here.

I pushed back from the table, stood, and motioned to Wilco. "We're not going to get anything from her today. She can dry out overnight in holding. We'll try again tomorrow morning."

CHAPTER 13

Dee's bridal shower was that Thursday evening. The event room she'd originally booked had found out we were Travellers and had canceled her reservation, so we ended up in the basement of the church.

A luau-themed party: bikini tops and grass skirts and high hair, dark-lined eyes, and whitened teeth that stood out like neon against fake tanned skin; brightly painted nails and even brighter leis piled high on cleavage; drinks and drinks, strobe lights and swaying hips; crepe paper–covered tables, pineapple candles, and fake hibiscus centerpieces—*anyone bring a limbo stick?*—and enough booze to stock a pub. Ironic, since a couple days ago I'd been here for a sobriety meeting. And the music? Real Don Ho-ish, heavy on the steel guitar and ukuleles, spurring an impromptu line dance. *A hookie, hookie, hookie, hookie lau . . .* I eyed a table of sweet little girlie drinks with paper umbrellas and twisted fruit. The smell of rum hit my nose. . . . *Want, want, want . . . Stop. I'm sober now. At least since yesterday.*

I can do this. I can.

Someone brushed against my arm. Mrs. Black, eighty-two

years young, her wrinkled hand clutching a drink, and a coconut bra stretched over a T-shirt with LEI ME printed in sparkly
letters.

Being sober sucks.

I wore my habitual jeans and T-shirt. Plus sandals and the
three leis that had been plopped over my head the moment I arrived. No coconut boobs for me, thank you.

At least I'd had the foresight to leave Wilco tucked in the
trailer for the night. Traveller parties were always light on clothing and heavy on strobe lights, sort of like an unwritten rule—
Travellers have a lot of those—but like lightning flashes, Wilco
couldn't tolerate strobes. And a freaked-out dog wouldn't mix
well with this crowd. The strobes didn't settle too well with my
own IED memories, either, but I could deal with it. Maybe. I
rotated my neck, rubbed the suddenly tight muscles in my
shoulders, and took a deep breath. . . . *Calm. stay calm. . . . This
light show is for fleshy dancing, not for melting flesh.* Still, my
anxiety heightened with every strobe. I inventoried my options—escape to the ladies' room or take the back exit? *Leave
or stay? Leave or stay . . . ?* Then I saw Meg waving at me from
a corner table. I shrugged, cast one last glance at the exit before
snatching a couple skewered meatballs from the buffet and
joining her.

"Where's the guest of honor?" I asked.

"Dee? She's over there."

I looked around, didn't see Dee, but caught Nina slinking in
the shadows, a large woven straw bag, like the ones islanders
might use for shopping, slung over her arm. But she wasn't
shopping. Well, in a way she was. She was pilfering as she went
along: a corkscrew, a pen, a small bobblehead hula dancer. *What
does she want with that? And . . . oh! There's Dee.* Someone had
set up a photo-op corner with white sand, a beach umbrella, and
a blow-up plastic palm, where Dee posed with a couple of her
friends, who were all fake smiles and . . . *Aloha, all!*

I turned back to Meg. "Can't believe Dee's getting married in a couple days."

Meg began worrying one of her red curls, her gaze falling to the table, freckled shoulders slumping forward.

"You okay, Meg?" Two years ago, she'd lost her own husband. She had tried again last year but had picked the wrong guy. Watching her friend get married couldn't be easy.

"Yeah. Just remembering better times. You know, before . . . before everything."

"I know."

"And now Gran. I'm worried, Brynn. She's not going to come home."

"We don't know that for sure."

Her eyes watered. "Don't we?"

I reached over, touched her hand, and murmured all the right things, then stopped short when Mo appeared at our side. She looked pissed.

My mouth went dry. "Hey, Mo. What's—"

"Is this how you treat your own?" She was in my face, darkened lips hovering inches from my eyeballs, her breath like hot, minty onions.

Meg scowled. "What's your problem, Mo?"

Queenie, the ever loyal shadow, stepped up. "She's upset—"

"Upset? Yeah, I'm upset." Mo's voice was high and strained, too loud.

The music died down; faces turned our way.

Fight's a-brewing.

Mo continued. "They came and hauled Hughie off. Right in front of the kids. You could've warned me, Brynn, but no, you just sicced your copper buddies on us."

"Easy, Mo. I didn't know—"

"Like hell. You turned on me. Is this how you treat your own?"

"No . . . I . . ."

"The girls were screaming for their daddy."

Queenie pulled on her elbow. "Calm down, Mo. You're going to ruin Dee's party."

Mo shook her off. "They threw him down and cuffed him right in front of my girls."

"Mo, I swear, I didn't know." *In front of the kids? Harris probably. What a jerk.* "Did the officer state the charge?"

"What do you mean?"

"The reason they were arresting Hughie."

"Yeah. Suspicion of murder."

What happened? When I talked to Pusser, he didn't have anything on Hughie. Definitely not enough for a warrant. Did Silvas play into this somehow?

Mo crumpled into the chair next to me. She'd gone from angry to broken. The onlookers lost interest. *Nothing to see here, people. No fight. Try next time.* The music started up again. I could barely hear Mo's sobs over the strains of ukuleles. Queenie disappeared and came back with a plastic cup in hand.

"Here, Mo. This'll calm ya."

Mo sipped, leaving a burgundy lip print on the cup's rim. Her muscles relaxed. She used a party napkin to dab at smeared mascara. "He's the love of my life. All I got."

Except when you were ridin' off with cowboy, I thought. *Or looking for your "chance to get outta this hellhole" of a marriage.* I bit my lip and took a deep breath. "I want to help you, Mo. I do. But you have to come clean."

She took another gulp from the cup. Less crying, more serious now. "What do you mean, come clean? What are you saying?"

I leaned in. "You cheated on Hughie. And the man you cheated with is missing. Hughie's going to be a prime suspect . . ."

"But you know he wouldn't have . . ."

"I'm trying to help you, Mo. Now think. Did they ask Hughie any questions?"

She finished off the drink. "No. Just came in and cuffed him."

"They take anything?"

"Some of his tools."

Pusser suspected this was a matter of clan justice. I looked around. Whispers, intense stares, nods of understanding. Not of accusation against Hughie so much as of the rightness of using tools to exact justice from the man who'd beat his wife. Clan reality. Clan justice.

Maybe Pusser was right.

Echoes of Hawaiian music followed me outside the back door and mixed with the chirping chorus of crickets. The sun hovered low on the horizon; the dusky sky was blanketed in warm pink hues. I inhaled balmy air laced with the smell of fresh-cut grass and pulled out my cell to call Parks. I needed info on Hughie's arrest, but I pocketed my cell when Colm pulled into the lot.

He parked and came over. "Been reading about the case. Any leads?"

"No. Ears and now a tongue, and we got nothing." Except Hughie, but he didn't do this. I knew the guy. He didn't have the heart for it, or the back.

Colm shook his head. "They're saying eyes next."

"That's how the proverb goes."

"People are worried."

"They should be. He'll strike again. No doubt about it. Unless we already have the culprit in custody. But we don't have proof. Not yet." Both Silvas and Hughie stuck in a cell gave some small comfort, but only if we could nail one of them—Silvas—to the crime.

"That's a lot of pressure." He shifted, lowered his chin, drawing my gaze. "It'd be a lot for anyone. Especially someone fighting to stay sober." My face burned hot, and he noticed. "How are you doing, Brynn?"

"I'm fine."

He studied my eyes, my face.

Okay, so I'd fallen off last night, but it couldn't show, shouldn't show, I thought.

He persisted. "Are you sure?"

"Just drop it, will you?"

"Sorry." He backed off a step, took another tactic. "Your grandmother . . . I just saw her."

"Oh yeah? How was she?"

"Okay. I didn't stay long. Your cousin was with her."

"Meg? I don't think so. She's here at the party."

"No, not Meg. Your other cousin. 'Second cousin,' she said. I'd never seen her before. Didn't get her name. Long blond hair. Said she was from Augusta."

Blond? Augusta?

Katie Doogan.

Gran's room was dark. I left the door open a couple inches for light and went straight to her bedside and peered down at her face. Her chest rose and fell in raspy breaths, and tiny slobber bubbles formed at the corner of cracked lips. But she was okay.

On the nightstand I saw a black baseball cap, the same one Katie had worn that day she tried to run me over. I picked it up, crushed it in my hand.

Gran's eyes flicked open.

I bent, brushed aside a swatch of her gray hair, and kissed her forehead. Her head lolled to the side. She saw the hat in my hands and squirmed, drool sliming her lips as she worked her mouth. No words came out. Frustration stung her eyes. She was paler this evening. Not well.

"It's okay, Gran. It's okay. Don't worry. I'll take care of this. She won't be back, I promise." I pushed a button on the rail and lowered her bed. I snatched a tissue from a nearby box and wiped sweat from her face. "Just rest . . . It's okay."

Her head shrank back into the pillows; her eyes were sunk in two gray pools of puffy skin.

Light flooded the room. I turned as Sadie entered, wheeling a monitor cart. "How are you tonight, Mrs. C.?" She looked my way. "Oh. I didn't know you had a visitor."

"Was someone else here earlier?"

She looked at the computer screen. "Looks like OT came in this afternoon and speech therapy—"

"No. I mean a woman. Blond, petite, pretty?"

"I don't know. I just came on shift. Why? Did something happen?" She paused at Gran's bedside table, threw away crumpled tissues, and cleared a container of uneaten gelatin.

Gran's eyes widened; bloodshot lines radiated from the pupils. Sadie and I both fussed over Gran; then Sadie bent to straighten the blanket. Gran flinched and recoiled, then thrashed her legs. I tried to touch her, calm her, but she was too agitated.

Katie had done this. She'd crossed the line. Anger swelled in me. *If she comes near Gran again, I'll kill her.*

Sadie dimmed the bedside light. "Don't let this upset you, Brynn. It's common for patients like her to have bouts of anger and frustration. It happens all the time."

"I think she's upset about a visitor today. I don't want anyone allowed in here except me and my cousin, Meg. And her priest. That's it." I was going to need someone to stay with her around the clock.

"Okay. I'll make sure the staff knows. I'm sorry if someone upset her. The doctor's prescribed a sedative as needed. I think she'd sleep better . . ."

"I think that's a good idea. I'll stay with her for a while." I sat on the edge of the bed, next to Gran, and stroked her hand, but as soon as Sadie left, Gran pulled away and raised a shaky finger, pointed to her bedside table. Her lips constricted over and over, but no words formed, only growl-like noises, which she emitted in airy, snorty spurts.

"What is it, Gran?"

What is she trying to tell me? I searched the bedside table for her pad and pen, found them, held the pad in front of her, and positioned the pen in the crook of her hand. She strained to connect the pen to the paper. It fell from her grip; I replaced, then again, before she managed a small squiggly S-like mark. Nothing. She fell back against the pillow, her features sagging along with our hope for any sort of communication.

"I'm sorry, Gran." I stretched out next to her, pulled her face nearer until our foreheads touched. "I'm sorry. I'm sorry," I whispered over and over, until I felt her hand, rough and calloused, brush against my cheek. She stared into my eyes. My world slowed, and I saw joy and sorrow, sincerity and truth, Gran's inner essence, a glimpse into a beautiful soul, a flicker of light, and a whisper of hope.

CHAPTER 14

Later that night, I went back to the trailer, went to bed but hardly slept. I rose at dawn, walked Wilco, and sucked down three cups of coffee before heading into work. Fridays were doughnut day, so I headed toward the break room, thinking Parks would be there. I wanted info on Hughie's arrest.

But Harris got to me first. "Got somethin' that might interest you."

"Oh yeah? What's that, Harris?"

He had a mug of coffee in one hand, a breakfast burrito in the other. Wilco sat at his feet, snout raised, drawing in deep breaths of spicy sausage, tangy green peppers, and milky eggs. "Tracked down the registration on the van that tried to kill you. Guess who? Kathleen Doogan. Augusta."

My morning coffee curdled in my stomach. *Stay calm. All he has is a name. Nothing.*

Harris talked with his mouth full, yellow chunks of egg rolling between his tongue and teeth. A bit of egg came out, stuck to his lower lip. He brushed it off. Wilco snarfed it off the floor. "She's married to Kevin Doogan. Your old boyfriend.

Imagine that. Looks like you were screwing around with a married man."

"You don't know anything about it, Harris."

"I know that he disappeared right after Costello's place burned down. There's still a warrant out on him." He scrutinized me. "You're still seeing him, aren't you? That's why the wife is out to kill you."

"No."

He raised his brows. "You're lying. I can tell. You knackers are all about protecting your own, but that ain't goin' to happen this time, Callahan. You're in this deep. I can sense it. And I'm going to find out how."

Parks was in the break room, ripping open a sugar packet. She glanced up, gray shadows arched under her eyes. "Hey. Harris find you?"

"Yeah, he found me."

She looked around, leaned in close. "What's going on, Brynn? Harris's talking about the hit-and-run driver and how she's one of you and that you got a personal connection to her husband, the guy we got pegged for Dublin Costello's murder. Heard him talking to Pusser about it first thing this morning. You got some sort of trouble, Brynn? You can talk to me. I'd understand."

"I did have something going with her husband. Didn't know he was married at the time. As soon as I found out, I broke it off."

"You know about anything that happened between him and Costello?"

"No."

"You haven't seen him since then?"

"No."

She emptied another sugar into her coffee and stirred. "Then why's she coming after you now? After all this time?"

"Hell, I don't know, Parks. She's a freakin' nutcase, that's why. Who knows what she's thinking?" Parks's stare was hard. She held it steady for a couple of beats. Blood rushed through my ears; my throat tightened. There was a half-eaten doughnut on the counter. I picked at it. "What's up with Hughie Black's arrest? What do we have on him?"

"A witness placed him at the bar that night."

"What? Who?" It was unlikely anyone other than a Pavee would recognize Hughie.

"One of the girls at the party that night. Nina's her name."

Of course she gave him up. Nina had a record for stealing. Cops coming around and asking questions would make her nervous. She felt vulnerable. Probably had a load of stuff in her little place, including that haul she had made just yesterday from the luau. It wouldn't be hard for her to give up Hughie to save herself. "What'd she say?"

"She saw him when she was leaving to go home. He was lurking in the parking lot."

Mo would have been in Walker's vehicle out in the lot, making out heavy by then. "Just lurking? No argument or fight?"

"No. No report of fighting. Nina saw Hughie standing by his car out in the lot, waiting around for Mo. Their girls were in the backseat. He questioned Nina about Mo, and she told him that Mo had already left. He got back in the car and drove off."

"You don't believe her?"

"He could have caught up with them somewhere else later. Or could've doubled back. Found her there in the parking lot with Walker, gone off on him, killed him."

"Where's he at?"

"County lockup."

Pusser walked in. I braced myself for an onslaught of questions about Katie Doogan but got something different. "There's a woman up front. Says her husband's missing. Could be tied into our case somehow. You two go talk to her."

* * *

The woman was hunched over the conference table, filling out forms. A couple of flesh rolls filled the gap between a midriff shirt and jean shorts cut indecently low. In the chair next to her, a dirty-faced kid sucked his thumb. I caught a whiff of sour diaper.

Parks and I sat across from her.

"Deputy Parks, and I'm Deputy Callahan."

"Kimber Bannock." Her lips pressed into a thin line as she eyed Wilco, who was sitting between Parks and me. "That dog don't look friendly."

Neither did she: dark hair, hard mouth, a defiant stare.

I shot Parks a look. She was busy scribbling notes, her head down. I kept the conversation going. "You told the officer that your husband is—"

"Ex."

"Excuse me?"

"Ex-husband. Reed. He comes every other Thursday to pick up the kid for the weekend. This is my weekend off, and he ain't nowhere around. The lazy SOB has done this before. I'm sick of it."

I looked at Parks again. "My partner probably gets that. She's got kids of her own. Isn't that right, Parks?"

Parks nodded. Then went back to her notes.

"Yeah? Then you know."

"She knows what, Ms. Bannock?"

"How much of a pain in the ass they are."

My eyes darted to the kid, who was wide eyed, innocent, too thin. He caught me staring, squirmed, and started whimpering. He reached for his mama and got his hand slapped.

"Stop fussin', Noah."

But he kept on. And Kimber grew still and dark, the quiet before the storm, a buildup of electric-like anxiety. I straightened; Wilco's ears alerted. The boy sensed it, too, and came unglued, wails interspersed with little hiccup-like sobs.

Kimber slammed her hand down. "Shut up. Shut up. Shut up . . . !" The words exploded from her mouth. Little Noah shrank back in his chair, trembling.

Parks came alive instantly. "Calm down. You're scaring him." She scooted closer to the kid, touched his hair lightly. Her maternal instinct filled the air with a palpable balm. The kid kept his head down, but his gaze angled up at Parks, and he soaked up her warmth like dry earth sponging up the first rain.

Wilco, never one to miss lapping up positive energy, leaned closer on Parks's other side.

The mother snapped, "Don't tell me to calm down. You don't know nothin' 'bout us." She pushed back from the table, jerked Noah away from Parks, and stood.

I rose up and got in her face. "Sit back down, Kimber." *Wonder how this chick would like it if I picked on her like she picks on her kid?*

She plunked back down and released the boy's arm. Noah sat again, away from Parks, but shot glances her way. A lifeline had been cast, and I knew Noah inwardly clung to it.

I looked over her missing person's form. "You didn't put how long Reed's been missing."

"Well, he was 'pposed to pick up his kid on Thursday, but when he didn't show, I called his work. He works over there at the Oil & Lube on Franklin. You know it?"

"Yeah."

"Well, they said he ain't been there all week, which makes me think he's still up in that hollow. His boss probably fired his ass by now. And he made good money, too. I tell ya, if he don't give me my child support, I'm going to start sellin' some of that crap he's got stored over at my place."

"Hollow?"

"Lickhog Hollow. He spends most his weekends up there."

I knew the area. Thick, dark woods; full of criminal types, mostly moonshiners and small-batch meth operators. Meth. Was that the connection here? "You heard the name Randy Silvas?"

"No."

"Chance Walker?"

Kimber stiffened. "I don't know any of these names, okay?"

"What's Reed doing in Lickhog Hollow?"

"He's an outdoorsman. Likes to camp and stuff. Probably takin' a woman up there. He's got a lot of women."

A lot of women? Is one of them Mo? Could Hughie have gone after two men, both of whom were bedding his wife? I didn't want to believe it, but—

Kimber sneered. "Just like him to do that. Gets whatever he wants from them women, too. A smooth talker."

Yeah, well . . . maybe not now. Hard to smooth talk your way into the girls' pants if someone's cut out your tongue.

CHAPTER 15

The ATVs roared to life, and we fell in line behind Pusser as we entered the narrow trail one by one: Parks, Harris, and me. We were heading into Lickhog Hollow to question some folks Pusser knew and try to get a fix on Reed Bannock. Two things about Bannock's disappearance pointed to the Walker case: Lickhog's reputation for meth operations, which also synced with the Silvas connection, and the timing of Bannock's disappearance. Not much, but at this point, it was all we had. Silvas was still clammed up with his attorney hollering about insufficient evidence. And, from what Kimber had told us, Bannock could be a womanizer on a hell-raising bender. Or he could be hiding in these woods from Kimber—I'd run and hide from that woman—or he could be lost or injured. Could be that he was the second victim or the murderer himself. Only one way to find out.

Two minutes into the woods, my thighs burned from gripping the seat. The terrain was rough, with roots, rocks, and pitted ground tossing my vehicle around. In the carrier attached to the back of my ATV, Wilco hunkered low, head down, but eyes and nose alert. Above us, patches of blue sky peeked through the dark forest canopy like shards of stained glass. Branches whipped by; bugs pelted my sunglasses and stuck to my lips like crunchy crumbs. We continued for about two miles before the trail dwindled and the woods became unnavigable. We cut the engines, got off our ATVs, and regrouped.

Pusser held binoculars to his face and surveyed the woods around us. "The river's just ahead. We'll follow it downstream about a mile. If I remember right, that's where we'll find the Ridleys."

Parks swiped at the beads of sweat on her forehead. "Who are these people?"

"An old family who's lived in this hollow since as long as I can remember. They don't come out much," Pusser said.

Harris spat out a stream of tobacco juice. Wilco scurried for a sniff. "Didn't know we had another clan of crazy-ass gypsies out here."

Pusser's eyes darted to me. "These aren't Travellers. No one knows rightly where they've come from. Maybe they're a mixed people, part black, part Native American, and something else. Dark skinned and blue eyed. Melungeons. They keep to themselves."

Melungeons. Outcasts, like me.

Harris hitched his pants. "My daddy seen a Ridley once when he was out huntin'. Said they look like crazy-eyed inbreeds." He squinted my way. "That's what you get when cousins marry cousins. A bunch of retards. Anyways, my daddy says he don't care to ever see one again."

Pusser dripped sweat. "Don't really give a shit what your daddy thinks, Harris. These people know everything that happens in this part of the woods. If Bannock is up here, they'll know it. And they'll know where he is and what he's doing. Hell, bet you ten to one, the Ridleys already know we're here. Probably watching us, as we speak."

We fell silent. Mosquitoes buzzed, water babbled some-where in the distance, and a high-pitched screech of a bird sliced through the air. Harris set his jaw and puffed out his chest, but the white-knuckle grip around his rifle and his dart-ing eyes gave him away: all bravado and no balls. A dangerous combination.

Pusser shouldered a heavy pack, slid a toothpick between his lips, and headed through the thicket. "Let's go, people." Parks and Harris followed, but I hesitated, scanning the dark shad-ows of the woods and rubbing down the prickles on my arms.

It wasn't the Ridleys or anything Pusser had said, but some-thing felt off about our search. I looked to my dog for cues, as he tended to sense subtle things, but Wilco pushed past me, carefree and eager for adventure, and bounded ahead, ramming his snout between roots and into crevices and stopping to pee here and there, before moving on to the next interesting scent. I shouldered my own pack and followed.

Five minutes later, we came upon the river. About a quarter of a mile downstream, a young boy popped out of the brush with a rifle in his hand. He was maybe ten, barefoot, dark brown skin creased with dirt, and blue eyes partially concealed behind a long lock of jet-black hair. "Whatch ye be wantin' here? This is Ridley land."

Pusser held up his hands. "I'm a friend of your father's."

"What be your name?"

"Pusser. Frank Pusser."

Another kid, this one younger, shot out of the woods and ran past us in a blur. The first kid kept the rifle trained on us. His eyes, large and curious—not scared—took us in; his cheeks reddened as he skimmed over Parks and me.

A few tense moments later, the young kid returned with an older man, bone thin, with strong features and gray-streaked hair.

Pusser stepped forward, hand extended. "Gideon."

"Frank." He took the sheriff's hand, glanced our way but didn't stare. Didn't bother with introductions, either. Just turned and motioned for us to follow.

We did. In silence. Not another word was spoken until we broke into a clearing by the river. Several shanties dotted the opposite shore, slanted and weathered; smoke swirled from a central campfire in gray curlicues against the azure sky. We crossed a hand-fashioned bridge that spanned a narrow part of the river, and approached the encampment. A half-dozen kids milled about, playing and wading in the river shallows, but all activity stopped when they caught sight of us. Wilco sniffed at one of the toddler's feet. He burst into tears and ran to his mother's arms.

Out of one of the shanties came a woman, plump, with a tight gray bun and a face like dried potato peels. I guessed her to be Gideon's wife. We settled in some chairs on the porch, a shallow overhang providing relief from the sun's glare. The woman sat on the ground, gawking at Parks and me, her eyes taking in every detail of our clothing and hair, then getting stuck on the gold band on Park's left hand.

Pusser yanked off his pack and unzipped it. "I brought some things for your family."

Gideon leaned forward, lips widening over broken teeth. Pusser pulled out several pairs of socks, spices, a package of hard candies, and a pair of leather work gloves. Gideon handled each item with care. "Thank you, my friend." He looked to his wife, who gathered the things with a grateful nod and took them into the shanty.

After she left, Gideon turned to Pusser. His eyes grew thoughtful. "It's been a long time."

"I know."

"You used to come by for visits now and then. Been so long that my boys don't recognize you no more."

Pusser's gaze flicked my way, then to the ground. He blinked a few times, as if blotting out a distant memory.

Gideon spoke softly. "You ever find her?"

Pusser's features sagged. "No. Never."

We sat silently, their cryptic conversation sinking into our minds. They were talking about Jo, Pusser's missing daughter. I was surprised Gideon knew about Jo, since Pusser rarely discussed her. Grabowski knew about her. He'd been on the force with Pusser when she went missing. He had let me in on a little bit of the story, had said that Pusser suspected Jo's boyfriend, a boy from our clan, a Doherty, one of Dee's cousins, had taken her away or killed her. No one had been able to prove anything, though, and Jo had never been found. If it was true, no one would likely ever know. It'd been over twenty years now, a long time, but the pain my boss carried was still fresh. Grief was like that. The pain of profound loss messed with a person's sense of time.

Gideon offered a brief smile. "Don't you be givin' up hope, Frank."

Pusser nodded and cleared his throat. "We're looking for a man named Reed Bannock." He held up a photo we'd been able to get from Kimber. "His wife says he's been coming to the hollow for a while now. Have you seen him?"

Gideon took the photo between calloused fingers, squinted, and then raised his other hand and made a motioning gesture. The boy who'd held us at gunpoint earlier came forward. "You seen this man, Asher?"

Asher stared at the photo for a few seconds and nodded.

"Where'd you see him, boy?"

"Down yander 'bout two mile. He was carryin' a large pack and heading into the woods by where the river forks off to the Li'l Branch."

Parks took out her notebook and scribbled notes.

"When was this?" Pusser asked.

The boy jammed his hands into his pockets and lowered his gaze. "A few days back, there 'bouts. He'd been actin' like he plum out of his mind."

"How's that?"

"Lookin' over his shoulder like he was runnin' scared. Cryin' like a girl."

His daddy asked, "Any critters 'bout? Bear?"

"Naw. Weren't nothing after him, Pa. Just him jabberin' like there was someone with him, but there weren't nobody there."

Jabbering meant his tongue was intact, at least at that point. Maybe Bannock was just a negligent parent, after all. But running scared? Like a hunted animal? If negligence was his only crime, he wouldn't be running scared like that.

But a potential victim would.

CHAPTER 16

Gideon sent Asher with us to search for Bannock. The boy slipped through the woods like a sparrow flitted through underbrush. Kid had to keep stopping and wait for us to catch up as he led us from the Ridleys' settlement to where he'd last spied Bannock. We went upriver about a half mile first and continued to the point where the Jones River forked. Then we followed what Asher had called the Li'l Branch, a slower-moving tributary.

We walked the edge of the river where possible and trudged the shallows when the bank was too narrow or corroded to navigate. My boots were mud-caked, my socks were soaked through, and the stench of stagnant, slimy river water coated the back of my throat. Parks looked sick to her stomach, Harris cursed with every step, and Pusser struggled to keep up the rear. A fine-looking bunch of law we made.

Only Wilco looked happy with this woodsy trek. He stayed right behind Asher, slightly ahead of me, his three paws sloshing along the riverbank as he bent here and there to lap at the water. The rest of the group fell farther behind.

"Hold up a minute, Asher," I said.

The kid turned and cocked his head at me, gave the group a look. He nodded. The others slowed, with a look of gratitude. Pusser was fatiguing, his breath coming in raspy spurts and his face drained of color. He was too out of shape to keep up. Dead weight. And he was on me for my issues? He needed to take a long look at himself.

That's unfair. Pusser's been good to me. More so than most settled folks. He could have canned me a long time ago for my drinking. This bit with the addiction meetings was his way of trying to help me. That's all.

Yet just a couple days ago, I'd lied to him about the whiskey I'd sucked down. I shook my head. *There's no saving someone like me.*

"What are you thinking, Callahan?"

I turned around and looked at Pusser, who'd finally caught up. "What do you mean?"

"You're shaking your head."

"I was thinking about what the kid said." I pointed up ahead, past Asher, who was scouting the riverside. "That Bannock left the river and moved into the woods. Stupid thing to do. Leaving his water source, especially in this heat."

"On the run maybe. Gideon's boy said that Bannock seemed scared of something."

"Here!" came Asher's voice.

I raised my hand. "This way, everyone." I moved ahead and then squatted where Asher stood, pointing at the ground.

Asher looked at Pusser. "This is where that man left the river. I 'member them trees"—he pointed up—"and the man headed right through there."

I looked about, saw the disturbance on the forest floor, a couple dislodged rocks and, a little higher up, a bent sapling, a few broken twigs. I turned back to Pusser. "Looks right."

The boy was already turning to leave.

"Asher," Pusser said to stop him. "Thank you, son."

The boy's brow creased, whether in acknowledgment or discomfort, I couldn't tell. Then he turned and headed back the way we'd come.

"Prints?" Pusser turned to me.

"No. Snapped branches and disturbances in the ground cover, but no prints. But he could have come through before the storm the other night, and the rain washed away the prints." I got a visual fix on Wilco, motioned for him to come closer while I pulled a water bottle from my pack, then took a swig, cupped my hand, and poured some for him.

We continued tracking for another mile or so, deeper into the woods. The trees became denser; the forest closed in, shutting out the sunlight. Vultures circled overhead. I looked up, wondering what they'd ... Then it hit me. A smell. Like a mix between rancid meat and feces. Decay. But not human decay, because Wilco didn't react, but something else.

Harris gagged. "What's that smell?"

Pusser spit out his toothpick. "Something dead."

A few more steps and we heard the electric buzz of flies. Thousands of flies.

I watched the ground, picking my steps carefully, almost running into Pusser's back when he stopped.

"No one move." His face drained of color. "It's a damn punji pit. This trail's rigged."

I pulled my rifle forward, on guard and ready. Parks did the same. I scoped the woods, my blood pulsing, my breath like a tornado inside my head. We were vulnerable; anyone could be out there, ready to pick us off, one by one.

But there was nothing. No movement, nothing but a small breeze swaying the forest canopy, and with it the lingering smell of rotting animal, and something else ... wood smoke.

"Campfire. Not far," I said.

I zeroed in on Wilco and motioned him to my side. He loped over, head high, sampling the air as he moved. Not a care in the world. As soon as he reached my side, I squatted and attached his lead and reeled him in close.

I looked over Pusser's shoulder. The razor-sharp chiseled points of a dozen or more sticks poking up from a hole in the ground had impaled the fly-infested carcass of a large animal. Fleshy meat still clung to the animal's rib cage; severed flesh dangled around a headless neck; four hooved legs stuck out straight to the side. If Wilco had fallen in that pit . . .

Harris and Parks lowered their weapons and picked their way toward us.

"Damn," Harris said. "It's a big animal. It's a . . ."

"It's a horse," Pusser said.

Parks covered her mouth. "Why would someone kill a horse?"

I pointed at the neck. "And then take its head? Another animal didn't do this. Those cuts along the edge of the neck bone look like chop marks. A hatchet probably."

Pusser shook his head. "Someone take a few photos. Then let's stay on track. Exercise caution, people. We don't know what we're up against."

CHAPTER 17

Parks snapped a few photos with her phone, and then we moved on, single file, Pusser and I and Wilco in the lead, then Parks. Harris took up rear guard. The path narrowed, almost fading into nothing; brush and branches scraped at my body like a thousand sharp claws. Shades of green foliage surrounded us, and everywhere I looked there were clumps of sticker bushes, and as my dog moved through them, his fur snagged the stickers up like a magnet. Another hour of grooming tonight.

I knew more than most deputies might about tracking, though my experience worked better in desert sand than in mountainous deep woods. Pusser had been certified in tracking who knew how many years ago, though I doubted he'd kept up any practice, considering his, well, lack of finesse, let alone stamina, on this hike. Thankfully, Bannock had even less finesse: his path remained clear enough for some time. Only the farther we went, the denser the vegetation, with underbrush and a lot of forest-type litter: leaves, twigs, fallen branches . . . ideal for hiding traps, more punji sticks, or trip wires. So, we slowed our pace and moved low and fluid, like snakes slithering through the underbrush, our eyes scanning the ground for both tracks and traps.

"Shh!" Pusser motioned to us.

We stopped. Overhead, distant voices carried through the trees. A low mumble at first, then growing more distinct as we moved forward. Just chatter. Nothing that indicated stress or agitation or alarm. Our presence had gone undetected.

We came upon a web of zip lines strung between trunks, homemade tree stands, then sheets of plywood propped against tree trunks. The setup reminded me of the equipment used for military combat drills. A little farther up the trail, an old Buick, maybe ten years old, not even as old as my station wagon, sat peppered with rusting bullet holes. Whoever was up here, they took their training seriously.

The breeze picked up again, and the smell of burned coffee reached my nostrils. Wilco's too. He lifted his snout and took a deep drag. The sounds were louder now and more distinct: voices, a man laughing, a small engine revving. . . . We were close to encountering the target.

Pusser motioned for us to spread wide, a flanking maneuver of sorts. Harris and Parks provided cover, while Pusser, Wilco, and I went straight in and attempted to make peaceful contact.

A sharp rattling sound pierced the air, like a thousand rattlesnakes trapped in a metal drainpipe.

We froze. Coiled concertina wire, partially hidden by brush and laced with rock-filled beer cans, spread before us. Parks was on the ground, her leg caught in the barbs of the wire. She wiggled silently, trying to free her skin from the metal claws.

I dropped Wilco's leash and rushed to help her.

Gunfire cracked overhead.

We crouched low, weapons drawn. I drew my pistol and crouched over Parks, shielding her. Wilco, deaf to the sounds, remained rooted, his snout raised, muscles quivering. I searched the surrounding trees. Nothing. Harris started to move, and a shot zinged overhead, splintered bark off a nearby tree.

"McCreary County Sheriff's Department!" Pusser yelled. In the next second, we were surrounded by a half-dozen heavily armed men in full combat gear.

Pusser shouted again. "Sheriff's department!"

A bearded man spoke. "No shit? We thought you might be forest fairies. You're outnumbered here, boys." He looked at Parks and me. "And ladies."

They remained in formation, weapons raised. They were a motley group: old, young, short, tall. And there was a woman, jeans and T-shirt, a long ponytail, mean face, with silver-ringed fingers clasping an AR15. She worried me.

So did Harris, who stood off to the side, shoulders back and chest puffed up, like he was ready to take on the whole damn crew.

Pusser stood up straight and lowered his gun. "We came to talk, that's all."

I holstered my pistol. If these guys were going to kill us, they would have already done it. Or if they wanted to, my pistol wasn't going to be much defense against a dozen or more automatic rifles. I turned away and untangled the wire from Parks's leg. A moan rumbled deep in her throat as razor-sharp barbs tore at her flesh. Sweat stains grew along her hairline; she went pale; a bloodstain seeped through and spread over her pant leg.

"Easy, Parks. I've got something to take care of this." I motioned for Wilco, removed some antiseptic and a leg wrap from his vest pouch, and went to work on the injured leg.

The ponytailed woman inched toward me and zeroed in on Wilco, her left eye twitching.

Another man stepped up, buff, buzz cut, and an unwavering gaze. He carried an AR15 with a customized mag, a Glock in his waistband, a bowie sheathed on his right outer thigh and, if I was right, a smaller-caliber pistol concealed on his left inner ankle. This man left little to chance.

He gave Harris an up and down, smirked, and then addressed Pusser. "What do you want here? This is private property, and we're within our constitutional rights."

"Understood. We're not here to argue that. We need to speak to whoever is in charge."

"I'm in charge."

"Don't trust them, Viper." The woman's knuckles were white around the grip of her gun. The barrel bounced nervously.

I finished with the leg and slowly stood.

She shook her gun at me. "Stay back."

I raised my hands. "Hey, relax. Okay?"

"Ease up, Crystal." Viper's eyes took me in, moved over my scarred neck. I kept my posture neutral, but the assessment unnerved me.

Pusser spoke up. "We're here looking for a couple missing men. We have a report that one was seen heading toward your camp two days ago." He slowly opened his jacket, with two fingers pulled out a printout of Walker and Bannock, and held it up.

Viper squinted at the paper. "I've never seen these men."

Wilco moved closer to Crystal and inhaled the air around her legs. She frowned and shuffled back.

Pusser held up the printouts. "Anyone else seen these men? Their names are Walker and Bannock."

Grunts and murmurs, but no solid answers.

Viper looked around, then back at Pusser. "Looks like you got your answer. No one's seen them. You can go back now."

Pusser didn't seem satisfied. "You men have horses up here?"

Viper shifted. "No."

"There's a horse carcass about a mile down trail. Headless."

"I've seen it."

"No idea how it got there?"

"No."

"It's on your land."

The bearded man spat out a line of dark saliva. "Someone must've been trespassing. Sort a like y'all are doing right now."

The air crackled with tenseness. Viper's jaw tightened. "No one here knows anything about the horse. Or the missing men."

The sound of Wilco's growls drew my attention back. His ears flattened; his tail went rigid; his eyes trained on the woman. I glanced around. The leash was on the ground on the other side of my dog. I reached out to tap his haunches and get his attention so I could rein him back.

The woman misread my movement and panicked. "Don't move!"

I didn't.

Wilco, his back to me, sensed something. His stare locked on the woman; his lips curled as he snarled.

"Get," she said. Then louder. "Get, dog!"

"He can't hear—"

She kicked out her leg, and her foot connected with the tip of his snout. A sharp yelp cut through the air, followed by a series of snarls.

"Stop! He can't hear you."

Wilco snapped at her leg.

She leaned back and aimed the gun. I lunged forward and knocked the barrel away as I stepped in and threw my other elbow at her face. It connected with a loud thunk. Her head jerked back, eyes rolled, arms went slack, gun fell to the ground, legs buckled, and down she went.

"Crystal!" The bearded guy ran over and crouched by her side. "Crystal, baby."

I took the opportunity to grab the lead and pull Wilco back. He still snarled at the downed woman.

Viper had his gun raised again, trained on Pusser. "Now would be a good time for y'all to leave."

A few hours later, I was back at my desk, a strange brew of anxiety and anger zinging through me like a thousand tiny lightning bolts. I'd run into these paramilitary types before, and for the most part, they were law-abiding citizens, but I wanted more information on this particular group.

I bent down to where Wilco was curled at my feet, and ran my hand along his back, snagged a couple cockleburs, and gave them a yank. His head whipped around, jaw snapping. I jerked back—apparently, Wilco was in a bad mood, too. I turned to my computer; my fingers stuttered over the keyboard as I plugged key terms into the search venue of one of our databases. Several names popped onto the screen: Mountain Militia, Three Percenters, Black Robes. . . .

"Heard what happened out in the woods today." Jake Sheehan pulled up a chair. "Glad you're okay."

The punji pit; the speared horse; a dozen or more well-armed men; and the crazy ponytailed woman, Crystal, or whatever, garbed in military gear . . . "Nothing I couldn't handle."

"That's right. You were a lady Marine."

"Marine."

"Huh?"

"Marine, just Marine . . . Never mind. Is that why you're here? To see if I'm okay?" My tone was pissy. Anxiety did that to me.

His brows shot up. "No. I came by to see about the case."

My eyes grazed the curve of his lips, his jawline, shoulders, his chest. I'd been ticked because he'd pretended to be checking on me. Now I felt angry because he wasn't. Poor guy wasn't going to win. Apparently, I wasn't, either.

I tried to get back on track. "The group looked part military, part survivalist. Probably ex-military or trained security. A dangerous mix, if you ask me."

Yes, a dangerous mix . . . just like my Vicodin-depleted brain and your hot body. Dangerous for me, that is. That slip with the whiskey had set me back. And now a clawing need for another fix kicked my brain into overdrive. Sex opened the floodgates of hormonal dopamine, but that kind of chemically induced fix was coupled with nasty social stigmas and guilt. Even worse: entitlement and expectations from the other half of the equation. The last thing I needed now. Yet here he was. . . .

Wilco whimpered. I blinked, shifted, and looked down. Head tilted, ears cocked, brown eyes wide with question, he'd sensed the shift in my emotions.

Jake leaned in and looked over my shoulder. "What'd you find?"

I cleared my throat. "Local militia groups."

Wilco got up and sniffed Jake's hand, then nudged it with his nose, drawing Jake's attention away from my screen and from me. A stupid streak of jealousy set my nerves on edge. "Who do you think we're dealing with?" he asked, running his fingers between Wilco's ears. Fingers that could be running over my . . . *Stop it, Brynn!*

"We don't have a fix on who they are or their motive. Remember that strip mine that was slated for the southern part of the county a few years back? There was a huge opposition to it. The opposition organized, things got heated, and the mining company hired that group . . ."

"Patriotic Security Force." He settled back in his chair and nodded. "Highly skilled. Intimidating as hell. I see what you're saying. They served their purpose. Maintained the peace until the problem was resolved."

"Yeah, and the county didn't have the manpower to cover the situation."

"You think Bannock's involved with that group?"

"We're not even sure that Bannock was with that group in the woods. The head guy, Viper, said he'd never seen him."

"You believe him?"

I shrugged. "Pusser has someone else working that angle. I've been looking into connections between Bannock and Walker."

"Found any?"

I shook my head. "Nothing distinct. They're both home-grown boys. Went to the same high school, but different years. That's all I've got."

"That's not much. We've got just one high school. Everyone goes there. I went there."

"Did you know these guys?"

"No. I was ten years out of school by that time."

I looked up, a bit surprised.

He grinned. "I'm old."

Looking good to me. I avoided his grin, got back to the subject. I explained to him about Silvas and the possible meth connection, especially if Bannock was spending time in Lickhog Hollow, but maybe there was a paramilitary connection, though neither guy's background check showed military service. Then there were the women: Nikki the prostitute, and Kimber, and my own friend Mo, all more connections to consider. And Hughie . . . "What's Hughie's status?"

"Still in custody. We haven't filed official charges yet." He slowly stood.

My eyes slid down to what the bad girl in me wanted most, and I shot my head back to the computer screen. *Get your head on straight, Brynn.*

He said, "I'd better get back to my office. Want to do dinner later?"

Tempting. So tempting. "Can't tonight. Sorry. One of our witnesses was transferred from holding last night. Suicidal. Parks and I are going to check in on her before going home." And I needed to see Gran. And talk to Meg. And . . .

"You and Parks?"

"Yeah. Why?"

"Just saw her. She didn't look so good. Said something about heading home."

"Her leg got chewed up by some barbwire." We'd patched it up, and she seemed fine. . . . Something niggled at my mind.

Parks had been tired lately and sick to her stomach. Not that I was surprised, considering what we were dealing with, but I wondered . . .

"Tomorrow maybe?" Jake asked.

I tilted my head, saw the bland, casual look to his hazel eyes, as if a steak and fries were all he had in mind. Like he hadn't been thinking the same things I'd been thinking. Maybe he hadn't. Then again, maybe he had. "Sure. But I pick the place. Wear a suit. I'll pick you up at four."

He turned, with a slow grin.

CHAPTER 18

Harris and I met up Saturday morning to interview Nikki. She was standing at the hospital room's sink, looking into the mirror. The room stank. No amount of antiseptic could cover the chemical tang of her body sweat.

"Ghost." Her voice was weak, barely a whisper. "Look at me. I'm a ghost."

I looked back at Harris. He was round eyed and flushed, fidgeting with his utility belt. "I'll handle this," I told him.

Nikki had spent the past twelve hours on suicide watch, having been transported from her holding cell to McCreary County Hospital after she became despondent. So, we were back for round two with Nikki, walking a fine line between not wanting to upset her more and getting information from her that may uncover a killer or even save someone's life.

Wilco would have helped me walk that line. I'd seen it before, the calming effect he had on people. I'd seen him terrorize people, too, but he seemed to sense the difference between the good guys and the bad guys and knew when someone needed unbiased affection or simply something soft to touch. But the hospital was a hotbed of decay: cadavers, blood and body fluids, and strips of flesh and surgically removed organs . . . all too much for his nose. So, I'd left him secured in the cruiser, with the air running.

My own fingers itched for his soft fur as I crossed to the vanity and stood next to Nikki, studied her face in the mirror. Gaunt, hollow, yellowish gray, with bloodless, cracked lips . . . death warmed over. *Yes, Nikki, like a ghost.*

She coughed, deep and dry, then gagged.

I reached out. "Nikki, are you . . . ?"

She bent forward and spat into the sink. *Plink.* A tooth, yellow and brown with rot, stuck in the drain stopper. She stared into the mirror, then bent forward until her nose touched the glass, her eyes owl-like, dark and dead, her breath making a foggy little circle as she said, "Demons are comin' to kill me."

I know the feeling. "Not today. Not here in the hospital. You're safe here, Nikki."

She didn't move. Just stared at herself with that blank expression. Like a zombie. Maybe the final apocalypse has nothing to do with bombs or global warming, but drugs. Life-sucking drugs that leave their victims catatonic. The real walking dead.

I placed my hand gently on her upper arm. "Come on, Nikki. Let's get you back in bed."

She flinched and recoiled at my touch. I pulled my hand back and folded my arms, then leaned against the counter. The hospital room was bleak, curtains drawn, lights dimmed low. The television on, tuned to a cooking show, the volume nothing but a low hum, which blended with the chorus of hissing machines and beeping monitors.

"Nikki. Officer Harris and I are here to ask you a few more questions."

"I saw 'em, the evil one, in my cell, sniffing round my bedsheets, tryin' to get to me."

"Just bad dreams, Nikki. It's the drugs. Your mind's playing tricks on you." I waited for a second, letting it soak in, hoping that I was getting through to her. "Let's talk about Chance Walker, your boyfriend. How'd you two meet?"

She reached into the sink, picked up the tooth, and rolled it between her thumb and forefinger.

"Was he a client?"

She laughed, then stopped and stared blankly at the tooth. "I was just tryin' to forget. That's all I was doin'. That's why I tried it in the first place."

"Meth?"

"It grabbed hold of me like nothin' else. I can't shake it."

That's how it works. Take the wrong thing, and there's no going back. My meds were different, were needed, designed to help people like me. That's why I could quit. But dabble in meth or heroin, and you're screwed. Luckily, I was smarter than that. But I wanted to see this woman live. I thought about the group, about Josh and Juan and even crazy-eyed Mitch. They were making it. *Maybe . . . just maybe . . .*

"Nikki, there are people who want to help you. I want to help you."

Her gaze turned hard. "You're lyin'. You don't want to help me. Nobody does. I'm gonna get killed. That's what's gonna happen to me. They're gonna kill me dead."

I glanced at Harris. He shrugged.

"Who, Nikki? Who's going to kill you?"

She stiffened; a tremor overcame her. "I don't mind dyin', I don't. If someone was to say that there ain't no heaven, I'd laugh at 'em, I would. I know there's a heaven, cuz I've seen hell, and if there's evil, there's got to be Jesus, right?"

Harris rolled his eyes.

I turned back to Nikki. "That's right. And you can get better. It'll take hard work, but—"

"I got strong belief in Jesus, I do. That's why I told what I did. Shouldn't have. I know that now. Yes, I do. Cuz they're comin' for me now."

"Who?"

Her eyes darted back and forth. "Jesus, sweet Jesus!" Was she answering my question or just scared to death now?

I shook my head.

Harris stood. "She's nuts. Let's go. I got better things to do."

"Yeah, me too." We all had better things to do. Harris probably had a date. I had a wedding to go to. I leaned in and wrapped my arms around Nikki. She didn't recoil, just sort of sank into me. "We'll come back soon, okay?"

I looked back as we left. Nikki was looking in the mirror, mouth open, trying to stick her tooth back into the gum.

CHAPTER 19

Dee's wedding day, and it was raining. A torrential downpour, actually. Bad luck, as most Pavees would say—we're a superstitious lot. Each drop of rain supposedly marked the future tears of the bride-to-be. There was talk that the ceremony might be postponed, but in the end, Dee listened to the well-meaning advice of those around her.

"Don't put it off, Dee."

"No, dear."

"You remember what happened last time."

Like she could forget. The marriage arranged, the dowry paid, and there stood Dee at the altar, by herself. Jilted. Poor Dee. That was ten years ago. No one could even recall the guy's name . . . something Hurly—he was from another clan—but they remembered Dee standing there alone, mascara stains on white lace, while her mother struggled to make excuses. Dee had gone down in Traveller history as the "bride who wasn't," a legend or a stigma. It was hard to say which.

But however you looked at it, today was her chance for redemption, and the rain wasn't going to stop her. Her family had spared no expense. Travellers had come from around the country for this wedding, extra RVs, campers, and trailers clogging up Bone Gap's roads. It was *krosh*, the season of coming and going, when our men travelled for cash-paying jobs, but still, they came to Bone Gap today to help Dee celebrate. The clan was that way. Like one big family. A dysfunctional family, but still . . .

And here we were. I'd chosen a back pew. Out of sight and out of mind, or so I'd hoped. Not true. Heads turned, then bent inward, and whispers passed through tight lips, peppered with such words as *graansha, buffer, gorger*. . . . Whatever name came to mind, they all meant the same thing. *Outsider.* I should be grateful they weren't meant for me. Not this time. And they would never be meant for the "good girl" Meg, who sat to my right. No, these barbed words were aimed toward my guest, Jake Sheehan.

He fidgeted with his tie and leaned in close. "You sure I should be here? This wasn't what I had in mind when I asked you out."

I stifled a smirk. An evil part of me enjoyed seeing the discomfort any buffer felt in our midst. The same kind of crawling-skin feeling I felt in the middle of settled folk half the time. *Buffer.* The term fit Jake in other ways, too. I glanced over, saw the way his suit fit his body—*nice*—and caught a whiff of his cologne, woodsy and spicy. I had left Wilco home but knew his nose would have enjoyed the scent, too, though not for my salacious reasons. "Yes. I'm sure."

He'd dressed up, as directed. A nice pale gray suit, dark blue tie, something sharp for most occasions, but dull at a Traveller wedding, where men and women created a collage of sherbet colors with sprinkles on top. Hats and hats; and dresses of every shade, low cut and bedazzled; Caribbean brown spray tans and glistening jewels.

I'd borrowed one of Meg's dresses, sage green and sleeveless and off shoulder. The bodice and waist were formfitting; the bottom hem skimmed mid-thigh, modest by the standards of the women around us. Not exactly my style, though I had no idea what "my thing" in a dress might even be anymore. Too many uniforms had filled my past wardrobe. My neck and some shoulder scars showed, but the overall effect felt, well, presentable enough. A touch of mascara and lipstick, a little more back-combing at my stubborn cowlick, and I'd figured I wouldn't stand out too awkwardly. Unlike Mo, whose presence felt like a black eye on a princess. She sat with her head down, wearing a black lace shawl over slumped shoulders. A dark dot in a sea of color, Mo was flanked by Queenie, her loyal friend, and Nina, the backstabbing traitor who had ratted out Hughie. Nina leaned into Mo and whispered something, caught my stare and wheeled back around.

That's right, Nina. I know what you did.

The bride's family, the Doherty clan, took to the left side of the sanctuary, a large family and large people, happy and jolly and dark and hairy, most of the men with long, curly beards and the women with flowing dark locks. Black Irish? Lots of speculation there, but no one really knew for sure. On the right side, their antithesis, the groom's family, the O'Neils. A skeletal people, blondish-red hair, almost a pinkish color, which seemed to blend with their skin. Monotones. In appearance only, though. Their tempers flared red hot.

If ya know what's good for yer, don't cross an O'Neil.

I glanced up at today's keynote O'Neil: the groom. Baby-blue tux hanging on his thin frame, white shirt unbuttoned low, and a heavy gold chain with a crucifix cradled in a tangled nest of reddish-gold hair. Riley O'Neil was dressed to impress.

The organ started up, and a hush fell over the church.

The double doors in the back of the sanctuary opened.

And we stood, heads turned, and excited murmurs filled the church.

First, the flower girls, princess-styled hair, makeup, high heels wobbling down the aisle, and rose petals scattering. A slicked-up boy, pillow in hand and a devilish grin on his face, and then a stream of crimson red ruffles floated down the aisle. Dee's first cousins, five in all, big dresses, big hair, and big smiles—everything about a Pavee wedding is big—and then the moment, Dee herself, an angelic vision in lace and sequins, on the arm of her proud father.

I caught a flash of movement behind Dee, in the back of the church. A figure, short and petite, hair and face partially obscured behind a dark chapel veil. My heart kicked up. It was Katie. Our eyes met. A taunting grin, and then she was gone, having slipped back through the door like a ghost. And not the holy type, but the devil herself.

Jake noticed me looking. "What is it?"

"Nothing." Oh, it was something, alright, but nothing I could do anything about at this moment. My gut churned. She'd tried to kill me, and she'd intimidated Gran. The last burned me the most. But if I jumped up now and ran to find her, I'd only make myself the object of scorn. She knew that. And she'd be long gone by the time I catapulted through the wedding spectators.

I turned back to the front. Prayers and more prayers, songs, and bells, standing, kneeling, sitting, more kneeling, vows and rings, and Holy Communion, and we were almost there. Dee glowed; Riley blanched. He looked sick. About to faint?

Too late to back out now, buddy. You're trapped.

And then it was done. A final blessing and the couple faced their guests. Whoops rang out, and music started up, bold and lively, all in anticipation of what was to come.

The party.

* * *

The reception was held in a hotel in downtown McCreary. Dinner was served and cleared away, and the music started. Dee and Riley's reception was in full swing: thumping music, hazy chatter, bodies gyrating and swaying and touching, lots of touching. Jake was touching me. His hand on my shoulder at first, a quick squeeze, and a look, the type of look that lingers and searches and invites. Then a slower song, and his hand moved to the small of my back and lower. I let him. It felt good, flattering.

After the song, we found a table in the corner. He disappeared and came back with a couple drinks. "Your friend knows how to throw a party. A lot of booze here."

I glanced at my drink, hopeful, but it was just water.

He smirked. "I think it's a good thing I'm here with you."

"Might be."

"Is that a problem? Do you wish I wasn't?"

"No. Not at all. No problem." But another hour from now and we'd be the only sober people in the room. Then it might be a problem. I kept my eyes on the new Mrs. O'Neil. Dee didn't look all that happy. Regrets already?

Jake and I talked about Bone Gap and my friends and growing up Pavee and his childhood, which was the opposite of mine, normal and happy, with two parents and a nice house. Probably had a damned white picket fence, but I didn't get a chance to ask, because a ruckus broke out across the room, where a swishing of colored dresses circled like a corona around a brewing storm.

Dee's voice rose loud and clear above the commotion. "Don't run your mouth about me, girl."

Dee had made it clear that Riley's "bitch of a sister," Elva O'Neil, hadn't been invited, apparently to avoid conflict, but slighting Elva had only fueled an already building maelstrom, and here she was, tall, stringy, unhappy, and verbal. "The truth hurts, don't it, Dee? No one else would have you." Onlookers gasped, a couple giggled, and Elva drew a deep breath and went on. "Papa didn't give Riley any choice, and you know it, or he'd never have married a leftover bride like you."

Dee's cheeks puffed, and she spat out, "Riley and I love each other, and we're married, so deal with it."

With that, Riley stepped forward—finally—and stood his powder-blue-tuxed self in front of his bride. He looked down at her, and after a blink he said, "That's enough. Leave, Elva."

Dee took her husband's arm, cast a final dismissive nod toward Elva, and the cluster of spectators dispersed like clouds after a storm. And just like that, the parameters of their marriage had been set.

A Pavee wedding never went off without some sort of drama.

I turned back around. Jake grinned, shook his head at the scene, and then the conversation found its way back to the case.

"How'd your interview go with Nikki?" he asked.

"Not good. She's pretty messed up." I told him about her hallucinations, her fear of evil people coming after her. "She's paranoid and suicidal. I feel bad for her."

Jake responded, but I wasn't listening now, as my eyes widened at the sight of Kevin Doogan talking to Meg across the room. There was a warrant out for his arrest. Why would he risk coming out in the open like this? And here I sat with the assistant DA.

Jake followed my gaze. "What is it? Is something wrong?"

"No. Nothing. Sorry." I looked him straight in the face, gave a slight smile, to pull his gaze from where Doogan stood. It worked. Until someone approached, and Jake looked up.

It was Meg, thank God. I introduced her to Jake, shot a quick glance across the room. No Doogan.

"Dee wants to talk to you," she told me. "Said to meet by the restrooms. It's something important. Can't wait." Meg never lied. Never. I took "Dee" not as our newly wed friend, Dee, but as *D*, the first letter of Kevin Doogan's last name. I excused myself.

No one was waiting for me by the restrooms, not Dee or Doogan. I lingered for a moment, not sure what to do, then noticed an exit door at the end of the hallway. It was propped open. I headed that way and found Doogan outside, in the back alley of the hotel.

"What are you doing here? You're wanted for—"

"I know. I had to talk to you. It's Katie. I think she's here and I wanted to warn you."

"Oh, yeah, she's here, alright. I just saw her at the wedding." Doogan took a quick look around. "She's really crazy, Brynn."

"I can take care of myself. But she was in my grandmother's room at the nursing home."

"Is your grandmother okay?"

"Yes. I've got someone with her around the clock. But if she hurts Gran, I would—"

"I talked to my mother. I'm driving down to Augusta and getting the kids. I've got a friend in Texas. I'm taking them down there for a while."

"Kidnapping?"

"What the hell am I supposed to do? Can't trust Katie with the kids, and what type of judge would give me custody? I'm a convict, on the run. She has no record."

"She's stalking me."

His features softened. "Brynn, I'm sorry I pulled you into this mess. Katie was always . . . different. After our youngest was born, it got worse. She didn't sleep enough, wouldn't take the antianxiety meds the doctors prescribed, and she had a breakdown. She still needs help, but she won't get it. I don't know what to do anymore."

"What is it that she wants from me?"

"In her sick mind, she blames you for everything that's happened between her and me. She blames you for wrecking our marriage."

"You're the one who wrecked your marriage. I didn't even know you were married. Have you told her that?"

"I tried."

"Really? Because she's trying to kill *me*, not you." We stood next to a big Dumpster. The smell of rotten garbage rose up and settled around us. "And now you're what? Running away to Texas, while I stay here and deal with your lunatic of a wife. What you did for Gran was noble, right, and I'll never forget it. But now?" I turned away, ready to head back inside. "You're a coward, Doogan."

He grabbed my arm and spun me back around. My foot slipped on the trash at my feet, and I bounced against the Dumpster beside us. I heard a mouse or rat or something scurry away.

"Listen to me," he said. "I'm not a coward."

I tried to pull back, but his grip tightened.

"You don't understand, Brynn. Something like this happened before."

"She tried to kill someone else?"

He dropped my arm. "Not exactly. She goes to extremes to stop anyone from taking someone she loves. Last year, after I got out of the pen, I wanted to give my boy something special. So I bought him a puppy. And he loved it, took good care of it, too. But Katie ... Well, she hated that dog. Every accident, every time he chewed someone's shoe, she'd fly off the handle. She wanted to take it to the pound, but the boy pitched such a fit. Then one day he said he loved that dog more than anything ..." Doogan looked out over the alley, his next words slow and methodical. "And she believed him. The next day, we found the dog dead."

"She killed your son's dog? Why . . . ? Who would do such a—"

Then it occurred to me that Katie stopped by the wedding for one reason: to confirm that I was there and not at home with my dog.

Wilco!

CHAPTER 20

Some dogs get ticked when their owners leave them home alone. They plot revenge: dump the garbage, pee in the corner, chew sofa cushions. When I left Wilco home—which was rare—he waited, loyal and happy, nose pressed against the front window, tail high and swishing. Not tonight. We pulled up to the trailer; the lights were on, the curtains drawn, but no Wilco.

And the front door stood ajar.

I jumped out of the car and raced inside, Jake right behind me. "Wilco! Wilco!" He was deaf, couldn't hear me, but still I screamed, my throat constricting with emotion, my calls turning raspy and wet. "Wilco!"

"He's here, here," Jake called from my bedroom. I rushed in. He stared at my bed. Wilco's body lay twisted in my bedsheets, a lump of still fur.

I flew to the bed and tore at the sheets. "He's not moving! Jake, help. He's not moving. Wilco. Wilco . . ." His body was limp; he wasn't responding to me. I ripped off the last sheet, and a cheese cube fell to the floor. I pocketed it and placed my ear against Wilco's heart, felt the shallow rise and fall of his chest. "He's barely breathing. Help me get him to the car."

We rode to the vet, Jake driving, me in the backseat with Wilco slumped over my lap, head lolling and shifting with every wild turn. I steadied his head, my hand under his neck, fingers entwined in his fur. I bent forward and placed my face against his. Warmth and softness and my everything. Piece by piece, my outer wall crumbled. I fought to keep it intact. *Stay calm. Don't cry. He'll be okay. He will. He will.* My chin trembled. I swallowed hard, squeezed my eyes tight. *Don't cry. Don't cry. . . .*

"You're crying, Callahan."

"Aye, Drill Sergeant."

"Is this too hard for you?"

"No, Drill Serg—"

"I know just what you need, crybaby. Petty Officer, get over here."

"Aye, Sergeant."

"Take Callahan over to the mess hall and get her a nice cup of suck it up, will ya?"

"Excuse me, Sarge—"

"I said, get this sissy bitch off my line."

"I'm not a sissy bitch."

"What?" Jake eyed me through the rearview mirror.

I swiped my cheek. "Nothing."

"He's going to be okay, Brynn."

Was he? Three tours of recovery missions, grueling environments, debilitating injuries and he'd stayed by my side, through it all, even the worst of it. After the explosion, they'd told me that Wilco, rear leg blown off and bleeding out, fur and skin melted, dragged himself to my side and lay by my unconscious, broken body. He did that for me. He did everything for me. And we were still broken, both of us: night terrors, flashbacks, all the mind shit that went along with sniffing and poking through piles of rot to scoop up mutilated, putrefied bodies. But Wilco had persevered through all of it. Together. Always together. I ran my hand down his back, over his short nub and limp tail. "Don't leave me, buddy. Don't leave me."

Jake shot a glance at me in the mirror again, careened around a corner. We were almost there. I took a breath. *Suck it up, Brynn. Get it together.* I clung to my buddy, clenched my teeth, and forced my mind on the task, like the corps had drilled into us like a screw to the brain. Fear hardened to resolve; horror bled into an image of one person, one task. An icy spike bored through my spine, stiffening, strengthening. I had one task after this: find Katie Doogan. *I'm going to gouge out her eyes and cram them down her frickin' throat.* Eyes. A cold sneer crept past my lips at the irony. Settled law would never dole out a punishment to reconcile my loss. My own form of justice would be swift and merciless and, in my mind, commensurate with the crime.

The ears, the tongue . . . Suddenly I understood the motivation behind those crimes. Like a shift in sand, the crimes became the sanctification, the sacrifice required for redemption, the wrong morphed into right. When something so dear is ripped from your life, the soul screams for justice. Something vital for life itself had been torn from someone. Something loved without question, cherished . . . a child. I stroked Wilco's fur, felt a thin thread of life in his shallow breath. I had two tasks now. To mete out justice for this crime. And to find the person who had loved a child more than anything, someone who could carry out such a heinous act of payback. A father.

Wilco was whisked into the surgery room at the back of the clinic: sterile, with white walls, white cabinets, and rolling trays of medical instruments. He lay motionless on a cold stainless table, the vet listening to his heart. Thin, barefaced, with a gray ponytail, she had been called in during off-hours and had met us at her door, rushed us in with barely a question. She'd been in the community only a year or so now, so maybe her quick response came from still integrating herself into the town. Or maybe from Wilco's notoriety as "the dog on the force." Did I even care why? *Just fix my dog. Please.*

A tech stood by as the doctor called out orders. Another tech had taken the cube of cheese for analysis.

"Let's get an IV started. Prepare for a gastric lavage." She turned to me. "How long ago did he eat the poison?"

"I . . . I don't know. I left our trailer at four. He was there alone." Had Katie poisoned my dog before coming to the wedding? Or right after she sneered at me from the back of the church?

The vet checked the wall clock and turned back to the tech. "It could have been almost anytime, then."

A patch of fur was shaved from his leg, swiped with antiseptic, catheter placed, a monitor set. Wilco never flinched, his muscles noodle limp, eyes open, nostrils distended, lips flaccid. Words floated through the air: *orogastric tube, charcoal, sorbitol, fluid, intubate . . .*

The vet moved with a frantic rush, like a medic on a front line. "Check stats."

"Heart rate ninety-two. Respiratory rate ten. Blood pressure is one-ten over fifty."

The other tech came into the room. "There was a white pill in the cheese. Looks like trazodone."

The vet looked up. "Do you give your dog antianxiety meds?"

"No. Nothing."

"Would anyone living with you have sleep medicine that he could have gotten into?"

"No. Absolutely not."

Wilco was pulled to the end of the table, his snout was lifted, his jaw was opened and taped in place, and an intubation tube inserted. Next, the vet placed two more tubes, and the tech pumped an object that looked like a tire pump, but instead of air, it moved water up one of the tubes and into Wilco's stomach. The vet massaged his underside . . . like she was giving him . . . a belly rub. My heart ached.

Doc kept one eye on the monitor, one eye on Wilco. "Come on. Come on." Liquid flowed out the other tube and into the second bucket. The tech jostled the tube, and a milky liquid oozed from Wilco's stomach, foul smelling and slimy. Wilco's stomach lurched, and his gag reflex kicked in, throat constricting uselessly around the tubes. My own stomach roiled from a putrid mixture of anxiety and anger and hatred.

"Is he going to be okay?" My little girl voice. *Where's my mommy? Why don't I have a mother, like the other girls?*

No one had answered me back then, all those years ago, and no one answered me now.

"I need radiographs. Let's make sure nothing got into the lungs." The vet removed the tubes. Clear liquid dribbled from Wilco's slack mouth.

I found my voice. "Is he going to be okay?"

The vet gave me a sympathetic look. "All we can do is wait and see."

Black shadows and silence hung like shrouds in the corners of the trailer. I sat in Gran's chair, a bottle in my hand, my gun on the table next to me. Wilco, all I loved, had almost died today.

I brought the bottle to my lips, gulped, relishing the burn of the liquid against my swollen throat. I was back to drinking again. I'd regret this later, but now . . .

Headlights bounced through the window; on, then off; the slam of a car door; the clicking of heels on the front steps. Meg was home. She hummed softly as she made her way to the trailer, up the steps, then stopped. She pushed open the splintered door. "Brynn?"

"Here."

The light flipped on. "There you are. Why were you sitting in the dark? The door's . . . What's going on?"

"Someone broke into the trailer."

A small gasp. "What? When did this—"

"Sometime while we were at Dee's wedding. Wilco was poisoned."

"What . . . ?"

"He's okay. Weak. But alive. They pumped his stomach. Someone fed him cheese laced with trazodone. Enough to kill him."

She came over, knelt by my chair, rubbed my arm, her touch light and soothing. Always the nurturer, the gentle one, the steady one. "But he's okay."

"He could have died."

"But he didn't."

"Meg, I couldn't live without—"

"Shh . . . shh . . ."

"Or Gran."

"Stop it. Gran is going to be okay." Her gaze crept over the bottle in my hand. She frowned and reached for it.

I hugged it to my chest. "Let it be, Meg."

Her lips pressed into a thin line. She turned, looked at the door, then back at me, her gaze steady. "I don't understand. Who would want to kill Wilco?"

I took another swallow. She watched, not saying anything, just waiting. Gentle, steady.

Today it was Wilco poisoned and almost killed, but it could have just as easily been Gran. The hat left behind in Gran's room had been an overt message, Katie's way of demonstrating that she had complete access to Gran. Control over our lives. She had poisoned Wilco, and she could have easily done the same to Gran. Maybe she would next time. Retribution. In her sick mind, I'd destroyed her family, and she was out to destroy mine. Gran, Wilco . . . I looked at Meg, her striking red hair backlit by the room's single lamp. Would she go after Meg next?

She crossed her arms, turned from pacifier to interrogator. "What's going on that you're not telling me, Brynn?"

So much, Meg. So much. The bottle felt hard and alien against my chest, a weight that threatened to sink me. The booze, the pills, always the comforters I chose to numb myself, escape the realities instead of facing them. But Katie was smart. She knew me and my weaknesses. My past solace now served as anchors around my ankles, secured there by a madwoman.

My grip loosened on the bottle. I handed it to Meg. "I'm done. Will you take this and dump it out? I'm going to fix some coffee. We need to talk."

CHAPTER 21

Pusser was drinking coffee at his desk when I arrived Sunday morning. His reading glasses were perched on the end of his nose; papers and chewed toothpicks were scattered at his elbows. He looked up, mumbled something about the hot weather, and tipped a brown bag my way. "Bagel?"

"No thanks."

"How's Wilco?" Jake had insisted I file a report. Officers had been by; investigators sent to the vet clinic.

"He's okay. The vet kept him overnight for observation."

"You have any idea who would go after your dog?"

"Katie Doogan, I believe."

"What makes you say that?"

Careful, Brynn. I couldn't tell him that she had a history of poisoning dogs. I'd gotten that information from Doogan, a wanted felon. "Nothing was stolen. The act was deliberate and personal, vindictive. She's crazy like that, so it seems to fit."

"Vindictive because of your relationship with her husband?"

"Yes." I let it go at that. So did Pusser.

"There's been a warrant out for his arrest in connection to Dublin Costello's murder."

"I'm aware of that."

"You and Kevin Doogan . . . Well, that was last year. Why would the wife wait so long to get revenge?"

An echo of Harris's words. He'd gotten to Pusser. "Maybe she just found out about it."

"Could be." Pusser straightened some papers. "You stayin' sober?"

I'd anticipated this question. "No. Not completely." I'd thought this through, too. My failure at sobriety or harboring a felon—neither was good. Both could jeopardize my career. But falling off the wagon was the lesser of the two evils, and coming clean about something maintained some credibility. "I had a rough patch last night. After my dog . . ." I drew in my breath, looked down. "Just a bit of whiskey. My cousin set me straight. Today's a new day, and I'm committed to this."

Pusser sat back, his gaze sinking into his pockmarked cheeks. "It's normal to slip."

"That's what they said at the meeting. That it happens to most drunks." I said it straight, but the word *drunk* tasted like one of the shit balls Wilco gobbled up sometimes. "What's important is that I get back on track."

"That's right." Pusser looked satisfied, happy even. My answer must've scored points. And he'd moved on from asking me about Kevin Doogan. *Good.* "I called you down here because there are things we need to discuss with Grabowski."

I glanced toward the door—*Grabowski's back?*—then saw Pusser pick up the phone and punch in a number. "She's here. I'm putting you on speaker."

"Hey, Grabowski." I'd missed the guy. Go figure. "How are you feeling?"

"My physical therapist thinks PT stands for 'pain and torture.'"

"That bad, huh?"

"Yeah. But other than that . . . I'm surviving. Frank filled me in on Wilco already. I'm sorry, Brynn. Glad he's okay."

"I think it was Katie Doogan."

"Do you have a direct connection? Proof?"

"Not yet."

"Any other leads on her?"

"Nothing. But we'll get her." *One way or the other.*

Pusser opened a file folder. "I do have something from the body-parts case. ME says the tongue is a clean cut, like the ears. So a sharp, precise tool, like a scalpel. We could be looking for someone in the medical field."

No comment on that from Grabowski. Instead, "How about that group out in the woods?"

"The Feds got a fix on them," Pusser said. "The group is small and newly organized. They call themselves the Tennessee Security Force, but word is that they've become more radical lately. Nothing links Reed Bannock to them."

"Except Kimber Bannock's testimony," I said. "She says he spends a lot of time in the hollow."

Grabowski disagreed. "That could mean anything. Maybe he enjoys the outdoors."

"We're surrounded by outdoors, Grabowski. It's everywhere. Why that hollow?"

"Doesn't really matter." Pusser checked the file. "That militia group is operating legally, on privately owned land. It's listed under an umbrella organization, National Security Corp. They buy up large blocks of land across the states to use as training grounds for their people, mostly ex-military and law enforcement." Pusser sat back and stuck a fresh toothpick between his lips. "Bannock is neither. The guy works at the local Oil & Lube, divorced, one kid. No record. No firearms permit."

"Sounds like your run-of-the-mill thirty-year-old," Grabowski said.

I shifted. "Except for maybe his missing tongue."

The room grew quiet. The toothpick slid back and forth in Pusser's mouth.

Suspicion crept in, or maybe paranoia. "What is it?" I asked. "What aren't you guys telling me?"

Pusser pulled a piece of paper from the file, a yellow copy of a car service invoice from the Oil & Lube. "Parks went over to where Bannock works and asked around. One of the guys said they get a lot of gypsies in there. We pulled this invoice from their records. The customer's name is Hughie Black."

Damn.

He passed it to me. "Take a close look."

I skimmed the paper, found what he was talking about at the bottom of the sheet. *Serviced by: RB.*

I shrugged. "Okay, he may have come in contact with Reed Bannock. So what? Bannock comes across a lot of different people at work. I mean, what would Hughie's motive have been for cutting out this guy's tongue? A bad oil change?" I tossed the paper back on his desk.

"Did you see the service date? The day after Walker disappeared and the day before Bannock disappeared. The timing doesn't look good for your friend. If Hughie's wife had a thing going with Bannock as well as Walker . . . Well, like I said, it doesn't look good."

No, it doesn't.

Grabowski spoke up. "There's something you should still consider. Bannock might not be our victim. He could be the perpetrator in all this."

Pusser made a note. "I've asked for consent for a DNA sample from the kid. When the results come back, we'll know if he's our vic."

"Only if it's a match," I said.

Pusser narrowed his eyes. "What do you mean?"

"We don't have a control variable, or whatever. Hell, I'm no scientist. But what if the kid's not even his? I met Kimber. She's not exactly loyal wife material."

"She's right," Grabowski said. "A negative wouldn't rule

Bannock out as the vic. Still, a positive match would tell us something. What's happening with Silvas?"

Pusser answered, "He's got multiple drugs charges against him. He'll be a guest of the system for some time. But nothing concrete to connect his meth business with Walker, and the guy's got a solid enough alibi for that night, though an attorney might be able to shoot holes in it."

Pusser tapped his pen. My tongue flicked across my lips. I eyed Pusser's coffee. I'd been up late talking to Meg about Katie. A few lies, an omission or two. But the bottom line read right: Katie was Kevin Doogan's wife, and she had it in for me and my family, blamed me in her screwed-up brain for losing her husband. I had said nothing about Katie's possession of the gun that Gran had used to kill Dublin Costello, even though it was in self-defense. The fewer people who knew, the safer Gran would be.

The sound of Grabowski drawing a deep breath filled the room. I imagined he'd raised his finger in that "I'm about to make a point" pose. "Here's what I think."

Yup. Here it comes.

"Dismemberment is an act of dehumanizing the victim. It's also a form of dominance. In particular, in these crimes, whether the victims are dead or not, the dismemberment and the display of the body parts are very theatrical. It's one thing to dismember a body to hide it. Another to display pieces of it. Agreed?" Grabowski couldn't see our nods, but he continued, anyway. "The only benefit for Silvas to display like that would be to warn others not to snitch about his meth manufacturing, assuming Walker had done that. But he wouldn't display publicly, as that would only jeopardize his meth business. He'd be more personal about it, like packaging them to use as a warning for other buyers who didn't pay or as a display of power for competitors. I think one of the main points here is that the perp feels the need for dominance over the victim, whether it's for the purpose of revenge or something else. The perp is asserting his power. That's why the militia angle makes sense. Think about it. The militia is all about protecting the public for the good of all, and through force, if necessary. For a guy who likes to dominate his victims, that type of power is pretty heady stuff."

Dominant personality. Militia, sure, but that also describes every male Pavee I know. My mind flashed back to the decapitated horse. *Or maybe this guy's just into cutting up things.*

Crazy is as crazy does.

My hand fell to my side, twitched for my dog or a drink or both. Definitely, I wanted both. But what I really needed was my dog.

Later that day, I called the vet at home. I apologized for calling on a Sunday afternoon but explained that the department had official business, so I needed to get my dog back now. Which was sort of true. I didn't need to tell her I had to have Wilco to keep me sane through another night. But when I arrived and wrapped my arms around his neck, biting my lower lip to keep from crying, she probably knew, anyway.

Wilco's vitals were back to normal, no kidney damage, breathing and heart rate good. His wet nose against my neck, and his wagging tail and sloppy tongue, told me what we both knew: we were lucky. Wilco was released, and we headed home to Bone Gap.

CHAPTER 22

My trailer was a smoky haze of short skirts, runny black eye-liner, and emotional women. Queenie was in the recliner, sucking on a cigarette, a butt-filled ashtray on the side table next to her.

I coughed. "Damn it, Queenie. You're stinking up the place."

She stubbed out the cig and looked at the television. The news was recapping the case. A picture of Bone Gap flashed on the screen and then a mug shot of Hughie.

Meg sat on the floor, cross-legged, with a throw pillow in her lap, her lean fingers worrying the fringe trim. Wilco was curled by her, his snout resting on her leg. Mo slumped hunch shouldered in the corner of my sofa, a black lump of polyester ruffles and spent tissues. She stared straight ahead, wide eyed and lips quivering. Next to her, Nina leaned forward, hands hovering over my coffee table, her sticky fingers touching everything: a stack of mail, the television remote, one of Gran's paperback novels, a small bird Gramps had carved for Gran. . . .

"Why are all of you here?" I asked.

"We're keeping Mo company," Queenie said. "She's lonely without her man."

"And I want to talk to you about Hughie." Mo's thin voice cracked.

"I'm sorry, Mo. There's not much I can tell you about the case."

Queenie pulled another cigarette from the pack in her front breast pocket. "Just hear her out, Brynn."

I glared at the cig dangling between her lips. "Light that cig, and I'll shove it up your nose."

"Calm down, will ya? I ain't gonna light it. Just holding it. It's what I do when I'm stressed, okay?"

I looked back at Mo. "What do you want to know about Hughie?"

"When can he come home? The girls miss him."

"I don't know, Mo."

"Will he go to prison?"

Meg pushed Wilco off her leg and went to Mo. "That's not going to happen." She patted her hand and shot me a look. "Is it, Brynn?"

"I don't know. He might."

Mo burst into tears, and Nina, little Miss Fidgety, picked up the carved bird and nervously rolled it between her fingers.

"Look, Mo. Maybe if you come clean about that night—"

"I've told you everything."

"I need to know about the marks on your neck. What *exactly* happened?"

Her face turned red; eyes darted immediately to Queenie.

Queenie leaned forward, flicking her lighter over and over. The unlit cig bobbed between her lips as she spoke. "The guy got violent."

"Mo can answer for herself."

Mo swiped at the snot dripping under her nose, and Meg scrambled to snatch more tissue from a nearby box. Mo sniffed. "It's like Queenie said. Chance got aggressive. I didn't like it."

"So, you fought back?"

"No. I . . . That's not how it happened."

"Was Hughie there?"

"I didn't see him."

"Well, someone else did, and"—I glanced at Nina—"they reported it."

Nina squirmed.

Mo trembled.

The sharp flick of the lighter drew my attention back to Queenie. She blew a stream of white smoke through her nose and walked to the sofa, then took a long drag before handing the cigarette over to Mo. "Here, hon. Take a few puffs. It'll help calm down those shakes."

White haze pervaded the room. Wilco's eyes followed a smoke trail.

Mo inhaled and let out a long, smoky sigh. "Chance got mad cuz I changed my mind. I wanted to leave. He didn't like that, and things got a little rough."

"You changed your mind?"

"Yeah."

"Did he force you?"

"No. But he would have. I know he would. He wasn't anything like I thought. I was so stupid."

"What stopped him?"

"There was someone walking around the truck."

"Hughie?"

"No. A woman."

"A woman? Why is this the first I'm hearing about this? What'd she look like?"

"I dunno. It was dark outside by then. Blond hair. I think."

"Short, tall, skinny . . . ?"

"That's all I know. I didn't wait around long enough to get a good look at her. As soon as he saw the woman, he let go of me, and I bolted. What does it matter?"

"She might have been the last person to see Chance alive. Think, Mo. Do you remember anything else about her?"

"No. I'm sorry . . ." She wrung her hands. "They got the wrong man. Hughie would never—"

"We think the tongue belonged to a guy who works at the Oil & Lube in town." I knew they hadn't released that to the news yet, but it was sure to hit tomorrow, anyway.

"So?"

"His name's Reed Bannock." I watched for a reaction. Didn't see one. "Did you know him, Mo?"

She shook her head, but no other reaction, not the slightest twitch. No way had she been involved with Bannock, or I'd have seen something.

"What's that guy got to do with my Hughie?"

"He serviced Hughie's vehicle prior to disappearing. That connects Hughie to both victims."

Mo went stock-still, her cigarette burning down, ash dangling precariously.

Queenie snatched up the ashtray and held it out. "Here, sweetie. Let me take that from you." I expected Queenie to stick the stub in her own lips, but it met its demise in the ashtray as her other arm went around Mo, her friend. They sat like Siamese twins, joined in sorrow and pain. Queenie was a loyal friend through hard times. Despite a childhood of abuse and pain, she maintained her compassion.

Some people were like that. Some not. Like Katie Doogan. For her, only the suffering of others assuaged the distress of her own losses and failures.

CHAPTER 23

Pusser sat at his desk, working over a toothpick. "What's your take on those militia people?"

It was Monday morning, and I was back in my boss's office, discussing the case. "I can't figure out a motive. They're just a bunch of good ol' boys playing war games out there in the woods. And there's nothing that connects Walker and Bannock to them."

"Then why would Bannock have been going up there?"

I shook my head. "I don't know. There must have been something else up there."

Wilco, still tired from the ordeal at the vet, circled a spot by Pusser's desk and plopped down. He yawned and made a long whiny sound, then swiped his tongue over his lips before settling his head down and closing his eyes.

Pusser tossed his toothpick and replaced it with another. "Damn woods. Forty percent of my county is wooded. Trees as far as you can see. I used to think the forests were beautiful. Not no more. Them woods out there ain't nothing but cover for a bunch of criminals and weirdos."

I agreed. I slumped back in my chair. Things had caught up to me, too. My weary eyes settled over my boss's desk. The framed photo of his long-missing daughter was in a different spot than usual. He'd been looking at it recently. Probably spurred by Gideon Ridley's mentioning of her. Jo's disappearance had never been resolved. No body, no answers, no closure. Much like our current case.

"The Ridley boy didn't mention a horse. Just Bannock, on foot," I said.

"That's right. But whoever he thought was after him might have been on a horse."

"And the horse ran off and got snared in that pit trap? But why sever its head?"

Pusser's eyes narrowed. "Because it was of value to someone?"

"Like a pet. But then what? Pack it out of there? And what about Bannock? Dead or alive, he would have needed to be transported out of the woods. My dog didn't pick up anything. No human blood, no flesh decay."

"So, Bannock walked out of the woods alive."

I nodded. "If he was being forced at gunpoint, I don't think the assailant would have taken the horse head. It'd be too much to juggle with a gun. Not to mention a saddle and bridle. The horse didn't have either, so if it was ridden into the woods, those things would have been removed. And I don't think the perp would have risked returning for them later."

"What are you getting at, Callahan?"

"Two possibilities. Whoever chased Bannock never did get the guy, and Bannock has kept running. Or someone walked him out of there while someone else packed out the horse head and tack. Or rode out with it on another horse."

Pusser tore the toothpick from his mouth. "So, we could be looking for two perps."

* * *

I spent the next two workdays at my desk, compiling research and chasing leads, none of which got me anywhere. Pusser had asked me to follow up on anyone Bannock knew, although we'd pretty much done that already. If he'd made it out of the woods on his own and run, he'd have been looking for help, because the guy didn't have enough money to last long on his own. Since neither his bank account nor his credit card—he had only one, and it was close to its limit already— had been tapped since his disappearance, it seemed unlikely he was still alive and running.

That left us with the possibility that he had been escorted out of the woods alive.

The other possibility, of two perps, didn't give us much to go on. As for accomplices, Silvas's operation was pretty much a one-man show. Besides, I agreed with Grabowski that Silvas didn't seem the type to want to advertise his business by dangling body parts in public places. Hughie had way too many potential accomplices. The only thing in his favor on this count was that after his accident, he couldn't mount a horse any more than he could his wife. Which didn't rule out him walking in and out with a friend. But taking a horse head? Why?

Parks's photos of the horse included a partial brand that was still visible, so I spent way too much time trying to figure whose horse it was and came up with nothing. Was the horse even related to the case? The only indication that it was related came from the severed neck. The ME had looked at the photo and had verified that the horse's head was removed by a human, as evidenced by the apparent hatchet marks, not by a bear or a coyote or any other animal. Other than that, not much of a connection.

That led me to an even bigger question: Was Bannock's disappearance even part of the case? We wouldn't know anything until forensics could compare his DNA with the tongue. I just knew I'd wasted my time in this stifling office, on an investigation that was going nowhere, my gut begging for another slip, as in sip, off the wagon, while Katie still posed the greatest danger in my life and Gran's.

CHAPTER 24

Tuesday evening Wilco and I were in Jake's car, parked outside the church, the three of us splitting Chinese takeout. He'd called to offer to pick some up for us. Maybe a subtle reminder for me to make the meeting? No matter. It was good to see him, and I was hungry. Wilco wolfed down plain chicken and rice, while I forked in some moo goo gai pan.

Cars pulled in around us: Ashley was first, in a berry-red Volkswagen Bug, fruity and light bodied, the same as she liked her wine. Then Josh ripped into the lot, stones spitting under the tires of an older black Camaro, fast, dark, and deadly. Heroine and hero on wheels. Pavees noticed these things. We were a culture on the move, always wheeled, even if we were a little less mobile in Bone Gap. Roaming was in our blood. And a person's car said a lot about them.

I glanced at the adjacent parking spot, at my own vehicle, an out-of-date station wagon, cracked windshield, dents and rust, seats worn to the padding . . . case in point.

Jake stabbed at a piece of chicken. "So, how'd your research on the militia go?"

Wilco stuck his nose between us, his tail whapping against the backseat. *Whap, whap, whap.* . . . I shoved his snout away. "Just what we figured. Nothing but a bunch of guys playing war games." And Crystal. But she was hard to explain. "Organized but harmless, and not breaking any laws. No connection I could find to either Bannock or Walker."

Crazy-eyed Mitch pulled into the lot and parked cockeyed, taking up two spaces with his older-model Jeep Renegade—banana yellow, lifted and topless, with oversize chrome-studded wheels—base thumping as he blew vape smoke like jet propulsion. *Uh-huh.*

Jake talked with his mouth half full. "So, you believe the militia people when they say they've never seen the missing men?"

"They were convincing."

He gnawed on a long piece of gristly chicken, red sauce glistening on his lips like blood. Like . . . like . . . *Ooh.* Like the blood-crusted tongue that hung from the pavilion rafter.

I tossed my plastic fork into the take-out bag. "All full. The rest is yours."

He pulled the container close to his chest and went for it. "If Bannock wasn't in the militia group, then why was he heading up there?"

"Running scared probably. I think he knew that whoever mutilated Walker was coming after him, too. There's a connection between the two men. It's just a matter of finding it. We've interviewed neighbors and friends, checked financial records . . . nothing so far."

Lily eased into the lot, dark eyes serious and focused, behind the wheel of a new white Prius, a sleek capsule on wheels, calm and contained, like a pop of Valium.

I chuckled.

"What is it? What's funny?" He snatched a napkin and wiped his mouth.

"Nothing." Jake drove a black BMW, classy and meant to impress. "We should head into the meeting."

We cut across the lot and through the haze of cigarette smoke outside the door. Toby, the skinny, schizy guy in our group, took his last drag, flicked the butt, and followed us down to the basement. The full circle of metal chairs was set up in the center of the room; there were no new members. I took the same chair as last time; Wilco, tightly leashed, settled at my feet. A group huddled in the corner, last-minute chitchat. Colm came in, Bible tucked under his arm, and took his seat next to Margaret, our licensed social worker.

He straightened his collar and cleared his throat. "Everyone take their seats, please."

The *cha-chink* of butts settling into metal chairs, laughter, and a dry, hacking cough, body odor, stale tobacco, and some sort of pungent spice smell. I looked to my left. Lily. Dark pupils peered from under short stubs of lash, studying—no, judging—me. Noise to the right. I turned, expected to see Jake, but it was crazy-eyed Mitch. How'd that happen?

Jake sat next to Volkswagen Ashley, blond and pretty faced. I shifted and crossed my arms. *I hate this.*

Colm prayed, introductions were made, and Margaret kicked things off. "We have a guided discussion this evening, and our topic is 'slips and relapses, how to say no to that first drink or hit or whatever.' You fill in the blank. Who wants to start?"

Ashley tugged the hem of her skirt, an extra-short mini, and crossed her tan legs. "I joined an online dating site. And it's been tough." Her lips went all pouty. She shifted to the right, closer to Jake. "All the men want to meet for drinks."

Give me a break.

"That must be difficult, Ashley." Empathy from Colm. Priests were good at that, but how often do they really mean it? "How do you handle that situation?"

"Not well, I'm afraid. I slipped and had some wine the other night. But I remembered what you said. We are not defined by our mistakes, but by how we handle them." *Click, click, click . . .* Snaps all around. Ashley raised her hand, hushing the room. "So I got out of there and called my sponsor. She talked me through it."

Back to the snaps again, only louder now. *Oh, yes, the miracle of sponsors, where one addict commiserates with another. Charming.*

"Meth is different." The snaps stopped. All eyes on Toby. He looked bad today: sallow and shaky. His left eye was puffy; his lips were cracked. "It takes over. There are no slips, only falls. And if it's around, you take it, all of it, until you run out. Then you crash, wake up, and start looking for more. I'm clean now, but the cravings . . . They make me crazy, man. I swear, if someone handed me some right now, I'd slam it." He faked like he was injecting. "I'm serious, man. A needle full right here . . . I'd do it."

I glanced around, but no one else looked at anyone. They all felt the same and knew it, but they didn't want to show it.

Finally, next to me, crazy-eyed Mitch shifted and leaned forward. "Time, man. The more time clean, the easier it'll get. Just don't slip up."

Nikki. This is what it's like for Nikki. All or nothing, and going without was unbearable. She wasn't strong enough. Weak. Not like me. I'd slipped, sure. A bit here and there. Okay, a lot the other day. But I was back on track already. Wasn't I?

Lily's voice cut through. "You almost need superhuman strength to conquer the demon."

Toby shrugged, smiled, looked at Colm, and pointed to the ceiling, a questioning gesture, as if he was uncertain whether God was really there for him. Or if He was even enough.

Colm nodded in that reassuring way he had. Then his eyes moved to me, his gaze intense, his hand resting atop his Bible.

Snapping started, quiet at first, then growing more intense. My heart kept tempo. *Snap, snap, snap, slip, slip . . .*

"I slipped."

The snapping stopped.

"Oh, so Miss I'm Better Than You *does* have a problem. Wow."

I jerked to the right. Crazy-eyed Mitch looked straight ahead. *Not enough nerve to look at me when you say that, huh, buddy?* I stared him down. The inside of his ear had a glob of yellow wax with tiny spikes of black hair, like whiskers growing out of a piece of caramel. *Yuck.*

"Shut up, Mitch." Lily pushed her glasses up her nose. "Let her talk."

I looked at the floor. *I've already said enough.*

Juan's voice floated across the room. "Aye, *cariño*. We all screw up. It's okay. Tell us. We're here to help."

"My dog." The words were out before I could stop them. "I came home, and someone had poisoned my dog."

"Bastard."

"Damn."

"What the hell?"

"Motherfu—"

"I'm sorry, Brynn." I looked up. Colm's face was twisted in pain. Empathy again? Real this time? For me?

Mitch bent over, all his macho bullshit slid away, and he ran a gentle hand along Wilco's spine. "Glad he's okay." Wilco raised his snout and licked his hand. Mitch smiled.

Wilco could melt the hardest of hearts.

Ashley, with those legs again . . . crossed, uncrossed, crossed. "So, you drank?"

"Yeah. A few shots of whiskey. Maybe four."

Josh sat up straighter. "Damn, girl! That's a lot."

"We don't pass judgment here, Josh." Lily, such a rule follower.

"It was just booze." *Not like the stuff you're into, Josh.* "But I stopped."

"That's important." Time for Margaret's input. "There's a difference between a slip and a relapse. A relapse is when you don't stop. A slip is temporary. It can be a learning point. We can come back stronger, more educated. Like Ashley did."

Yes, yes. Like the wine-sipping, Internet-dating Ashley, our shining star. Thank you for your sage advice, Margaret. And such a moving example. Okay. Move on, people. Who's next? I looked around the circle.

"Did you learn anything from your slip, Brynn?" My eyes snapped back to Margaret, with her gray hair in an angular haircut and her pinched mouth.

Why, yes, Margaret. I learned that Black Label whiskey is worth every damn penny. . . .

Another voice. "You need yourself a good man. Someone like my Lucinda is to me."

I looked at the guy, button-down shirt and phone clipped to leather-belted khakis. *Tom . . . ? Jack?*

Colm dipped his chin. "How does she support you, Alan?"

Oh yeah. Alan. Booze. Or pills. Pot? I couldn't keep it all straight. These people were so screwed up.

"She scares the shit out of me." Chuckles came from all around the circle, and Alan continued, "Once she told me that if I started back up drinkin' again, she'd cut my fingers off. I believed her."

More laughter and a round of snapping. Except from Margaret. No chuckles there. Not even an itsy-bitsy smile. Definitely no snapping. *Jeez. Lighten up, lady.*

Lily's eyes widened behind her black-rimmed glasses. "Maybe she's the one the cops are looking for."

Was she serious?

"No, *chica.*" Juan was weighing in on this one. "They got

their man. One of them pikeys. Heard them people are into that type of thing."

Colm cleared his throat. "We don't pass judgment, remember?"

"I ain't judging nobody, Padre. That's the God's honest truth. Them gypsies are crazy."

My jaw tightened. Snaps sounded throughout the room. My face burned hot. I slipped my foot under Wilco. *Stay cool, Brynn.*

Juan continued, "I'm just glad they got that knacker. We'll all be a lot safer now."

Snap, snap, snap.

"Maybe we should let the courts decide his fate." It was Jake. I exhaled. *Thank you, Jake.*

"Courts?" Crazy-eyed Mitch shook his head and grabbed his crotch, gave it a squeeze. "Ask me, it serves that bastard right if they cut off his—"

"Alright. Let's wrap it up, folks." Colm bent his head in prayer. Everyone followed suit. Except me.

I stared straight ahead, my mind reeling. Poor Hughie. Condemned by both sides, cheated on by his wife, sitting in jail, alone and abandoned. And Mo. Yeah, she wasn't the ideal wife, but deep down she loved Hughie. She and the girls needed him.

"Things got out of hand tonight." The meeting was over. Colm had motioned for me to stay back as the others left. He folded and stacked chairs. "I'm sorry, Brynn."

"Wasn't anything I hadn't heard before."

"Still, I'm sorry."

He handed me a folded chair. I stacked it with the others and thought of something. Colm was good with these people, had a calming effect on them, knew how to talk to them. And I remembered Nikki spewing some religious talk last time I saw her. So, maybe he could get Nikki to the point where I could get something more out of her.

"I have this friend in the hospital. I thought maybe you might be able to visit her."

"Sure. What's going on? Is she sick?"

"She's a meth addict. Bad off. She's the girlfriend of one of our victims. Things are rough for her right now, and I'm worried about her. She's been on suicide watch."

He handed me the last chair, his features masked with concern. "I'll be glad to try. I don't know exactly what I could do to help her, though, if she doesn't want help. When did you need me to go?"

Tomorrow would be busy for me again, with the case, interviews, reports to file. "Can we go now?"

"Sure. Let's go see her."

CHAPTER 25

But she saw us first. And let out a bloodcurdling scream.

Nurses came running, soft-soled shoes squeaking like a herd of rubber duckies and one of them burst through the door.

"She's worse than when I saw her last," I told Colm.

Something white flashed in my peripheral vision. I ducked, and a foam cup hit the wall behind me, ice and water splattering everywhere.

Nikki shrieked. "Get out! Get out!"

Colm staggered backward. "What's wrong with her? Does she think I'm going to hurt her?"

"It's not you. She's hallucinating."

The nurse looked at me. "What have you done? We had her calmed down."

"I'm with the police. We need to question her."

"You won't get anything from her. Not in this condition." The nurse went to her and shushed her, speaking in subdued tones, and then flipped through the stations on the television until she got to a mixer spinning and humming while a large dark-haired lady added flour and salt to the bowl and explained, with a soft golf announcer–type voice, the importance of room-temperature butter. Nikki quieted, her body twitching and jerking, her eyes taking on a blank look as she absorbed the spinning mixer.

The nurse pulled us aside. "She's experiencing episodes of psychosis. She's incoherent. We see this in severe cases of meth addiction. The chemicals have damaged the brain."

"Permanently?" I asked.

"The brain might heal itself, with the right care. But it can take months. We can't handle her here. She'll be transported to a different facility soon. I don't think it's a good idea to question her now. It doesn't take much to set her off." She motioned toward the door.

I pointed to Colm. "The priest needs to minister to her."

The nurse sighed, glanced over her shoulder at the blank-faced woman in the bed. "You'll have to keep it short."

We promised, and she told us she'd be back in ten minutes. Ten minutes. Not much time.

I approached the bed, weak legged, wishing Wilco was with me. Wilco, my stabilizer. I needed him. "Nikki. It's Brynn. I brought someone to talk to you."

She rolled her head my way; her muscles twitched; her limbs jerked. "I ain't goin' back to no jail. I can't."

"I understand."

"I'll die there. Dead. Red dead. In bed. He said." She giggled, a wire-thin, twangy giggle. "I'm a poet."

Yeah, a regular Dr. Seuss. "You can beat this thing, Nikki. You've been clean for a few days already. That's something, but you need help, support. I brought Father Colm. He leads meetings at St. Brigid's for people who have the same type of struggles as you. When you get out of here and—"

She raised her chin, pinched her eyelashes, plucked a couple, and carefully placed them on her bedside tray. Black lashes were piled like grass clippings.

I cringed.

Colm dragged a chair over and sat down next to her bed. "Hi, Nikki."

Her pupils darted under raw pink rims from me to Colm, to the television, to me, back to Colm. "Y'all can't do nothin' for me."

"I can pray with you." Colm's voice sounded soft like a hymn, and his hands were folded softly into each other. The picture of serenity. And hope.

A flicker of that hope popped into her eyes, brief and shiny, then was covered over by darkness. She tipped her head back and laughed, the air filling with sour chemical breath. My stomach churned. Colm recoiled. Ammonia, brake fluid, nail polish, cold pills, battery fluid . . . mixed and cooked, and ingested, snorted, smoked—however she got her rush. Her organs had sopped up the chemical brew like dry cookies in milk, and the toxins gnawed her from the inside out. Meth rot.

Colm persevered. "Let me pray with you, Nikki."

She stopped laughing and flashed a brown, gooey smile, ran bony fingers along her chin line, and salaciously batted what lashes she had left. "Got any smokes, Father?"

"Afraid not."

Pluck, pluck, pluck . . . The pile of lashes grew; the rim of her right eye was searing pink now.

Colm swallowed hard. "Do you have family? Anyone you want us to call?"

Her face twitched. Her eyes were flat. "Mama's dead. Died in a hospital bed."

Back to the rhyming.

"I'm sorry." Colm paused then, took in her wasting frame, skin that sagged and hung like strips of toilet paper on a thin wire, attenuated and translucent, with a pulsing network of blue veins. Her grotesque deterioration didn't scare or repulse him. Instead, his eyes softened, and he moved closer and spoke softly. "You miss your mama."

"Yes." One word, barely whispered, yet I knew it was the most coherent thing she'd said in a long time.

Colm smiled. "She was a good mother, then?"

"No." Her eyes darted to the television; she jerked back, mouth twisting open, then shut, then slowly open again. She leaned forward, her eyes popping. "Did you see that? She can't do that. She can't do that!"

We followed her gaze, looked at the television chef. "She's just chopping an onion," I said.

Nikki sprung from bed, ran to the television, screaming, "Her fingers. Her fingers. She's cutting them off."

Colm reached for the bedside controller, fumbled, hit the wrong button, and turned up the volume. Nikki's eyes bulged, veins like a red spiderweb over a hard-cooked egg. She covered her ears, and her knees gave out. "Round and round they go, cut off the ears and no one will know."

I crossed the room and yanked the television cord from the wall.

"Round and round they go . . ." Nikki repeated the words like a mantra, sinking all the way to the floor and drawing herself into a tight ball. She clutched her legs close to her body and rocked, chanting, "Round and round they go . . ."

I knelt by her. "The woman on television is fine. It's your mind playing tricks on you. You're seeing things."

Nikki rocked back and forth. "Round and round . . . Why her hands? She wasn't even there."

"Where?"

"They got to her. They gonna get to me, too. Because I know."

Colm and I exchanged a look. The room filled with the sound of Nikki's bizarre chant. "Round and round, round and round, round and . . ."

Neither of us knew what to do next. I drew in a deep breath, placed my hand on her shoulder. "Nikki."

She recoiled. "The blood. It's everywhere. I smell it."

"There's no blood."

"It's all over me." She uncoiled and swiped at her shirt. Frantic. "Get it off me!"

"It's okay, Nikki. We're here."

She jerked back, raised her hands, her eyes wide with terror. "Blood."

Colm came over and crouched down. "There's nothing here, Nikki. Your hands are clean."

"My fault. It's all my fault. His blood is on my hands." The rocking started again. "Round and round they go, cut off the ears and no one will know."

"Who cut off Chance's ears?" I asked.

"Round and round . . ."

"Nikki. Do you know who cut off Chance's ears?"

"Dead, dead, in a hospital bed. Dead, dead—"

"That's enough!" The nurse was back. "You'll have to leave now."

CHAPTER 26

I pricked my egg, released the yolk, and sopped it up with buttered toast. I was in my usual booth at the McCreary Diner, the one overlooking the parking lot. Wilco was curled under the table, also in his usual spot.

Meg was working the breakfast shift. She slid onto the red vinyl seat across from me with a plate of crisp fried bacon. "Hey. I've got a couple minutes, unless things pick up in here." She snatched a piece of bacon and ducked down, popped back up, and wiped her hand on the napkin. "He's hungry this morning."

He chomped and slurped, then came out from under the table, his tongue scouring the floor for fallen bits. Then a thump, thump of the tail and needy eyes begging for more. I scowled. Meg laughed, snapped another piece of bacon in half, gave him one piece, and popped the rest in her mouth.

"Yeah, he worked up an appetite. We trained early." I'd taken Wilco out for a little scent work that morning. I'd connected with a midwife in town who gave me donated placenta. Last week, I had placed a placenta in a weighted pillowcase and had thrown it into about five feet of water off the bank of the Nolichucky River. It'd had plenty of time to ferment. This morning, after a few times back and forth, Wilco had hit on it.

Such a good dog.

I scooped up a forkful of hash browns and eggs, shoveled them in, and washed them down with a sip of coffee. Guess I'd worked up an appetite, too. "How was Gran last night?" I asked.

Meg ran her finger along the top of the table.

"Meg?"

"Her speech should have improved more by now. I'm worried."

"Me too."

"Have you seen Katie Doogan again? Or heard from her?"

"No."

"Makes you wonder what she's up to." A guy in the booth across from us cleared his throat and tipped his mug toward Meg. She held up one finger, leaned in closer to me, and lowered her voice. "I'm thinking we ought to move Gran to a different facility."

The guy with the empty coffee mug grumbled, then turned his focus to the corner-mounted television, where yesterday's press conference played on the local news. Pusser's face filled the screen. Reporters fired off questions. He did his best to answer: "No, we have not recovered any bodies . . . The suspect in custody has not confessed . . ." I tuned it out and slipped the rest of the bacon under the table to Wilco.

"Where would we put her, Meg? There's nothing else between here and Greeneville."

"That's where I'm thinking. I've already checked into it, and—"

"No. She stays here. Where I can keep an eye on her." My eyes were drawn back to the television, to a reporter talking about the ears, the tongue. . . .

A low murmur erupted around the diner; all faces were tuned in to the news.

"Mark my word," someone said. "It's one of them pikeys cutting people up. Those gypsies are into some weird things."

"That's fine if they want to mutilate each other, but keep it in their group," someone else responded. "Damn crazies. Leave us normal folks alone."

Meg shrank a little. Like me, she straddled both worlds: the Pavee world and the settled world. All Pavees did to some extent. We relied on settled money to feed our families. But most of our people took to the road for cash jobs, moving on before folks caught on to who we were. Meg didn't have that luxury. A widow, she didn't have a man to rely on, and as a single woman, she couldn't take to the road. Very few diner customers knew she was one of us. She needed to eat, so she intended to keep it that way.

A siren sounded, distant but quickly coming closer, and then a county cruiser popped into view, approaching from the left and heading up the street our way. A mass of folks rushed to the window.

What is it?

Speculation broke out among the diner crowd.

"Another piece of a body . . ."

"Eyeballs . . ."

"Thought they had the bastard."

"Waitress, bring me a doggie bag."

Meg slid out of the booth. "I'm back on. I'll catch you later."

"I gotta go, too. Don't do anything with Gran until we have a chance to talk, okay?" I gulped down the rest of my coffee, threw down a bill, and tapped Wilco with my foot.

Bills were paid, purses gathered, keys rattled as the mob moved toward the door. Gawkers. They couldn't wait to see the next tragic event play out.

Out in the lot, I punched my cell. "Hey, Parks. What's going on?"

Her voice was shaky. "We got a body. But—"

"I'm on my way."

Sanitary workers had found a man wedged behind an alley Dumpster downtown, not far from where Dee's reception had been a few nights before. Harris had taken the call. No word yet if the victim was missing ears or a tongue or anything else.

By the time I arrived, half the force was already there. Harris found me immediately.

"Callahan, you're here."

"Yeah. I was at the diner, saw the cruisers. Parks said a body was found."

"Really?"

I squinted.

He frowned. "You shouldn't be on this call, Callahan."

Down the alley, three or four guys huddled together, while a photographer squatted near the edge of the Dumpster. I headed that way, Harris on my heels. The recent heat had ripened the decay. I dipped my chin and gagged a little. Wilco was in the back of my car, going nuts, barking and clawing, slobber coating the inside of my windows.

"Give me a break, Harris. This is my case. Who is it? Walker?"

Harris snagged my arm. "Wait. I don't think you should—"

"Don't tell me, the guy's missing his eyeballs. Don't worry. I can handle it. I see a lot of that type of thing in my line of work."

"Wait."

I turned back. "What?"

"That's not it."

"Then what?"

Harris's face was a mixed bag of emotion, tight and tense, and hard to read. I didn't have the time—or the interest—to sort out his latest joke. "Don't know what your problem is, Harris, but I got a job to do."

The corner of his lip twitched. "Suit yourself. You ain't gonna like what you see, though."

"It's a dead body. What's to like?"

I approached the scene. The huddled guys turned and eyed me strangely. *What's up with them?* I spied Parks. *She'll fill me in.*

I kept walking, danger creeping over me, and . . . and . . . I gritted my teeth. *Don't, Brynn. Not now. Not now . . .* But my senses slowed, and I knew what was coming.

The first time was during a recovery mission outside Kabul, a suicide bomber on motorcycle, everyone shouting, running. And me? I went into system overload, and just like that, I detached, floated above myself, watching my life unfold like a film playing in slow motion. One of my shrinks had a fancy name for it: depersonalization, a coping mechanism that occurs during high-anxiety moments. Whatever. It wasn't a problem when I took my meds. Since quitting, it'd started up again.

It was happening now.

Me: Slow motion, one step at a time, left foot, right . . .

Parks: Looking up, surprise registering on her face, and slowly her lips parted, and words poured out like slow-moving syrup. "Nooo . . . Brynnn. Don't . . . come over . . . here . . . Stay . . . baaack . . ."

Me: Walking, walking.

Parks: Reaching out, arms treading thick air, head shaking back and forth.

Me: Pushing her aside, lowering my eyes, taking in the blood, the gun, the blood-soaked hair, the gunshot wound, and the victim's face, torn apart, the skull fragmented, blood and brain matter, but the features . . . the features . . . Kevin Doogan.

I instantly snapped back into my body, my surroundings, all

my senses acutely aware. And the pain of loss and regret overwhelmed me. I fell to my knees. "Doogan."

"She can't be near the body." It was Harris. His hands clamped under my arms and pulled me backward. "Help me get her out of here. She's connected to the case. She can't be here."

Two other officers dragged me away from Doogan. Harris bent over me. "I tried to warn you, Callahan. Sorry about your friend, but at least we got a few answers here."

I blinked. "What?"

He sneered. "The casing found by his skull, it's thirty-eight special. I'm betting that we've found the weapon we've been looking for."

I didn't know what to say. Didn't know what to do. Didn't do anything. *Doogan . . .*

The officers helped me up and took me to their cruiser. I sat in the back, while they hovered nearby.

"I want my dog."

They shifted but stood their ground.

"Did you hear me? I want my dog."

One of the officers spoke over his radio, looked over at the other guy, and shook his head. I got out, headed for my own car. He stepped in front of me. His name tag said WILSON. A municipal cop. Never seen the guy before.

"Move out of my way."

"We have orders to keep you here, ma'am."

I pushed past him, started for my car. He grabbed me from behind. I turned, swung, and ended up with two more guys on me, each tugging at my arms. Parks was yelling something at me. I ignored her and went after one of the guys, caught him in the jaw.

"Shit!" He reached for his Taser.

"You going to tase me? I'm one of you. Let me at my dog."

I heard tires screech and Pusser's voice. "Let her be!"

The guys backed off. Pusser came over, put his face in mine. Not angry, but concerned. Sad. "It's okay, Brynn."

Brynn. He never called me by my first name.

"It's okay." He placed his hands on my shoulders as he whispered, "Don't cry, Brynn. Not now. Not in front of these assholes."

"My dog," I managed.

"I'll get you to Wilco."

"It's . . ."

"I know. I'm sorry. I'm so sorry." He pulled me close and embraced me.

I melted into him: the smell of hard work and cinnamon and something greasy, his strength, his comfort.

Like a father.

CHAPTER 27

I was eleven the first time I heard the word, and it made me feel dirty. I was at a slumber party. Me in pigtails, pink polka-dot pajamas, and a pink striped sleeping bag; and Riana Meath, the most popular girl in the trailer park, wearing a short silky nightgown and flanked by her two besties, explained to me how babies were made. She was an authority, because the night after Jimmy Gorman's whiskey-infused funeral wake, she'd caught her father bending her mother over the kitchen table. Her parents in the drunken throes of passion, and Riana just around the corner, suspended in fascination. But *sex* wasn't the word that made me feel dirty. I'd heard about it before, maybe on television or in a song or something. It was the other word that she whispered that night. *Bastard.* Which was what she said could have happened if that man hadn't been her father. "No bastard babies in our household," she said with a cruel slant of her eye. I didn't know what she meant or why she'd said it, so later that week I pulled my friend Queenie behind the jungle gym at recess and begged her to tell me. She did. I was a bastard child, conceived by a sinful mother and an unknown father, and everyone knew it.

It shattered me. And I ran to the one person who I knew could pick up the pieces. Gran.

Just like I ran to her now.

It was a little after nine in the morning when Wilco and I arrived at the hospital. Gran was still sleeping, her brother in a recliner near her bed. He stirred and opened one eye. I touched his shoulder.

"Thank you, Jarvis. We'll sit with her for a while. Go get some breakfast."

He stood with a grunt and a cluster of knee pops, scooped up his crossword puzzle book and bottled soda, and shuffled out. Jarvis could talk. I had just rarely heard him speak.

I usually didn't bring Wilco into the hospitals; the smells overwhelmed him. But Gran would need his comfort. As did I. He went to her right away and nudged her hand. Her eyes popped open and registered alarm at first, then became soft and warm. She lifted her hand and swiped gnarled knuckles over his fur. If she could, she'd smile.

I moved in closer. "Gran, Doogan is dead. His wife murdered him." *With your gun, Gran.* But I didn't say that.

Her eyes popped, and her stroke-inflicted mouth fell open, a sort of distorted, slack-lipped gape that reminded me of that painting *The Scream.* That was what it was: a silent scream. Then she let out a thin, high-pitched grunt and tears fell and Wilco whimpered, his eyes on our faces, sensing our pain. I lifted the blanket and slid in next to her, then placed my head against her shoulder. The lace collar of her flannel nightgown tickled my cheek, a fleeting memory from long ago, warmth and comfort.

Kevin Doogan was dead. Gone. The man whose courage and kindness had helped save her from facing the heartlessness of the law was dead. The one man who had wanted to love me was dead.

I nuzzled deeper into the crook of her arm, *inhale, exhale, a muffled sob.* . . . Then my own tears fell. I cried until sleep overwhelmed me, an exhausted escape from a morning of trauma and a lifetime of hurt.

I woke up an hour or so later. Jarvis was already back in the recliner, nose buried in his puzzle book. I kissed Gran's cheek, slid out from under the covers, and headed back to work.

When I walked into the breakroom, Parks was sitting at one of the brown laminate tables, her head bent over a magazine. She looked up and frowned. "Hey, Brynn. About what happened earlier. When I told you a body was found, I didn't know—"

"I know. It's okay."

"No it's not. I'm sorry. When we answer a call, there's always the chance that it'll be someone we know, someone we love, but . . . well, I just can't imagine . . ." She shook her head. "Why are you here? Figured you'd go home and—"

"Pusser wants to see me."

"Do you know why?"

"Questions about Kevin Doogan probably."

She nodded and crumpled the edge of the magazine between nervous fingers. "Is there anything I can do, Brynn?"

"Help me find Katie. I want to bring her in, make her pay for this. Doogan didn't deserve to—"

"I don't think you understand."

"Come on, Parks. What's not to understand? She's a cold-blooded killer."

"But she didn't do this."

"She did. Trust me. She's crazy. She tried to kill me, ran over Grabowski, went after my dog, and now she's killed Doogan. She's got to be stopped before—"

"Doogan killed himself, Brynn."

The room spun. I tried to focus on Parks but couldn't.

"Brynn? Did you hear me? It was suicide."

"But that can't be."

"It's pretty cut and dried. The gunshot appears to be self-inflicted."

"It was set up to look—"

"No, Brynn. I'm sorry. It was suicide. There was a note."

I leaned over, my palms flat on Pusser's desk. Wilco paced at my feet, whining. He sensed my emotion, and it put him on edge. "There's no way Doogan killed himself. You hear me, no way!"

"Sit down, Callahan."

"Look, boss, I just need to—"

"I said, sit down."

I moved to one of the chairs across from his desk and sat. Wilco coiled on the floor at my feet.

Pusser's voice was softer when he said, "You need to take some time off, get a little perspective. This would be hard for anybody and—"

"Bullshit. You know me better than that. What I need is to keep working."

"Then show me that you're stable enough to be on the job."

"I want to read the note."

"No. Not yet."

"Why not?"

He smacked his lips a couple times, shuffled some papers.

"Boss?"

"You're not working Doogan's case. You're too close to it."

"Don't shut me out. Please don't—"

"You're not to go near Doogan's case, you understand?" He bent forward. "Harris is all over it. If you ask me, he's looking to connect it to one of you people."

Gran, actually. And he can. All the more reason I need to—

"Is there anything you want to tell me, Callahan?"

"Yeah. Suicide doesn't fit. Doogan's not the type."

"Things change. It's been a while since you saw him. Because if you'd seen him lately, you would have reported it. There was a warrant on his head in connection to murder. You wouldn't impede a case like that, right?"

We stared each other down. Little pricks of sweat broke out along my hairline. I popped my knuckles. "The autopsy?"

"It's scheduled."

"And if it's a homicide?"

"You'll know."

"The wife is over the edge. She's—"

"Careful, Callahan . . ."

A warning. Don't give yourself away. He knew. He was trying to help me. *Just shut the hell up. Anything I say could and would be held against me, etcetera, etcetera. Got it.*

"You should take some time off. Get some distance between you and Doogan's death."

"I need to work."

"I understand. And we need you. On Walker and now Bannock, because we got nothing, really."

I gritted my teeth, forced my brain to think about a case that meant nothing to me now, nothing compared to Doogan's death, to Gran's vulnerability. Pusser waited. I took a breath. "Not exactly true. There's a connection between Walker and Bannock. It's just a matter of finding it."

"Hughie Black. See what connections you find there, too." I started to speak, and he raised his hand to stop me. "You want to work, then work like a cop. Every angle. We know Walker and Bannock went to the same high school. Start there and go forward. But go home now. Get some rest."

"I . . ."

He stood. Wilco stood. I stood.

"Take the rest of the day off, Callahan."

CHAPTER 28

Pusser didn't give me much of a choice, so I left.

But on the way home, I stopped by the high school, picked up a stack of yearbooks and a list of staff who had worked during the years Walker and Bannock were in school. I needed something, anything, to keep my brain from flashing images of Doogan lying there. It was like being on a retrieval mission, where "Do your damned job!" became the mantra as you ignored the bile-inducing images assaulting you. Right now, I was allowed to do only one job: find the Walker/Bannock connection.

I spent the rest of the day researching, starting with the teachers. It'd been seventeen years, so many of them had moved on, a few had passed on, but a couple were still around. I made the calls, set up interviews.

We decided to start with Mrs. Handie, English teacher, retired.

Parks and I knocked on her door the next morning, at nine o'clock.

A woman with big orange hair held back by bright barrettes

answered the door and blinked twice at my dog. She hesitated, then invited us inside, served us sweaty glasses of sweet tea and butter cookies on doily-covered plates before settling into a pale blue recliner.

She regarded me with black marker eyebrows raised high on her forehead. "I hope the tea's not too sweet. It's hard to know how much sugar to add."

My glass had a lip stain on the rim, sticky burnt orange with a little shimmer. I turned it and pretended to sip from the other side. "Perfect," I said, my eyes settling on Wilco, who stood alert and hyperfocused on a cat sitting on the end table: long cream-colored fur and piercing blue eyes. Exquisite, except for the fact that it was dead and stuffed.

Mrs. Handie caught Wilco and me gawking. "Isn't she a beauty?" Gnarled-knuckled hands stroked the cat's fur. "Such a good girl, too."

Parks coughed and set down her glass. "I believe Deputy Callahan told you that we wanted to ask you a few questions about your former students Chance Walker and Reed Bannock."

"Yes. I remember those two boys." She continued to stroke the cat, her eyes sparkling with admiration, then she looked at my dog with disdain. "Princess doesn't much care for dogs."

Parks shot me a "What the hell?" look. I cleared my throat, bent forward, tapped Wilco, and motioned for him to sit down. "How long did you teach English at McCreary High?"

"Twenty-nine years. And just senior English." She squinted at Parks. "Do I remember you, honey?"

Parks squirmed. "No, ma'am. I didn't take senior English."

I cut back in. "And you remember Chance Walker and Reed Bannock?"

"Yes. I already told you that." She sipped her tea, and the glass came away rim kissed, with its own pair of shimmering burnt-orange lips.

"Do you know if the two boys knew each other?"

She put her tea glass down and sank back in the recliner with a couple rapid blinks. "Yes, they knew each other. They were both in my class."

"They were in the same class? I don't understand. Bannock was a couple years ahead of Walker in school."

"My summer remedial course. That's what we called it back then, remedial. It was a multigrade class. Summer school operated differently. If there weren't enough students for multiple classes, we combined them."

"Did they hang out together after class?"

Mrs. Handie stared, her gaze empty and distant, the right side of her face twitching. *Twitch, twitch, twitch . . .* She bolted upright, jerked around, looked at the cat, then turned back and zeroed in on Wilco. "Princess doesn't like you."

Wilco looked up at the woman's sudden movement and cocked an ear and whimpered a little.

Parks rubbed the back of her neck and sighed. "Mrs. Handie, were Walker and Bannock friends?"

Mrs. Handie stood. "Yes. I would say so. They were pranksters. Always causing trouble. Boys will be boys, you know." She tugged at her blouse, red polyester stretched tight over a sagging bosom, her eyes never leaving Wilco. "It would be best if you and your dog could go now. In fact, I insist. It's time for Princess's nap."

CHAPTER 29

For the rest of the morning, Parks worked the militia angle and conducted phone interviews with Bannock's work buddies, while I interviewed teachers. Most of them could remember one boy or the other, but no connection between them. I requested a roster for that summer school class and began calling students. Not many of them remembered Walker and Bannock. I checked out Hughie Black's school days, and his family hadn't even lived in the state back then, so that was a relief. I looked deeper into Mrs. Handie, too, but didn't find much other than that she was a crazy woman with a stuffed cat and poor cleaning habits.

Late that afternoon, Parks and I teamed up to go through the yearbooks together. We were in the department conference room, Wilco napping under the table and a half-dozen McCreary High yearbooks spread between us. Bannock was a year ahead of Walker, so we had five years to cover. We'd done a quick check to see if they were on any teams or did other organized activities together. No luck there. Now we were looking at the candid pictures to see if any included both boys.

Parks looked over at me and sighed. "That cat was creepy."

"It was." *Some people are just plain nuts about their animals....* I looked down at my own dog.

I was nuts about my dog.

Parks continued, "I don't know if we can believe anything she said."

"At least we have a connection." I hesitated, then said, "Today at Mrs. Handie's place, you said you never took senior English."

"No. I didn't make it that far in school."

"But you're a cop. You must've—"

"GED."

"Oh."

She picked up one of the books and flipped the pages, slid it my way. "Second row. Brace face."

I skimmed the page, landed on a younger version of Parks, thinner, with permed hair and braces. "Wow. That hair."

She giggled. "I know. Can't believe we did that to ourselves then."

I didn't. Wanted to, though. But Gran and Gramps had always said the money was better spent elsewhere. "So, what happened?"

"My girl happened, that's what. I was a sophomore. We'd just moved here from Asheville, North Carolina."

"That must've been hard."

"It was."

I slid the yearbook back. "So you didn't know Walker and Bannock?"

"I didn't know anybody. I was in school for only a month before I started showing. Just long enough to get a yearbook picture taken. The father was back in Asheville. Mama homeschooled me, and then I got my GED and went to community college."

"That's when you met John?"

"Yup. He's been the best daddy ever. To both the kids."
Something flashed in her eyes then. Regret? The nausea and the
tiredness, maybe it wasn't what I thought, but something else.
I reached for a book in the stack next to Parks. "Hey, Parks.
Are you—"

"I've gone through those already." She pushed the stack
aside.

"Thought I'd just do a double check," I said. We'd been at it
for a couple hours, and so far nothing.

Parks marked her current page and glanced at the wall clock.
"That does it for me."

"Heading home?"

"It's after five, and hubby gets all *hangry* if I push dinner off
for too long." She picked up the stack of books. "I'll take these
and go over them again tonight." She headed toward the door, a
slight limp still, and stopped. Jake stood in the doorway. The
two of them squared off for a second; then Parks dipped her
head and shuffled by.

Jake let her pass. "Yearbooks?" He walked in and looked
over my shoulder.

"We found a connection between Walker and Bannock," I
said. "They were in the same summer school English class.
That would have been the year before Bannock graduated. We
interviewed the teacher. She says they were friends. *Pranksters*
was her word. We're trying to see if they're pictured together
or maybe with someone else. We figure if there's going to be a
third victim soon, we'd like to get to that person before the
perp does."

"Get anything from the girlfriend yet?"

"Nikki? No. Not much. She's in bad shape." I scanned the
next set of photos and got distracted by a picture of a long-
legged girl wearing a super-short miniskirt. *And people think
our young Pavee girls dress provocatively.* I squinted closer. Oh,
I knew this girl, well, a woman now; she was married and lived

a few trailers down from me. *Okay, guess we Pavees do have a noticeable style.* I flipped to the next page. "What brings you by, anyway?"

"You."

I looked up.

He smiled. "I was driving by and saw your car in the lot. Thought I'd pop in and see if you wanted to go for dinner."

"Tempting. And thanks, but I want to finish this." I moved on to the next page. Pink balloons, glitzy dresses, twisted streamers looped from the ceiling, boys in tuxes, with dirty thoughts on their minds. Candids from prom. Glad I had skipped mine.

"You have to eat, Brynn."

"Uh-huh. There's a vending machine down the hall."

"I can do better than that. I'll get takeout and be back. Give me fifteen."

I shrugged and turned the page.

CHAPTER 30

Maybe he came back in fifteen minutes; maybe he didn't. I wasn't there.

Right after Jake left for take-out food, I got a call from Pusser. Nikki had bolted during the ride from the hospital to her new facility and was on the run.

She could be halfway to Nashville by now, or anywhere, but I knew from experience that the first thing she'd do was try to get a fix. And a fix cost cash. And the readiest supply of cash would be at Lucky's. Supply and demand. She'd said that the first time I interviewed her. Supply her customers; get cash; and fulfill her body's demand for a fix.

Twenty minutes later I parked in Lucky's lot and called in my location. Wilco was vested, on lead, and at attention. His nose twitched overtime as we worked down the line of trucks. Diesel fumes hung heavy in the air, along with the smell of grease and rubber and the zing of ozone riding in on the downdraft of a pending rainstorm.

I picked up my pace and headed down the next line of trucks. Another five yards and Wilco lifted his snout and drew in a deep whiff of air, lowered his head, spread his legs, and went low to the ground. The first drops of rain started to fall, and people dashed from the restaurant back to their rigs to beat what promised to become a deluge. The wind whipped at my hair. Then a sudden flash of lightning sent Wilco scooting under the undercarriage of a nearby truck. I yanked the lead. He gagged but didn't budge.

Damn it, Wilco. I got down on all fours, spread out, belly on the ground, and reached for him. My fingertips connected with a spike of fur sticking out from under the edge of his vest. I stayed like that, my cheek flat against the concrete, my finger-tips brushing against Wilco's neck, soothing and coaxing. His forehead wrinkled with worry; his eyes darted back and forth. I tapped him, tried to engage his stare. If he focused on me, there was a chance I'd get him out of there.

A high-pitched voice came from the other side of the truck, familiar and slightly slurred. Nikki's voice.

I rose up and gave Wilco's lead another yank. "Come on. Come on!" He didn't move. I dropped the leash—*Suit your-self*—and rounded the front bumper just in time to see Nikki climbing into the rig's cab.

Oh, no you don't.

I banged on the door. "Nikki!"

A face appeared, bearded and angry, and the window low-ered.

I spoke before he could say anything. "I want to talk to Nikki."

"Who?"

"The woman in your cab. It's police business. Tell her to come out here."

He looked me up and down. "Sorry, Officer. Don't know no Nikki. That's my girlfriend you saw. Ain't no law against my girlfriend visiting me now, is there?"

"Sorry to tell you, buddy, but your girlfriend's a known prostitute."

"What is this? Why you harassing us out here? I'm just—"

"Send her out. Now."

He looked over his shoulder, started talking. "Hey, dar-lin' . . ."

I radioed in for backup and was giving my location when the rig's passenger-side door popped open and feet hit the pavement.

I sprinted around the front of the truck, collided midway with Nikki. I clamped my hands down on her shoulders. "Hold up, Nikki. I just want to talk to you."

A hollowed-out face stared back, pale, with black-rimmed, lashless eyes, tightly drawn lips edged with little puss-filled sores. A whisper away from death. How was she even able to get from point A to point B, never mind from the hospital to here?

"I can't go back to that place." She was calmer, clearer minded than before. She had already had a fix, had got the meth pumping back through her blood. The first hit off the wagon was sweet but short lasting. She'd need to get more and fast, or she'd crash twice as hard.

She was desperate but at least coherent.

"Come with me, Nikki. We'll just talk. I promise."

"I already told you, I'm not goin' back."

"They can help you there."

"No. No. They want to kill me."

"It's hard to give it up, but—"

"It's my fault."

"That's the truth, Officer." I wheeled, surprised to see the trucker behind me. "I didn't know nothing about her bein' no prostitute. I swear."

"Shut up and get back in your cab, or I'll cuff you right now. You understand?" I turned back to Nikki. "You need help, Nikki. Let me help you."

"I just need some money."

"I didn't pay her nothing," the trucker said. "And you can't take me in unless money was exchanged. I know my rights."

Nikki's eyes darted; her muscles tensed. "Please. Just a little money. I've got to have some money."

A softer voice. Be gentle, Brynn. She needs understanding. "You can beat this, Nikki. Come with me. I can help you."

A flash of lightning and a crack of thunder. Nikki flinched, and rain fell hard.

"I gotta leave. Get away from here."

"Listen, Nikki. We'll make it work. We'll get you someplace else. Away from all this, so you can get better."

She met my gaze, pleading, scared. "You're not listenin' to me. I knew what happened to that boy . . . Chance told me what they did back then, and I . . . I told someone . . . It's my fault. What happened to Chance is my fault."

"What boy? What happened?"

The trucker started in again. "Nothing happened, lady. We weren't doin' nothin', I swear."

I whipped back around. "You just can't keep your mouth shut, can you?"

Sounds behind me. I turned back. *Crap!* Nikki was running for it.

I started after her and my foot slipped on the wet concrete. The momentum propelled me forward, my hands hit the pavement, and hot pain radiated past my shoulders and into my neck. I righted myself, looked left and then right, rows of rigs blocking my views, and then heard a scuffling sound off to the left.

I headed that way, skirted between two semis. *Where's my backup?* A small scream. More scuffling. I sped up. . . . *Nikki!*

I rounded a black rig with a jawlike grill painted with red and orange flames. A ways down, a man had Nikki pinned against another trailer. Her arms flailed, she thrashed back and forth, he got rougher, grabbing her by the hair and pulling her head back. Her throat swelled and was exposed.

He screamed, his voice rising above the pounding rain, "Where's my money? You took the stuff. Now pay up. Ain't nothing comin' for free around here."

I kept running. . . . Thirty feet, twenty-five . . . "Stop! Po—" Lightning flashed, and more thunder erupted. "Stop!"

The man released her hair. She stumbled forward, raised her hands, and went wild eyed as his hand flew up and cracked across her cheek. She careened back, slammed into the trailer, then crumpled to the asphalt, a pile of pale bones and wet clothes.

He reeled his leg back, nearby headlights gleaming off the steel toe of his boot.

"Nooo!" I flung myself and connected with a thump, my shoulder sinking into his back. We went down, and my neck snapped back, jawbone vibrated, teeth pierced the edge of my tongue, and hot, coppery blood swirled inside my cheek. *You son of a bitch!* I clenched, raised my arm; we rolled, pelvis to pelvis, his body on mine. . . . *I can't move. I can't move!* Car doors slammed, footsteps, and guys yelling . . . No, they were cheering, an audience of assholes. *Backup. Where's my backup!* He leaned in, a wiry beard, black nose hairs, snarling lips, chipped yellow teeth, hairy knuckles coming in fast, clenching my neck, squeezing my throat. I bucked, jerked my leg up into his groin, felt the satisfying connection of knee bone to meaty scrotum. He popped up, eyes wide and back arched. He clenched his crotch, howling like a wounded coyote, then plunged forward, eyes boring into me, nasty and angry, hands vise gripping my throat. *Oh shit!*

I tried to scream, to raise myself up, got an inch or so, and fell back again. More cheers, black dots. *Can't breathe. Can't breathe. Click, click, click* . . . I knew that sound: nails on pavement. *Click, click, click* back and forth, growls, deep and fierce. *Wilco!*

I raised my hand and motioned. . . . *Attack. Attack!*

A blurry arrow of fur, muscle, and teeth flew through the air and connected—*thunk!*—and then screams, high-pitched baby squeals mixed with low, undulated snarls permeated the air, along with hot dog breath and the ammonia sting of piss, dumb ass's, not Wilco's. I pushed backward, free and clear, and scrambled to my feet, wiped the blood from my lips, and sucked in air. Wilco stood with all three paws on the man's chest, his teeth buried in the guy's shoulder.

The air lit up with lightning, thunder boomed, but my dog didn't budge. "Good boy." I looked back toward the semi, through the pounding rain, past the crowd of onlookers. . . .

Nikki was gone.

CHAPTER 31

Reinforcements came, med transport was called, witnesses were interviewed, reports filled out, and a couple hours later, and well after midnight, the mess at Lucky's was a wrap.

Wilco and I were soaked through. I headed home for a hot shower, got there, and found Meg curled on the sofa, Gran's afghan pulled tight around her torso, red hair fallen over her features. I nudged her. She rolled her head, her eyelids fluttering.

"Meg. It's me. It's late. You should get into bed."

Her eyes opened, and she sat up. "Brynn. I wanted to talk to you."

I took a seat. The coffee table was littered with crumpled tissues and a spilled bag of potato chips.

"Is Gran okay?"

"No change. But the—"

"No change. That's good, right? She'll get better. Maybe we should—"

"That cop you hate came by this evening. Harris."

My jaw clenched. "What'd he want?"

"He had questions about things. A lot of things." Her fingers worked the loopy yarn of the afghan. Gramps's favorite. It still held the faint smell of the cigarettes he had enjoyed so much. The same ones that had killed him. "You haven't told me everything that happened with Dublin Costello, have you?" I blinked and looked away. My hand trembled. Booze-soaked blood had swirled around my nerves for years, calming them, numbing them; and now deprived, they pulsated in protest. I slid my quaking fingers under my leg.

There weren't many things I kept from Meg, but some things cut too deep. That day in Dub's trailer all those years ago, when I rejected him, refused to carry through with an arranged marriage Gramps had promised him, Dub forced himself on me and brutally took what he wanted, leaving me beaten and bloody and torn, raped of my innocence. I'd never told Meg. Couldn't. The scars from that rape weren't like my war scars. Yes, I carried both. But in war I was a casualty, and my scars were a banner of honor and bravery, but rape . . . those scars were different. I was the victim, yes, but in my mind, I replayed the trauma over and over: Could I have done more? Fought harder? Screamed louder?

I kept my gaze focused on the floor. "What type of questions did Harris ask?"

"He wanted to know if Gran still had a gun."

"What did you tell him?"

She stood and started pacing, arms wrapped around her midsection. "I didn't tell him crap. He's a copper. A musker."

Loyalty. Part of clan creed. It paired well with another clan trait: hatred for settled law.

She went on, "But why's he asking? That's what I need to know."

"What else did he say?"

"He had a photo on him from the newspaper. Back from that time when Gran waved a gun at the press. She was within her rights. They were trespassing. Looking in our windows and stuff."

"Yes, she was within her rights."

"That damn copper laughed at me." Meg was worked up. "He said that it didn't matter if I talked or not. He'd have it figured out soon, anyway."

Harris was getting closer. It was only a matter of time now before he connected Gran to the gun that had killed Dublin. Time I didn't have to spare.

CHAPTER 32

Every day Wilco watered the bush outside the department's main entrance. He took pride in his work: backside turned, little nub lifted high, a steady stream directly dousing the roots. His bush, his department. That Saturday morning we were at it early. He watered, while I checked out the parking lot, looking for Harris's vehicle. It wasn't there. I didn't think it would be. Harris wasn't the early bird type.

We headed in, passing by a few of the second shifters. The McCreary County Sheriff's Department Web site bragged that we were composed of thirty-two full-time staff members, all committed to keeping the county a safe place to live, work, worship, and raise a family. Actually, that number was stretched to include two janitors, dispatchers, and a couple civvies who worked the front desk. Then divide the remainder by the number of shifts it took to cover every hour of seven days a week and, well, we were lucky when not more than one crime was committed at the same time. Truth was, McCreary County was the smallest county in Tennessee, covering 186 square miles of the Bald Mountains and the Unaka Range, and last time I checked, it had under twenty-five thousand citizens, most of them making less than forty thousand a year. McCreary County was small and poor. The same could be said for the sheriff's department. Still, we ran a three-shift department. The sheriff, Wilco and I, Parks, and sometimes Harris made up the criminal investigative unit. We were on call 24/7 but reported daily at 8:00 A.M. with the other day shifters: patrol officers, clerks, dispatchers.

But right now it was barely 6:00 A.M., and none of those people were here. The department was quiet, one front-desk worker, a dispatcher, a janitor or two roaming about, but most of the deputies were on patrol. This should be easy work.

Wilco headed straight for his spot under my desk. I headed for Harris's spot. A few seconds were all I needed. A quick glance over my shoulder. No one. I focused on his desktop, cluttered and chaotic: computer; a stack of unfinished reports; a crumpled chip bag; foam coffee cup; a rec league softball trophy; and a pile of file folders, smudges of greasy chip prints on the ones most opened.

Another glance around, then file folders first. Three or four case files, but none of them Dub Costello's case. I moved on to the shallow center drawer: pens, Post-it Notes, loose change, a pack of gum, and . . . oh, a full prescription bottle. I checked the label. Vicodin. I didn't know Harris had anxiety. *And he takes the same pills that I do, or did . . . used to, might still need.* I twisted the top and took a few for myself and went on to the next drawer—a couple department manuals (no greasy fingerprints there), notepads, a half-empty twist-top soda—and then the bottom drawer.

This one had a lock, but Harris never bothered. I pulled it open. An extra holster, a couple ammo mags, busted flashlight, a department-issued Polaroid camera and, crammed way in the back of the drawer, a couple photos. The top one caught my eye. I hesitated. . . . *What the hell?* I pulled them out for a closer look. Nudes of two different women, each suggestively posed. I recognized one of them as Amber, our ditzy front-desk gal and one of Harris's old flames. He had many. The department used Polaroids because they were instant and tamper-proof, used mostly for documenting domestic abuse. This was abuse, alright—feeding Harris's perverted appetite was an abuse of the film. I thought of the picture my maimed body would produce, and a cold slime of disgust washed over me. Only one man had made my body feel whole enough, good enough, to touch. And Doogan was dead. I closed my eyes; a brew of guilt and grief bubbled in my gut. I shook my head. *Focus. Focus.* I started to set the pictures back and saw the corner of another photo.

I turned it over; my stomach churned. This gal was skinny, with greasy hair and a marijuana leaf tattooed under her left breast. I'd never seen her before, but she was young. *Too young.* And she was posing on a cot. Just like the ones in our holding cell.

I'd always suspected Harris of being a perv and knew he was a jerk and stupid, too, but not this dumb. My guess, he had shoved these in here just as a temporary place before he could put them somewhere safe, someplace accessible only by him.

My mind raced. Call Pusser and report what I'd found? Maybe. But I had a better idea. I pulled an evidence bag from my utility belt and dropped the photos into it, shoved it inside my bra, and moved to my desk to settle back in my chair.

An hour or so later, Harris swaggered in, coffee cup in hand and a blue file folder tucked in his armpit. He settled into his chair with a creak.

He put the file folder on his desk and patted it with a sneer aimed my way. "I've got a couple more pieces of important info about Dub Costello's murder. Real interesting information. Got it tucked right in here."

He set his cup down and paused; his chin sank into his chest as he surveyed the top of his desk. His hand hovered over his stack of file folders, then moved back and forth, like a psychic would when doing a reading. "Someone's messed with my stuff." He cursed and glared at me. "You been messin' with my things, Callahan?"

I kept my eyes on my paperwork, but my cheeks burned hot.

Drawers opened one at a time, and when he got to the bottom drawer, he stopped.

I looked over. "Something the matter, Harris?"

He got down on all fours and searched inside the drawer. More curse words, and then he plopped back into his chair, hard enough to send it wheeling back a foot. He swiveled and faced me head-on. Our eyes locked.

I flashed my sweetest smile. "What a weird coincidence, Harris. You and me, we've both got some important information tucked away."

At roll call, Pusser filled the others in on my ordeal with Nikki last night. "We ended up with a couple arrests, assault on an officer, a possession charge. But Nikki Russo is still on the run. So be on the lookout. She's in bad shape but still might be our best witness to the Walker crime."

Afterward, I came back to my desk to check the county booking records. It didn't take long to find the girl in Harris's picture: Alma Shelton, eighteen, picked up on a possessions charge, held overnight, released on bond the next morning. Young, but legally a consenting adult. Lucky for Harris. But now I had a name.

I also searched crimes reported during that summer Walker and Bannock were together in remedial English. And I found something.

I headed to Parks's desk. "Hey, Parks. Did you find anything in those yearbooks you took home?"

She looked up. Her eyes were dull and distant. "No. Nothing."

"Too bad. But I might have come up with something. When I confronted Nikki last night, before she ran off, she said something about how she 'knew what happened to that boy' and that she told someone. Check this out." I had printed the report and now slid the information in front of her. "I couldn't find a crime with a boy in their school. But I did find this. Zeke Farrell. Age seventeen. There's a death notice, but no obituary. At least not that I've found. According to the report, the death was ruled as rail suicide. Zeke was lying on the tracks on the edge of town. The conductor tried to stop, but it was too late. No witnesses. The ME didn't have much to work with, but they were able to identify him. Think it might be what Nikki meant?"

She shrugged.

I tapped the paper. "Looks like the municipal cops were first on the scene. Johnson was the reporting officer."

It made sense. He was a lieutenant now on the city cop force and likely was a beat cop back in the day.

Parks sat back and rubbed her temples.

"Are you sick, Parks? You haven't been yourself."

"I'm okay. This case is complicated, that's all." She smiled, but it looked forced.

"You've been working hard." I gathered the report. "Listen, I'll take care of talking to Johnson. I'll see if I can find out what he remembers about Zeke's death."

She grabbed hold of the papers. "No. I'll do it. I've got time."

"Okay. Sure." I leaned against her desk, thinking through the facts. "Zeke would have been about the same age as Bannock and Walker. Maybe they knew each other. The timing is right. Walker was going into his junior year at the time, and Bannock his senior year."

"True, but the report lists suicide as the cause of death. There was no evidence pointing to anything else." Parks shook her head. "A horrific tragedy. I can't imagine how his parents took it. His mother, especially."

Her eyes watered. A cop, yes, but a mother first. She'd seen her share of accidents, death, tragedies like this one, but when it involved a child . . . she had a mother's heart.

"Sure you're okay, Parks?"

"Yeah. Kids, you know. They're never easy. My daughter's been giving us a tough time. Out late every night and such a smart-mouth. She's driving me crazy. This morning I told hubby that I couldn't wait until she heads to school this fall, to get her out of my hair, but truth is, I can't imagine life without her. And if she ever felt so bad that she did something like that . . ."

Parks wasn't usually so emotional. "She's going to be okay, Parks. She's strong. Got a good head on her shoulders, like her mama."

She let out a long breath. "Yeah, I guess."

I pushed off the desk. "So, okay, back to Zeke Farrell. The timing and age are right. That's all we have. But it's the only thing we have. I'll go run it by Pusser and see how he wants us to proceed."

CHAPTER 33

Pusser wanted us to reopen the investigation into Zeke Farrell's death. It was kind of a long shot, based solely on the words of a strung-out junkie in a rainstorm and a string of loose facts, but it was all we had. Parks talked to Lieutenant Johnson but didn't get much. He remembered the case— "Gruesome," he said—but had nothing to add to what was already in the report. The school was a dead end, too. There was no record of enrollment for Zeke Farrell. No address, nothing.

Harris was going back to Walker's and Bannock's places of employment and interviewing people they had worked with, as well as Bannock's ex, Kimber. I tracked down the train conductor and called his number but wasn't able to reach him, yet. For now, there was only one other thing to do. Go back and see the crazy woman.

Mrs. Handie opened the door, wearing a housecoat and fuzzy slippers. Her eyeballs rolled around the porch. "You don't have that dog with you, do you?"

"I left him in the car."

"Come in."

A fat spider scurried on a network of overhead webs as we ducked into a waft of grease and dust, musty old newspapers and urine-soaked cushions. Crazy-woman smell. My gaze drifted to Princess, still perched on the end table, then back to Mrs. Handie.

Parks cleared her throat. "We've thought of a couple more questions."

I pulled out a picture of Zeke, a copy from the newspaper article on the incident, a boy with a lopsided grin. "Do you know this young man?"

She crossed the room to her cat. I followed. "Yes. We knew him, didn't we, Princess?"

The cat's dead and stuffed, lady. Get a grip. "Was he in one of your classes?"

"Oh, heavens, no." She ran long fingers over the cat's forehead and down its back. "He was our angel."

My jaw went slack. "Angel?"

"Guardian angel. If it weren't for Zeke, my sweet baby wouldn't be with me today." She bent in and made kissy noises. "How many times did Mommy tell you not to go outside? Such a naughty, naughty girl."

Parks had pretty much pressed herself up against the door, chin down. Stifling a giggle over the crazy cat woman or nauseous again? Hard to tell. But the stench was getting to me, too.

I kept on. "Um . . . did Princess get hurt?"

She scowled. "Why would you say that? She's right here. After the vet said, well, said bad things about my Princess, Zeke took her to his house for a bit and then brought her right back to me. See?"

Tread carefully, Brynn. I smiled at the stupid cat. "It's a miracle."

"Yes. A miracle."

She loved this cat so much, she couldn't bear to part with it.

Couldn't bring herself to believe that it had been hurt, let alone that a vet had pronounced it dead. And Zeke had stuffed the thing for her? No, this was a professional job, no kid's hatchet attempt. Zeke must have had some taxidermy training. This crazy woman probably thought he ran a cat spa or resort, and kitty came back all prim and glassy-eyed happy after a little retreat.

"How did you know about Zeke? That he could, uh, fix Princess?" I asked.

"The vet recommended him."

"Do you remember the vet's name?"

"Styles. Dr. Styles. Such a nice man. Do you know him?"

My mouth went dry. "Yes. He took care of my dog." And I took care of him. Rammed a knife into his stomach. Gutted him, as Pusser claimed. I'd taken justice into my own hands, the Pavee way.

At the mention of Wilco, Mrs. Handie became agitated again. We weren't getting much from her, anyway, so I wrapped up the conversation and thanked her for her time. Before I left, she insisted that I give Princess a quick scratch between the ears.

I obliged, the little beast's glassy eyes reminding me again of Styles's last wicked sneer as the life drained from him. I shivered. All that had happened two years ago. No need to think of it now. Or ever again.

CHAPTER 34

But it all came rushing back in my dreams that night.

I jerked awake, the sheet sticking to my sweaty back. My heart pounding against tightened chest muscles; my breath deep and labored; and inside my head, like ocean waves beating against my skull. Wilco shifted and sat up, whimpering, and sniffed at my face, hot tongue running over my cheeks. He had sensed my nightmare, my anguish, and now comforted me in the way only he could.

Bang, bang, bang . . . I flinched and tightened my grip on Wilco, placed my cheek along his, willing myself to calm. *Car doors, that's all.* I knew it. But to a war-torn brain, logic didn't always prevail. That was why I no longer slept with my gun on my nightstand. One night I had woken with Meg in my sites, when she'd come in after hearing my anguished nightmare cries. Now the gun lay in the top dresser drawer. The extra few seconds to retrieval was enough time to come to grips with reality.

Cold water on my face, that was what I needed. I threw my feet over the edge of the mattress and made my way down the hall, past Gramps's old room, where Meg now slept, to the bathroom. I splashed and dried my face and squatted on the toilet. Wilco came in, pawed at my legs, and sniffed the bowl. Gross. I nudged him away with my foot. "Get!"

Outside, more car doors, voices, car engines, the beep of a horn. *What's going on?*

I finished my business and made my way through the trailer, my whiny dog on my heels. As soon as I cracked the door, he pushed through, hobbled down the steps, and lifted his nub on a patch of weeds in the front yard.

There were a dozen or so people outside, adults and a few kids next door, at what had been Doogan's trailer. Talking and laughing, a couple of them crying, and all of them revolving around a tall middle-aged woman, who held her angular frame in a way that demonstrated her presence: the matriarch, not demanding attention but embracing what was expected—and given. Her red hair was pulled into a sleek ponytail, and a simple black dress served as the exclamation point to her position. I had never seen her before but recognized her instantly. How could I not? She had the same chiseled features as Doogan—his mother.

I shut the door and paced, my heart pounding. Doogan's family. *Why are they here?* No doubt to gather his things. It was logical, simple. *Let them do their thing.* Yet my nerves tingled. I couldn't let my last contact with Doogan, even if only through his family, slip away.

I wanted to meet them. Had to meet them. So back to the bathroom for a couple swishes of mouthwash, a quick comb through, then jeans and a T-shirt, Wilco's leash, and I was out the door. The woman I'd seen was no longer in sight. My dog wandered to a clump of men, muscle shirts and tattoos, hands in jean pockets, feet shuffling. One of them bent over to pet Wilco.

"This your dog?" he asked.

"Yeah. Sorry about that." I joined them and attached the lead to Wilco's collar.

The guy stood up straight. His eyes roamed from the front of my shirt to the raised, puckered skin of my neck. My scar itched. "You're Brynn." He held out his hand. "Sean. Kevin Doogan's cousin. Kevin told me about you. That's why I recogni—" His eyes darted back to my scar, then away.

Yeah, buddy. That's right. I'm the burnt-up woman who lives next door. Had this joker sat back and had a good laugh when Doogan described me?

I gritted my teeth and said nothing, but Sean found his voice and met my gaze. His hazel eyes were the same shade as Doogan's. "I think you should talk to my aunt Callie," he said. "Kevin's mom. She's inside the trailer, packing up his belongings. We're here to take his body home for the wake."

"I don't know." *I want to talk to her . . . don't I? That is why I came outside. But what would I say to her?* Wilco came to my side and brushed against my leg. I let my hand drop, felt his warm, wet nose against my palm. The other guys stared at me. Off to the right, a couple of kids kicked a ball around. Doogan's kids. I recognized the boy. A carbon copy of his father.

Sean pointed at the trailer. "She's asked to meet you."

She wanted to meet *me*? I agreed and followed Sean inside, to where Doogan's mother knelt in the front room of the trailer, rearranging items packed in a box. The trailer smelled of dust and wet carpeting, rusted pipes and dank toilet water. A baby slept in a portable crib in the corner of the room. Wilco sniffed the perimeter, then plopped on the floor nearby.

Sean put his hand on the woman's shoulder. "Aunt Callie. Kevin's friend Brynn is here."

She turned my way, her eyes swollen, glazed over, and intense. Unblinking. Her movements slow and deliberate. Shock numbed her brain, erected a protective wall, syphoned the pain that threatened to destroy her heart.

She held out her hand to me, and long ice-cold fingers enclosed mine. I knelt to her level. "Mrs. Doogan. I'm sorry for your loss." Inadequate, but I had nothing else.

"My son talked about you. You're a cop."

I swallowed and fought to keep my breath even. Doogan talked to his mother about me?

Her features tightened. "My son did not kill himself."

I nodded. Not sure what to say.

Her mouth twisted in anger. "It wasn't suicide. He was murdered."

"There was a note."

"The note is a lie. Those weren't his words. And there's no way he would have done that to his kids."

So, she'd seen the note. "What did the note—"

"I told that to those coppers. It was a lie. But they don't ever believe our people. But a mother knows her own son, Pavee or not." Her voice thinned out to a whisper. "Murdered. Just like my Sheila. Two children murdered. Two . . ."

"I'm sor—"

"It was Katie. His wife. She did it. *An bhitseach.*" That bitch.

"They were having problems."

"Yes. Since the beginning. I was against that marriage. But her mother and my mother arranged it long ago, and my husband was convinced that it'd be a good union, and good for the family."

Ah, yes. I knew those words. Katie came with a good dowry. Good for the family.

"But things went bad right away. And then my son got into trouble. He . . . he did prison time."

"He told me."

She nodded. "Then Sheila's death . . . murder." Her voice broke. "Kevin told me that you brought her killer to justice."

What I did went beyond justice. "Yes."

"And my son helped you with something, too."

So, he'd told her about Gran and Dublin Costello. "Yes, he did."

"My son cared for you."

"We didn't know each other for very long."

"But you . . . ?"

"Yes, I cared for him."

Her eyes, intense and determined, bore into mine. "You think she did it, too?"

I did. But I didn't answer.

"I want Katie to pay for what she's done to my son."

"We don't have proof that she killed him."

"She did. I know it. She murdered my son. You know it, too. And she needs to be brought to justice."

"She's the mother of your grandchildren."

"I'll see that they're taken care of. Believe me, they'd be better off with no mother than with her."

CHAPTER 35

Callie's words replayed in my mind as I drove to work that morning: *They'd be better off with no mother.* . . . The link between mother and child tore at the fabric of lives. My own mother, unmarried and pregnant at seventeen, in trouble with the law, and ostracized from the clan, had left Bone Gap and me behind. Had it been a blessing? Had I been better off without her, raised by Gran? I loved Gran with all my heart, yet I carried my mother's absence with me every day, and that void defined me. For the better? Worse? I didn't know. What would Katie's children suffer if I doled out justice to their mother, the woman who had killed their father? And what would they suffer if I didn't?

Parks met me outside the department at eight o'clock. It took about thirty minutes to get to Johnson City, and another ten or so to locate the train conductor's place, a ranch-style home, red brick with white trim and a screened front porch. Old but well kept.

A lawn mower sat mid-strip in the front yard. A man called from within the screened porch. "I'm here. Come on in."

We entered, Wilco at our heels. "Mr. Roger Meyer?" I asked if it was okay to have my dog with me.

"Call me Roger, and yes, I'm glad to see the dog. Used to have a dog. Duke. Best damn dog ever." He offered a pudgy hand, dirt creased and calloused. Gray tufts of hair poked out on either side of a cap advertising the local Ford dealership. He smelled like fresh grass and sweat. "So, what's the sheriff's department want?" He motioned for us to sit.

My shoes made a scraping sound on the green indoor/outdoor carpet. I settled in a folding lawn chair and explained why we were there.

Roger rubbed at his whiskered jaw. "I remember it like it was yesterday. Coal train, but ain't a lot of need for that now. They shut down the old Clinchfield line, you know? Don't think trains run through your parts no more." He picked up his coffee cup and took a sip. "Get y'all some?"

"No thanks. Can you tell us about that night?"

"Not much to tell. The kid was on the tracks. I couldn't stop in time, and I hit him. It's haunted me ever since."

"Is there anything in particular that stood out?"

"The whole damn thing." The cup shook in his hand.

"I'm sorry."

Parks hadn't said a word. She sat opposite me in a lawn chair. An electric fan hummed and clicked in the corner. Wilco lay directly in front of it, focused on the whirling blades, his fur rippling from the blowing air.

Roger continued, "About a month after it happened, the mother paid me a visit. I could hardly look at her, felt so bad for her."

"Was she angry with you?"

"She was. But I explained to her that I couldn't stop the train. She seemed to understand, but she wanted to know stuff."

"Like what?"

He stared at the floor. "Like if he moved or tried to get up before . . . before I hit him."

"Did he?"

His features darkened. "It was a high-speed collision. I didn't have time to slow the damn train down. It couldn't be avoided. And he was just a kid. It was awful. There was nothing left . . ." Sweat pricked his hairline. He set his coffee aside and swiped his forehead.

"I understand." And I did. The impact of that type of speed would be like bodies impacted by explosions: blood spray, flesh fragments, bones, and odd chunks of organs. "But the mother asked if Zeke had moved. Did he flinch? Anything?"

"No. Nothin'."

Parks spoke up. "Are you sure? It might have been difficult—"

"Listen, lady. I had full freight that night, 'bout seven thousand tons, and was travelling at 'round fifty-five miles per hour. It was near ten seconds from the time I applied the brakes until impact. The longest ten seconds of my life. I was locked on that boy. Didn't close my eyes or nothin'. Dear Lawd, the sound when I hit him . . ."

Wilco turned his head and whined.

Roger's eyes glazed over. "I'm tellin' ya, there weren't no movement. He was just lyin' there, stretched out straight across the tracks, with his arms at his sides."

That doesn't sound right.

Parks must've thought the same thing. She stayed quiet, folded her arms, and clenched herself. This type of talk about a kid must've bothered her.

I leaned forward. "His head didn't move at all?"

"Nothin'. Still as a dead man." He looked down and shook his head. "Poor woman got real upset after that. Kept sayin' that someone had lied about her boy."

"Lied about what?" I asked.

Roger still shook his head. "Didn't say. I didn't ask, couldn't. But I was the only one who saw . . ." He squeezed his eyes against seeing the horror once again.

I came to a silent conclusion: This didn't sound like suicide. If Zeke had been conscious at the time, he would have flinched or cowered before impact. It would have been instinctual. He couldn't have helped it.

Still as a dead man.

Was it possible that Zeke had been drugged prior to lying on the tracks? Was the lie about not finding drugs in his system or in whatever pieces of it they had recovered? That the mother knew her son took drugs, or suspected he'd been drugged? Or . . . was he knocked out or already dead before impact? His arms at his sides . . . Had someone arranged his body on the tracks? I'd seen posed bodies before, done for a purpose, whether ritualistic or to honor the dead. But the only reason to lay a dead body on railroad tracks would be to cover up the real cause of death.

I called Pusser on the way back from Johnson City, put him on speaker, and told him we'd gotten a break in the case. "I don't think Zeke Farrell's mother believed her son died by suicide." I told him about the body and how it was immobile before impact and positioned on the tracks. "Has Harris turned up any connection yet between Walker and Bannock and Zeke Farrell?"

"Nothing yet."

"Any luck finding an address for his family?"

"Harris pulled the death certificate. Mother was Georgia Farrell. The address of the deceased wasn't listed. We've checked with utility companies and the postal service and came up with four families in the area with that last name. We're checking them one by one. I should have something soon."

The low hum of food-place noises flowed over the line. It was Saturday. The Cuban sandwich special of sliced slow-roasted pork, glazed ham, Swiss cheese, and thinly sliced dill pickles layered with spicy brown mustard on sliced French bread. The

McCreary Diner's nod to an international sandwich. Ten to one, Pusser was in his usual corner booth. Was Meg working today? I couldn't remember, but lunch sounded good. My stomach growled.

I scanned the side of the road for food signs. "I don't get it. Roger said that he told all this to the cops at the time. I would have followed up on something like that."

"Maybe they did, and nothing came of it," Pusser said. "You know how it is. Witness testimony isn't always that accurate."

"Roger seemed pretty sure about what happened."

"Can't be an easy ordeal for him. Besides, it was seventeen years ago. And trauma does weird things to memory."

That's an understatement. "Do you remember anything about the case?"

"I remember that a kid committed suicide on the tracks around that time. That's about it. The local cops handled it."

Parks pointed out a place for lunch. She must have been hungry, too.

"We're pulling off for a bite to eat," I told Pusser. "We'll be back in an hour."

After lunch, I went back to the department and spent the rest of the day at my desk, digging back through the ME's reports and calling local taxidermy shops. Maybe Zeke had worked for one of these places and had taken Princess there or had learned enough to stuff her himself. But no one had heard of the kid.

When I finally left work, Harris was out in the lot, leaning against my car. "You like playing games, don't you?" he said.

I pulled out my keys. "Get off my car."

"What are you planning to do with that picture?"

"You mean the picture of the naked girl on the holding cell's bunk? *That* picture?"

He glared at me. "I found her name," I said. "Alma Shelton. Pretty young thing. Emphasis on *young*."

"All you got is a picture. You can't prove nothin' with that."

"I wouldn't waste my time trying. If it comes down to it, I'll simply turn it over to the district attorney's office. Let them take on the burden of proof."

His face went slack, then hardened again. "Do, and I'll report this." He stepped forward. Wilco, sensing the tension, moved in front of me, his ears back. Harris stopped where he was but pulled out a piece of paper, held it out at arm's length. A newspaper article. Gran in front of our trailer a couple years ago. I remembered when it happened. The press had been on us, and they had gotten a picture of her in front of our trailer, waving a gun, threatening them for trespassing.

"I blew it up," Harris said. "Made comparisons. That engraving on the grip is unique, that's for sure. It's the same gun, and it was in your family's possession." He got all smug-like. "There's going to be a lot of questions for your grandmother."

"She's sick, Harris. She can't even talk, let alone answer questions."

He smirked. "And then there's Kevin Doogan. I checked around. He was spotted in town last week, right before his death. There was a big wedding that day. One of your pikey friends was getting hitched. And you gypsies are big on weddings, everyone knows that."

Okay.

"So, I pulled the video surveillance from the hotel parking lot. And look who was there." He pulled out a still shot of Doogan, walking in the lobby. "At the same hotel, the same party as you, the same night he killed himself. How's that work?"

"You seem to think you know."

"I didn't. Not for a while. Not until the note."

"The note?"

"Doogan's suicide note."

My stomach turned; my heart kicked up. Anxiety. And he read it in my expression.

"You *should* be scared, Callahan. Because it's lookin' a lot like your grandmother was involved in Dublin Costello's murder." My blood boiled. I got in his face. "I don't know what you're hoping to accomplish, Harris. But you better be careful where you sling this crap. It might come back to hit you in the face." I jingled my keys. "Now get the hell off my car."

It all rained down at once.

Gran's stroke, Doogan's death, Katie's threats, Harris's accusations . . . I opened the door for Wilco and climbed into my car, watching Harris walk away, anxiety snaking through my body. Wilco stared at me from the passenger seat, watching and panting, slobber dripping onto my pants. I stretched out my legs, reached into my pocket, and pulled out the meds I'd lifted from Harris's desk. I sat for a while—couldn't get the shakes to go away—and looked at the pills. Relief, I knew. Sweet relief. My hand jiggled, the pills jumping like Mexican jumping beans—*Take me, senorita! Take me!*—and I licked my dry lips. I shifted them to my left hand, my right reaching for my water bottle. My hand brushed Wilco's wet nose, and he cocked his head at me. Deep brown, trusting, questioning eyes.

I shifted my reach, this time going for my cell, and dialed. "Jake?"

"Brynn. I was going to call and see—"

"I need . . ." What did I need? Every muscle ached with tension, tight and throbbing, called out for relief. Booze or pills, but that wasn't an option. I slid the pills into my glove compartment. Stored and locked away for now. "I need to see you. Can I come over?"

CHAPTER 36

Jake lived in a midcentury fixer-upper on the corner of South Main and Union, not far from the county jail and just a stone's throw from Hawg & Dawg. Before I'd arrived, he'd run over for a couple orders of barbecue, coleslaw, and baked beans. I found a spot for Wilco in the family room, got him settled with a bowl of water and some kibble that I kept in a baggie in my pack. Then Jake and I fixed our own plates. We ate next to each other on his sofa, feet propped on the coffee table, a baseball game on television. Jake was a Yankees fan.

"I played two years in college. Tennessee Volunteers. Catcher. I had big dreams back then."

I knew nothing about baseball. My people were into bare-knuckle boxing. Toe-to-toe, or strap fighting, an Irish Stand Down, whatever you called it, Pavee men fought raw and hard, smashed faces, broke teeth, and spewed blood. Baseball seemed like confessing a chocolate addiction to a heroin addict.

"Why law then?" I reached for a napkin. Wilco turned his head and watched my movement, saw none that indicated more food heading his way, and settled his head back down.

"That was Pop's dream. He was a lawman. Wanted his boy to be like him, I guess." Regret flashed over his features.

"You don't like your career?"

"I do, but it wasn't what I really wanted at the time. I . . ." He laughed. "I thought I wanted to coach kids. But my father was right. Law suits me. I've done okay for myself."

Had he? Jake had complied with what his family expected. I had rebelled against what my family expected. Two different paths followed, yet we had ended up in the same place. Both drunks.

He continued, "Another five years and I'll have the DA's position. I'll be fifty then. Not bad."

Hard to believe he had fifteen years on me. I stole a look at his body: strong build, tight abs. . . . Still looking good for his age. Not bad at all. Really good. That was what came from working at a normal job, behind a desk, with a gym membership, instead of dodging bullets and baking in desert sun.

"How about you?" he asked.

I raised my gaze. "What about me?"

"You were an MP. Now a cop. Is that what you always wanted to do? Or did your parents influence you?"

I almost laughed. If only he knew. The only law Pavees adhered to was a sort of pseudo-moral code set forth by our ancestors, intertwined with our culture and religious beliefs, so intertwined, in fact, that it was difficult to discern tradition from the tenets of our faith. Even more so for those of us who attempted to live in both worlds. "No, I didn't exactly plan for things to work out the way they did. The Marines was my way out of here. Then I got injured, and I . . . Well, police work is all I know."

"What happened to you must've been horrible."

"Yes."

He moved in closer. Close enough for me to breathe in the scent of clean shampoo and smoky barbecue and feel his leg touching mine. Shivers ran through me. I took a deep breath and shifted away.

"What is it, Brynn?"

"There's been so much, Jake."

"Your friend Kevin Doogan?"

"Yeah."

"He was more than a friend, wasn't he?"

"You've been listening to rumors?"

He shrugged.

Of course he has. He's pumping me for information. The chill of that fact should have shut down my thermostat completely—it cooled it a bit, but he still smelled too damned good. "We were friends at one time." *Tread carefully, Brynn.* I couldn't let my guard down. Jake was all friendly now, but if Harris got his way, he'd see to it that I was investigated for harboring a fugitive, or worse. Then the DA's office—Jake's office—would be coming after me. Jake could prosecute me. What a tangled web the cops and the DA's office made: they cooperated to bring criminals to justice, but as soon as a cop messed up, the DA turned on him or her.

He shifted and opened a bit of space between us. Teasing me? That stupid, human, all–too-needy female in me wanted him to close the gap again. I resisted the urge. Resented the urge. Why had I really come here?

He continued, "Have they found his wife?"

"No." I didn't want to talk about this. Doogan and Katie, and Harris's findings—they were too much. My anxiety kicked in again.

He sensed it and changed the topic. "You get a break in the case with that English teacher?"

"Mrs. Handie," I said. Then we hashed back and forth over the details. Most he knew. Some I filled him in on: my interview with the conductor and the position of Zeke Farrell's body on the tracks; Mrs. Handie's English class; the crazy stuffed cat; and the conductor's conversation with Zeke's mother, Georgia Farrell. "We're trying to locate their residence. Only four families with that name around here, but none of them are the right Farrells. We think Georgia probably lives somewhere in the hills, off-grid."

"There're a lot of those types around here."

"You mean my type?"

"That's not what I meant."

"It's fine. I get it. It's hard to understand what we're about."

He shifted, and our legs touched again. Something squirmed low in my belly.

"Why'd you call today, Brynn?"

"I've had a lot of stress. The case, other things, you know. It's been hard."

"Are you using again?"

"Came close today. Didn't."

"I'm glad you called, then. That's why we have sponsors. People you can call. It's different for everyone. Slips, relapses . . ." He ran fingers through his hair. "Was it bad today? The need for a fix?"

"Yeah. Pretty bad."

"Did you have access to something?"

"I can always get booze." *And I stole a few pills. Still have them, can get more if I need them.*

"So what kept you straight today?"

"The case. I need to be sober. There's a lot at stake. And . . . I keep thinking about that girl. Walker's girlfriend, Nikki."

"The prostitute?"

"Yeah. I can't seem to shake her. She's so messed up."

"You think that could be you?"

"I've never gone that far for a fix, but—"

"She's a prostitute, Brynn. You're not like that."

I looked at him and almost laughed. For all the talk in our

group about how addiction hit any walk of life, I couldn't believe he had just divided addicts into those "like that" and us.

"Yeah, she's a prostitute. I'm a Pavee and a cop, and you're a lawyer. You just don't get it, do you? When it comes down to it, we're all just addicts. Willing to destroy our self-esteem and worth and even lives for one more pill, drink, prick of the needle, whatever." I stood. It'd been a long day already. The last thing I wanted was an argument. "I should go."

Wilco came to my side. I reached down and buried my hand in his fur.

Jake reached out, pulled my hand to him, and tugged me gently back to the sofa. "Don't go yet. Let's talk more." His hand covered mine; his fingers worked against mine, not urgent but ready.

He rested his other hand on my thigh, and heat shot through me, a familiar aching settled between my legs. Sex could easily become my new rush, my new release, my new drug. I had known Jake was interested, had sensed it. Maybe he needed it, too. Two addicts satisfying their mutual need for a substitute for their chemical addictions. It'd be good between us, easy, fun. But nothing more than a shallow physical release, and each fix a short-lived stopgap. Never a relationship, no intimate talk afterward, no real connection. Because he was a prosecutor and I'd committed prosecutable crimes, I could never pour out my soul to him. I couldn't tell him about Dublin and the rape, Gran and what she'd done, my fears, my hopes, my desires. . . .

I'd told Doogan all those things, trusted him with my heart and my body. And he'd betrayed me. Now he was dead. Gone. And I had no one.

Didn't need anyone, actually. I shifted away and stood. "I'm going home."

He rose from the sofa and placed his hands on my shoulders. "Are you sure you want to go?" His voice was soft, coaxing.

"I don't want to do this, Jake. Not today." *Probably never.*

He threw up his hands. "Yeah, right. You were the one who called me. But that's fine. Go home." His jaw tightened with anger.

"It's been a long day, that's all."

He turned away, picked up the remote, and raised the volume on the game. I hovered, dismayed at his instant and silent dismissal. But what did I expect? One addict to another, we had needs and got pissed when they weren't fulfilled.

I motioned for Wilco and headed home.

CHAPTER 37

First thing the next morning, we navigated a private road that bordered Lickhog Hollow. I followed about twenty feet behind Pusser's cruiser, watching his undercarriage bounce over the pitted road. We'd received a call from the South County Volunteer Fire Department. They had responded to reports of a house fire a little after eight o'clock in the morning and had found something suspicious.

My arms ached from holding the steering wheel steady. Wilco whined with every bump. So did Parks. The two of them together were making me crazy.

A mile more and the air turned dark with smoke. An acrid smell seeped into my cruiser, Wilco pawed at his cage, and Parks covered her mouth and gagged. Humidity was high and thick; soot-laden air clung to my windshield, and my wipers were turning it into twin black rainbows. I leaned over the steering wheel and squinted. Ahead of us, a couple of fire trucks and a dozen volunteer firemen fought a blazing cabin. Flames engulfed the house, roaring and sizzling, popping and releasing tiny red embers into the air.

We parked a ways back, and I surveyed the rest of the property: a row of cracked solar panels shrouded in weeds, overgrown gardens, an open-sided horse shelter and, farther back, a cluster of white box beehives. A metal pole building stood away from the house. A couple men scurried about its perimeter, their gestures animated. I couldn't hear them over the roar of the fire or the blast of water from the hoses.

Wilco whined from his cage in the back of the cruiser. I walked around the car and opened the back hatch so air could circulate through the vehicle. He was frantic, pawing at the cage, snarling and snorting. Heat radiated from the blaze.

One of the men came our way. "Glad you guys got here. We were checking the outbuildings for the residents and found something in the barn. Soon as they get this burn under control, I'll show you."

Pusser, Harris, and Parks leaned against my cruiser to watch for a while. I hung back and rummaged through my pack for bottled water and Wilco's bowl, sweat dripping into my eyes. Wilco was cowering in the corner of his cage, panting, filling the cruiser with anxious doggy breath. He couldn't hear the roaring flames or the men screaming back and forth, but he could smell the smoke, see the reflection of flames in the car windows, and feel the heat. Every fiber of him quivered, and his eyes glazed with flashbacks of our own personal horrors. I'd hoped after that scene at Lucky's that maybe it was getting better for him. He had stood on that jerk's chest, teeth embedded in his shoulder, and had held steady against the lightning flashes without hesitation. A step forward, I'd hoped, but I suspected it was adrenaline that overcame his flashback and saved me. Thank God it had.

I crawled into the cage and placed the bowl at his feet and filled it. He looked at the water and whined, his tongue an unfurled strip, dry and crusty, his nose like a dried-out sponge. I cupped my hand, scooped up some water, and covered his snout. "Here, boy. Drink some. Come on." I curled up with my dog, held him, comforting him the way he'd comforted me over and over again. He was always there for me, strong and loyal. I wanted to be those things for him, too.

Parks peeked in. "How's he doing?"

"Stressed."

"Poor fellow." She had no idea. But I did. There was no rhyme or reason to what triggered a flashback. It struck when and how it chose.

An hour later, after the fire was under control, and Wilco, too, we gathered outside the steel pole building on the edge of the property. Wilco had gone from a ball of quaking fur to wonder dog. He was next to me, on lead, all three legs locked in stance, nose straight, back rigid, muscles rippling with anticipation. We stepped away from the other officers, and I motioned for him to sit, then I crouched low and unleashed him. Free to go where his nose led him, he was suddenly in the tall weeds that had sprung up along the side of the metal building. Back and forth, nose up, nose down, paws clawing at the ground. He was on a scent. I already knew blood had been found inside the barn. Human or animal, no one knew. But I kept my demeanor neutral, not wanting to interfere with Wilco's nose. I'd been there before, and it had cost me my dignity as a handler.

A search outside Bagram Airfield, in the armpit of Afghanistan: hot, sandy, and foul smelling. One body still not recovered, and it was late, and time was short. The sun burned low on the horizon; our minutes were numbered. I couldn't find a place to squat for a piss, and my flak jacket dug into my sweaty skin. I was short on patience and eager for the find. The search grid included a row of rocketed Humvees and a cluster of flattened huts. I focused my dog there, assuming a soldier under fire attack would have taken cover. Twice Wilco wandered toward the open sands. I called him back, kept him trained on the hut area. As the sun set, I was disappointed. No body, and our time was up. No soldier would be returned to his family.

Weeks later, I got word that he had indeed been recovered. Not from the hut area, but from the open land adjacent. Lesson learned: Never lead the dog. Let the dog's nose do the leading. There was no room in scent work for the handler's assumptions.

Now I kept my distance while Wilco's nose led him along the outer rim of the building. His tail went rigid, straight as a straw, with a slight kink at the end. A sure sign that he'd hit on a strong scent. Front to back, back to front, then inside the open door of the building. A couple seconds later I heard a series of sharp barks.

I followed inside and stopped short. Heads everywhere. Not human, but animal heads, some only skulls, bony white, with hollowed eyes. Front and center, a grand buck's cocked head, ten points, strong necked, eyes glossy bright, and pinkish tongue between brown lips. Behind that table a full-sized bear and a mountain lion that was perched on a log. *Fascinating.* Along the far wall, an antelope, a bobcat, more deer, and a shelf of smaller mounts: squirrels and a muskrat, birds of all feathers, a hawk midflight, and a slinky red fox. Wilco stopped, stared at the fox, and let out a long, deep growl. He got no response, and went back to work.

Pusser shuffled inside, Harris lurking behind him. "It's like a damn zoo in here."

Harris nodded. "Except nothing's alive."

Pusser turned. "Great detective work, Harris. No one else noticed that."

Harris glared at me, like it was my fault he was a dumb ass. It wasn't.

I watched my dog, nose to the ground, working the room.

A couple of firemen entered. One of them spoke up. "A fire was started over there, on that side." Black streaks marked the back wall, floor to ceiling. Sooty water dripped through cracks in the roof and ran along the facets. "They used gas, but not enough for this steel building. The fire didn't take like it did in the cabin. It was just smoldering when we got here. We hosed it down from outside, then entered to check for victims. That's when we found all this. Figured with the case you are working on, body parts and all, just maybe it connected."

I went to Wilco. As I neared, his tail thumped; then he lowered himself and flipped over, ready for his reward. I looked at the area and saw nothing, so I motioned him on. He obeyed.

One of the firefighters came in closer. "He find something?"

"Yes."

"I don't see nothing."

"If he alerted, there's something there."

"You sound pretty damn sure of that."

"I am."

Wilco continued to work, nose to the ground, while impatient stares weighed on my back.

Pusser crossed the room to a long workbench against the far wall. Stacks of clear-faced drawers held thread and needles; others were labeled EYEBALLS, CLAWS, BEAKS. Paints of every color. Boxes of foam and shelves of animal forms. He held up what looked like a plastic horse head partially covered in fur. "The missing horse head."

"Stuffed and mounted like Mrs. Handie's Princess." I shook off the memory. *So weird.*

Parks came in and stood on the periphery, quiet and still, a slick sheen on her forehead. She fidgeted in place, hands shoved deep in her pockets. She didn't look good.

"Parks, you feel okay?" I asked.

She swallowed. "I'm good. Smells horrible in here."

Pusser's eyes roamed over a line of tools hanging above the bench. He pointed out a scalpel-like knife. "Let's get the scene techs in here. See if there's latent human blood or other matter among all this. All these tools go to the lab." He shook his head. "They're gonna have a helluva job."

Parks nodded and pulled out her phone.

Pusser opened a drawer, pulled out a stack of papers, and let out a low whistle. "Bingo."

I started that way. "What'd ya find?"

"Shipping receipts. Looks like they're from different suppliers. All delivered here to Georgia and Buck Farrell."

"That confirms it's her place."

"Sure does. They run quite the taxidermy business here."

The firefighters got excited. "Hey. Your dog. What's he doing?"

I wheeled. Wilco was now in the back of the room, moving deliberately around a few large plastic barrels, head up, then down, poking his nose in the space between them. Then he froze. He backed up, sat, and turned to me, stared with eyes blazing. Another hit.

I clipped his lead and pulled him back as Pusser used his gloved hand to lift one of the lids. His face went slack and ashen, his Adam's apple wobbled, and then he gagged and turned away.

"What is it, boss?" I peered into the barrel. Red, murky liquid with floating fat, like boiled broth unskimmed. A rib bone floated on top. Acid and human remains married in a nasty stew. I looked away; my stomach churned; my head spun. "*Graltcha*, Mary . . ." A prayer from my youth, comfort from the past, but not enough to stop the bile rising from my stomach. I scurried, made it about five yards, bent over, and puked.

Harris chuckled.

Pusser wheeled. "Something funny, Harris?"

Harris's glare landed on me again.

I swiped puke-laced spittle from the corners of my mouth. I'd seen bodies shot up, blown up, burned up, and all that was expected during war, but placed in a fifty-gallon barrel of flesh-eating acid? Deliberate evil. And it was hard to look at.

Parks started toward us. "What is it?"

I held up my hand. "Stay back. You don't need to see this."

Pusser stepped between her and the plastic barrels "Parks. Check to see if the crime-scene techs are on their way."

"Yes, sir."

He pulled a toothpick from the cylinder in his pocket and crammed it between his teeth. "We've got to find this bastard fast."

CHAPTER 38

Things got hectic after that: the crime-scene techs arrived, followed by the coroner, with a couple of his assistants in full biohazard gear. I got Wilco out of their way and back inside the air-conditioned cruiser, with some food and water, suited myself up in plastic crime-scene overalls, and went back into the pole barn.

Pusser issued orders like a drill sergeant. "Parks, put out a BOLO on Georgia and Buck Farrell. And are the roadblocks in place yet?"

"Yes, sir."

"Good. The fire's fresh. They can't be far."

Unless they burned with the house, I thought.

"Let's find out if there are any vehicles on the property."

Harris spoke up. "Already checked. None. Nothing registered under their names, either. But a lot of mountain folk don't even have driver's licenses."

"Horses," I said. "If Georgia and Buck used horses to go after Bannock, maybe they used them now to get away."

Pusser gnawed his lip. "They'd want to get away faster,

but . . ." He called over one of the firemen and was told, yes, there was a horse shed on the other side of the property, but it had been empty. "So, they could be on horseback. Or just let their horses loose to avoid the fire."

A tech had a field blood-test kit and was working over specks of trace blood that had been found at the spot Wilco first hit on. He pressed a test strip against one of the specks and examined the results. "It's human," he said.

Another officer came in, notebook in hand. "We found a burial plot a couple hundred yards back in the woods. Zeke Farrell's gravestone is there. And the father's gravestone—Buck Farrell." He flipped a couple pages. "The date indicates that Buck died shortly after his son. In November."

"So, we're just looking for Georgia." I glanced at the horse-head mount, half finished, on the workbench. "It'd take a strong woman to live out here and do this type of work, but overpowering and dismembering a man and then chopping him up and stuffing him in those barrels . . . It'd be a lot easier with help."

Pusser agreed. "A boyfriend, you think? Kin?"

He squinted at Parks, who was standing by the door, arms crossed, head down. "Parks, you got that BOLO out yet?"

Her head snapped up. "I'll get right on it." She turned and slipped out the door.

"Sheriff." A female tech stood by a stack of storage cabinets lined up against the far wall. "I've got something."

We went over.

She used a gloved hand and shifted a framed photo of a teenager, dark haired, fat, and pimply faced, with dull brown eyes and a bucktoothed smile. "Zeke," she said. I nodded, recognized the lopsided grin from the newspaper clipping. "And there's more stuff in here. Tools and things. I can't tell."

Pusser peered inside the storage cabinet. There was a jumble of items, and everything needed to be processed. "Get all this stuff photographed and entered into evidence." He turned my way. "Callahan, get everything you can on Georgia Farrell. Next of kin, anyone whom she may be in contact with in the area. Where's the nearest neighbor?"

"We passed a place on the way. Maybe a half mile down the road."

"Go talk to them."

His radio bleeped. "County one-fifteen. County one-fifteen."

He answered, "One-fifteen. Go ahead, dispatch."

"Abandoned vehicle found one mile north of roadblock A. No plate."

"Ten-four."

"It's Georgia," I said. "It's got to be her."

Pusser shook his head. "Or whoever burned this place down, her with it." He glanced at the barrels. "Unless she's in one of those barrels."

"Whoever it is, they likely spied the roadblock, left the car, headed out on foot in the hollow somewhere. Georgia's lived out here her whole life. Knows these woods."

"I'll call in the reserve deputies. We'll get a search organized."

"By the time you get that together, half the day will be burned. She'll be so deep into these woods, we'll never find her. Send me in with Wilco. We'll get a jump start on the search."

"Not alone. Who do you want? Parks or Harris?"

Did he even have to ask?

CHAPTER 39

Fifteen minutes later, we were at the sight of the abandoned vehicle, an old-model Jeep, rusted and rebuilt with scraps. So far, we hadn't been able to tie it to Georgia. But I had no doubt it was hers.

The stench of acrid smoke still hung on my uniform, my hair felt sticky, and no amount of water got rid of the burnt taste on my tongue. I pulled a collapsible bowl and water bottle from my pack and squatted down by my dog. "Here you go, boy." He lapped it up, and I poured more, running my hand along his back. It came away black with soot. I looked over at Parks, who stood alone, her eyes scanning the tree line. She hadn't said much since the crime scene.

I finished watering my dog, then paced back and forth along the edge of the woods. After a while, I stopped and called out, "I've got something."

Pusser came over. I pointed out a couple smudged footprints and some snapped twigs. "Entry point," I said.

Pusser squinted. "Okay. Reserve deputies are en route. You've got about an hour's head start. Get a fix on the perp's location and call it in. Don't engage unless necessary. Radios will be spotty. You're good to go."

I carried an AR15 stuffed with a thirty-round mag, plus a couple extra magazines and a backup pistol. Parks was equally armed. We were leaving nothing to chance.

We entered the woods, Wilco off lead. The brush was thicker here, tree trunks were side by side, and branches a tangled mess of bark and leaves. The only thing a leash would get me was a thousand snags and tangles.

We spaced ourselves and walked single file in silence, me in the lead, Parks several yards behind me, and Wilco off to the left, bounding here and there, not so silent.

I gazed around, checking low to high for signs. "Keep your eye out for tracks," I told Parks, "or snagged hair, a bent leaf, a dirt smudge on a log, vultures circling overhead. Could be anything."

It worked for a while. But a quarter mile more and we lost sight of the fugitive's trail, wandered a bit, refocused, and canvassed the area in a grid-like pattern. Wilco busied himself peeing on tree trunks, a pee here, a pee there, here a pee, there a pee. . . . *How much pee does that dog have in him?*

I stopped between two narrow trees and leaned in closer. "This woman knows how to move through the woods."

Parks stayed a few yards back. "See something?"

"Broken branch."

"Could be an animal, like a deer or a bear."

"Could be." I moved in a wide circle around the tree, expanding my circumference each time, paying close attention to the ground. After the third pass, I squatted. "It's not an animal. I've got human footprints. Small. A woman's size. It's Georgia Farrell. I'm about sure of it. And the impressions are shallow. She's travelling light." My eyes swept to the front, right, behind us, searching for any signs of infiltration. I pointed out a clump of weeds a few feet ahead, the stalks bent and pointing west. "That way."

I checked our map. We were about a mile from a small stream, a possible water source. Other than that, there was nothing.

We continued. The terrain took a deep downturn, and the foot impressions became farther apart. Georgia had picked up her pace, maybe was running. *Why?*

Halfway down, we found a couple of overturned rocks and a deep gouge in the dirt. "She slid here and fell," I said. "Then went on. But her gait is different. Limping maybe."

Parks nodded, and we continued, aware that we could encounter Georgia at any time.

Another fifty feet, Parks stopped and raised her chin in the air, dark eyes scanning the woods. A twig popped, and I took a knee, shouldered my rifle, and skimmed the barrel over the woods, silently dominating my perimeter. For a few minutes, we remained motionless, in tune to nature and alert to any sound, smell, or movement: the soft motion of swaying leaves, the flow of water, the buzz of bugs . . . a rustling sound.

I swept my gun to the right, landed with Wilco in my sites, and lowered the barrel. He drifted along the ground, his nose working some sort of scent.

Then a whimpering sound, human, not from my dog, and mostly garbled by the babbling stream, but still audible. I turned, and turned again. *Where's it coming from?*

Parks heard the same and motioned for me to move right as she worked her way left. We walked stealthily stopping every few steps to listen, our guns raised. Movement caught my eye. It was Parks signaling me. Another dozen steps and I'd closed the distance between us. Parks pointed to a small rocky ledge just ahead. I nodded; we moved, our steps synchronized, my scope trained, finger caressing the trigger. I peered over the edge, and a face popped into my sight. My finger twitched. *Shit!* I lowered my rifle.

"Don't shoot, Parks!" I held my hand out. "Don't shoot. It's Gideon's son."

He half cried, half mumbled, faint and weak, head lolling to the side, his body sprawled on the ground some fifteen feet below us. We backtracked and found a safe path down to the ravine, Wilco catching up to us. I told Parks to remain on the perimeter, rifle ready and alert, covering us, while I knelt by the boy.

"Asher, it's me, Brynn. Remember me? I'm a friend." His black skin had turned to pale chocolate milk. His eyes were blank, and his lips bloodless. His left hand held his right forearm, fingers crusted with dried blood. Wilco bounded over for a deep sniff. Asher flinched, his eyes widened, and small mewling sounds came from his mouth.

"Easy now. He's not going to hurt you." I pushed Wilco away and reached for Asher's hand and gently lifted it. "I need to look at your arm, okay?"

The wound was grotesque, swollen and puffy, with jagged flesh surrounding a protruding bone. The mewling turned to moans. Then his stomach clenched up; he gagged and heaved. I turned him to the side and held his shoulders in place. He heaved again. Nothing came up. More heaves, over and over, wrenching and dry.

That was when I saw the other wound, a cluster of pellets embedded in the muscles, maybe deeper, on the left side of his back.

Someone had filled this kid's back with bird shot.

"Parks. Get over here. We've got a problem."

CHAPTER 40

"He's been shot."

Parks's knuckles blanched around the grip of her gun. "Shot?"

"Bird shot. But it's bad. His back looks like raw meat."

The heaves had stopped but were followed by rapid, shallow gasping. Shock, or the bird shot had penetrated deeply enough to collapse a lung. Deadly either way.

"We don't have much time," I said. "He needs to get to a hospital. We need a med chopper."

"Here? There's no place for it to land."

I searched the trees but couldn't get my bearings. "Where the hell are we, Parks?"

She spread the map on the ground between us, and her index finger tracked our route so far, then tapped our current location. "Here, I think. Two hours to hike this far in, more carrying the kid back."

The boy moaned, semiconscious now. I looked at Parks. She nodded. The kid didn't have that kind of time.

"Give me options. Any bare spot."

Parks peered at the map. "Negative."

"A wide riverbank, shallow river . . . No. Wait! I do remember something about this area. That militia encampment isn't far from here. Maybe a mile due north. They might have medical supplies." Then I shook my head. "Yeah, and guns ready to shoot us. Last time we met them, it wasn't pretty."

"But he won't make it." Parks stared at Asher. Saving a kid came first.

"Okay, let's go for it." The militia encampment was stuck in the woods—no clear space for a chopper—but they'd likely at least have some medical supplies. "Call it in and let our guys know what's up. Let's get him there."

I found a couple fallen branches, thin but sturdy enough, I hoped, to hold Asher's weight. Evacuation litters came as standard equipment in the Marines, no branches required.

Meanwhile, Parks worked her radio. "Nothing out here."

I unzipped my pack and pulled out a shelter tarp and nylon cord. "Over one branch and under the other. S shape," I said. We worked, folding the tarp over and under the branch poles.

As we worked, anxiety kicked in. My mind sought relief. I half grinned.

"What?"

"You know the joke. A gypsy, a Melungeon, and the militia meet up in the woods." I cut strips of cord.

Parks frowned. "No. What's the punch line?" We tied the cords off for extra security.

"Beat's me."

She shook her head. "Let's hope not."

Wilco paced back and forth by Asher, then stopped to sniff his wounds. I scooted closer to the boy, leaned in with a piece of cord, wrapped it around his body, and cinched it around the upper part of his wounded arm, a makeshift splint, but enough to stabilize the arm for transport. His eyes fluttered open, then rolled back in his skull.

"Stay with me, Asher. Stay with me."

"We can't lose him, Brynn. He's just a boy."

His eyes snapped back open. He groaned, his head rocking from side to side.

"He'll make it, Parks. He's a fighter."

She bent over Asher with a water bottle and tipped it to his dry lips. Asher gurgled and coughed. "Wo . . ." He sputtered some more; water dribbled over his lips and down his neck.

Parks looked at me. "He's trying to talk."

I bent closer. "What is it, Asher?"

Parks's radio crackled. The dispatcher's speech sounded fragmented. Parks barked our location and what we needed, over the static.

I stayed focused on Asher. "Asher. Is there something you want me to know?"

He licked his lips. "Woman."

"A woman shot you?" His eyelids opened and shut. I tapped his cheek. "Hey, Asher. Stay awake, okay, buddy? We're getting you help."

Parks pocketed the dead radio. "Don't know if it got through or not."

We half rolled/half lifted the boy onto the litter and used the last of our cord to secure his body. I shouldered my rifle and lifted my end; the improvised stretcher wobbled between us. We moved toward the militia site, zigzagging through underbrush, Wilco staying close to Asher.

We'd gone maybe half a mile when my foot struck something. I stumbled forward, overcorrected, and the litter slipped from my grip. Asher bounced and slid, the rope cutting into his wound. His eyes bulged; his mouth contorted with pain. His shriek, high pitched and thin, tore through me and echoed through the trees.

"Oh, crap." Parks put her end down.

Asher writhed, his nostrils flaring in and out as he struggled to take in air. Fresh blood oozed from his arm. Parks pulled a rain suit out of her pack, dropped to the ground, and pressed it on the wound.

My stomach churned. "Don't die. Don't die . . ."

Wilco whined, his eyes focused into the woods on the left.

"Stop there. Don't move!" The muzzle of a gun poked through the brush. The bearded guy whose nutty wife had tried to take me down stepped forward, gun aimed at me. "You and your mutt back for—"

"Hold up, Jed."

I whipped my head to the right. Viper stood behind Parks, and two more of his crew broke through the surrounding trees behind him, guns drawn.

Viper's eyes were already on Asher. "What do you have?"

I kept my voice low. "He's bleeding a lot. The bone's through the skin."

Parks shifted aside slowly, exposing the wound to their view. The big militia guy jerked back. "Son of a bitch."

"He's been shot, too," I said. "In the back. Bird shot."

Viper stepped in closer. "He's just a kid. Who would shoot—"

"We're tracking a fugitive," I said. "A woman, we believe. She's violent and armed. We think the kid came across her. We found him like this at the bottom of a ravine He was probably on the run and took a fall."

Viper scoured the surrounding trees. "And she's still out here somewhere in the hollow?"

"Yes," I said. "I believe so."

Viper's features turned dark. The muscles under his shirt twitched. Anger radiated from him. Three guns were still pointed at us. No one moved.

I broke the silence. "We can't get a chopper in here. Radio's dicey, too. Hoped you had medical—"

"No." Viper shook his head.

"What the hell do you mean, no?"

He ignored me, motioned to Jed. "Let's get them out to the landing area."

Landing area?

Jed stared a moment at his leader, gun still on me.

"Now!" came the order, and the guy lowered his gun, grabbed a radio, and started calling.

"We got a spot," Viper said. "Chopper friendly, but we keep it covered. Kid needs more than we have here." He knelt close to Asher, covered the boy's hand with his. "We got you, buddy. Hang in there."

Asher's eyes fluttered.

Jed spoke up. "They heard your call earlier. They're already in transit. Won't take long."

Viper nodded, motioned, and his men lifted the boy and headed out. They threaded easily through their territory to the rendezvous spot, Parks trailing them.

Viper stood in front of me. His intense eyes took in the scars on my neck in one fleeting second. Then he nodded. "You did good getting him here, soldier." And he turned and slipped into the undergrowth. I shifted my gun, took up the rear guard, and for the first time, my puckered skin felt like a badge instead of a maiming scar.

I motioned Wilco forward. "Let's fall in line, soldier," I said, then thought, *A gypsy, a Melungeon, and the militia meet up in the woods. . . .*

CHAPTER 41

I opened my eyelids. Fur. Nothing but fur.

I pushed Wilco aside and looked at the clock: 7:10 A.M. I'd lain awake half the night, my depleted mind stuck on an image: a wild-haired, evil-eyed madwoman, half Katie Doogan, half Georgia Farrell, pursuing her next victim—me, I was sure. Every creak of metal, every pipe gurgle, every little sound from Meg's room had sent my imagination into overdrive. I hadn't fallen asleep until the early morning hours, my gun tucked under my pillow and Wilco as my shield.

"Thanks, buddy." I patted my dog—my loyal friend—and rolled out of bed. Thirty minutes later, I'd showered, fed myself and Wilco, and hit the road.

News had spread quickly. It was all over the radio as I drove into work: "A house fire occurred at approximately 8:00 A.M. yesterday morning at a rural farm twelve miles outside McCreary. Two bodies have been recovered from the scene. Cause of death is unclear. The victims have yet to be identified."

"No doubt," I said to my dog. "Hard to identify a soupy

mix of acid, body fluid, and floating bones." My black humor was lost on his deaf ears. But seriously, the ME had his work cut out for him.

But I'd underestimated our ME.

"I just got off the phone with the medical examiner," Pusser said. He'd called Harris and me into his office first thing. I hadn't seen Parks yet. She must've been running late. "A titanium plate used in a knee reconstruction was found in one of the remains. The serial number is linked to Reed Bannock. The ME has also located a dental implant in the second barrel. He's tracing the device's serial number now. Hopefully, we'll have something soon."

"That second body is probably Walker."

"That's my assumption. But let's wait until it's official."

A quiet settled over the office. Wilco had curled up in his usual spot.

Pusser pulled up a file on his computer and accessed several photos of the taxidermy shop. He rotated his screen so we could see it. "Here's the crime-scene techs' analysis." He pointed out areas on the photos. "Traces of human blood here and here. We think this spot is where the victims were dismembered." He pointed to that spot where Wilco had hit on scent. "She probably used a tarp or something to collect the blood." He went to another photo. "These are the contents of the storage cabinets. Surgical gloves and a scalpel, which also tests positive for human blood. A large needle and twine, identical to what was used to secure the tongue and ears. And a framed photo of the boy, Zeke."

"Georgia's done it all to avenge his death," I said.

"And some poor bastard is about to lose his eyeballs." The gash on Harris's head had scabbed over. He picked at it as he talked.

Pusser sat back. "I sent out a fresh team this morning. If she's in that hollow, they'll find her."

"If she's there," I said. "She's probably long gone by now."

Pusser agreed. "She could be holed up with family. We're looking into possible kin."

I asked him about Asher.

"Still in ICU. I drove Gideon and his wife to the hospital last night. They're staying there with him. They're torn up about this. That boy means everything to Gideon."

There was a knock at the door, and Jake walked in. I shifted in my chair; my cheeks burned. Anger or embarrassment, I couldn't decide. Wilco moseyed on over and sniffed at his feet.

"Sorry to interrupt," he said.

Pusser leaned forward. "Pull up a chair. We're just discussing the Walker and Bannock case."

Jake nudged Wilco away and grabbed the straight chair from the corner.

Pusser continued, "You heard the ME's findings?"

"Yeah. I heard. Incredible."

Pusser filled him in on our prior discussion. Jake listened intently, not looking my way once. So that was how he was going to play this. Like I didn't exist.

"We need to shift our focus," I said. *Yeah, I'm here, buddy. Like it or not.* "The answer is in Zeke Farrell's death. We have two victims. And if we don't find Georgia, we may have a third on our hands soon."

"That's the idea," Harris said. "Find Georgia before she can kill again."

"Exactly," I said. Harris looked my way, as if surprised I agreed with him on anything. "Georgia Farrell isn't the type of woman to give up. And she's already lost everything of importance to her. Torching her own place came easy to her. She'll finish the job, one way or the other. So, if we find that third intended victim, we'll find Georgia."

"That's an interesting theory." Jake turned his focus back to Pusser. "But I actually stopped by to discuss another matter."

Pusser squinted. "Like what?"

"The results of the handwriting analysis your office did headed us in another direction on the Doogan case."

Pusser avoided the looks Harris and I gave him. What results? Why hadn't he mentioned that to us yet?

Jake went on, "Our office is investigating allegations against Ms. Callahan." He finally looked my way. "An anonymous tip came in yesterday, claiming that the gun found by Doogan's body belonged to your grandmother."

My eyes slid toward Harris. *Anonymous tip, my ass.*

His face paled.

"We know you had a personal relationship with Kevin Doogan," Jake said. "He alluded to it in his suicide note."

Pusser hadn't let me read it yet. I looked away. Blinked back tears. *Don't let him see you cry, Brynn.* "Yes. We were close." I met Jake's gaze. It burned with anger. Such a switch from a couple night's ago, when those very eyes burned with desire.

"We pulled Doogan's financials. He'd been in town for over two weeks. Did he contact you during that time?"

No mention of Dublin Costello's murder. Yet. Maybe they hadn't made the connection between the slug found in Dublin's remains and Gran's gun.

Pusser leaned forward, waiting for my reply.

Harris had video surveillance of Doogan at the wedding party. Had he showed them?

"Did someone say they saw me with him?"

Jake frowned. "Just answer the question."

"I broke things off with Doogan a long time ago. Didn't even know he was married at the time. I think they'd been having problems for years. Maybe you should be looking at the wife for this. She's been stalking me. We know she tried to run me down and put poor Grabowski in the hospital. The van's registered in her name. And I think she poisoned my dog, too. Have you matched the handwriting to her?"

Jake pressed me. "You didn't answer my question. Have you seen Kevin Doogan recently?"

"Am I being charged with something?" I looked around. "And why aren't we discussing the Farrell case? There's a killer out there looking for another victim." I was worked up. "And when is Hughie going to be released? Why are you still holding him?"

My questions rolled off Jake and went unanswered. Instead, he looked at Pusser. "It might be prudent for her to be pulled out of the field until this issue is resolved."

This was personal. Had I given in, would he be so hard on me now? "Like hell. You can't do this."

Pusser snapped back, "Easy, Callahan." Then to Jake. "Look, I need her on the Walker/Bannock case. Until you have something more substantial, she continues to work." He placed both palms down on his desk. "We're done here."

I caught up to Harris in the hallway and pulled him into a nearby conference room. "What gives, Harris? Thought we had an understanding."

"I didn't call in that tip. I swear it wasn't me."

"Why should I believe you?"

"I'm tellin' you, it wasn't me."

"And I should believe you because you always tell the truth, is that it? Nothing but the *bare-naked* truth."

His jaw went slack, and I knew this wasn't Harris. If he was going to bring me down, he wouldn't do it anonymously. He'd want credit for it. This was Katie. She had killed her husband, had made it look like suicide, had written the fake note, and had called in the tip about the gun. She played for keeps. *I could, too.*

I tapped Wilco between the ears and turned away. Watching Harris squirm was fun, but I had better things to do right now.

But Harris followed, cut me off, and hissed in my face. "What are you going to do? Give that picture to Pusser?" He was in close, and I could barely see beyond his sweat-filled pores and red-veined eyes. The air grew hot with the stench of sour stomach. "If I go to jail, you go to jail. And that grandmother of yours, too. She'd spend the rest of her short life there—"

"Are you threatening my family?" My voice was high, thin, strung out. He was pushing me too far. I was close to the edge.

He took a step back. Unsure now.

"Know this, Harris." I shook with anger. "I cherish my family. And if you ever threaten them again, in any way, I'll hunt you down and make you regret it, because I am exactly what you've said all along—a crazy-ass gypsy."

I sat in my car out in the lot, fist clenched, unclenched, breath in, breath out. My mind raced: *Harris, Jake, Pusser, Gran, Doogan dead, and Katie. . . .*

Wilco bounced between the front and back seats, his warm fur brushing against my bare arm. A feeling that usually brought me comfort. Right now, it irritated me. I pushed him back.

"Sit down!"

He was caught off guard, and his one rear leg faltered. He fell back, overcorrected, and slid forward toward the floor. He got stuck there, facedown, back nub clawing the air. High-pitched yelps echoed inside the car.

Wilco! I twisted, reached over my shoulder, and hoisted him from between the seats. I pulled a muscle; a hot twinge radiated along my spine. "Damn it!" Pain, pain, pain . . . too much pain for days now, from eating concrete to avoid the van, grappling with Silvas, and being battered by that truck driver, until every joint in my body had been slammed or contorted. I turned forward and reached into my glove department; shaking fingers struggled to pick up the small white pills. They fell. I bent, scooped them up, and popped them.

Instant guilt slid down my throat as I waited for relief.

I closed my eyes. Inhaled and imagined the pills inside me, dissolving, little white particles breaking away, being absorbed and feeding into my bloodstream, rushing throughout my body like sparkling glitter—happy, warm, magical glitter.

Wilco whined. I kept my eyes closed. Waiting for the warmth, the magic. He whined louder. *Be quiet, dog.*

Waiting, waiting . . . I'd been without for so long. My tolerance was low. It wouldn't take much time. . . . More whining.

"Shut up!"

My eyes snapped open and met his in the rearview mirror: brown, soft, worried. And mine: blurry blue, hollow, dead . . . ghostlike. *I'm a ghost, a ghost. Dead, dead in a hospital bed. Nikki and . . . and dear Gran . . .*

I opened the door, leaned over, and crammed my finger down my throat. One gag, two gags . . . I reached farther, pressed my tonsils, soft and spongy. My stomach heaved, eyes tightened and strained, bile rose, and chunky liquid splattered on the ground. . . . More heaving and heaving, a final dry gag, and then empty. My tongue was coated, foul, sour stickiness, like curdled milk and hot orange juice.

Wilco pawed my back. He was in the front seat now. I sat up, swiped my sleeve across my mouth, and leaned into my dog. "Let's go home, boy."

CHAPTER 42

A gunshot at 2:00 A.M.

I sat straight up in bed, pushed Wilco off my legs, and stumbled across the room to my dresser. Between the rolled socks and panties, my hand connected with my gun and closed over the grip. I squatted against the wall, one eye on my window, adrenaline surging hot through my veins. My door burst open. I wheeled, raised the gun, finger on the trigger. . . .

"Meg! Get down."

She fell to the floor and crawled toward me. "Gunshot next door, Kevin Doogan's old place."

"Get in the closet and stay there. Don't come out for any reason, do you understand?" I threw on a sweatshirt and pulled on sweatpants. Wilco stood by the bed. I made brief eye contact with him, then, staying low, made my way down the hall and to the back door. I cracked it open for Wilco, slipped through, and crouched by the steps.

A baby cried, its screams drowning out the usual night sounds. One by one, porch lights flipped on and windows lit up. I shuffled along the side of our trailer toward Doogan's place, stopped at the corner, stood, raised my gun, and scoped the area. Doogan's trailer was lit up like a nighttime convenience store, but quiet. No more gunshots. Nothing but a crying baby.

I crossed the yard and knocked on the door. "Callie! It's Brynn from next door."

The baby's cries grew louder, and the door popped open. Callie Doogan stood there, disheveled, in a pink robe cinched at her waist, her youngest grandchild on her hip. Kevin's other two kids hovered behind her.

"I heard a gunshot. What's going on?" I said.

"Katie. She was here in the trailer. Standing over me while I slept. Sean went after her."

"Where? Which way did they—"

Another gunshot. This time from down the street. I ran toward the gunfire. Wilco joined me, ran alongside me, his mouth open and ears back. We continued past a few trailers, saw nothing. Doors popped open, and people wandered outside, looked around. A woman came out of a nearby trailer, and behind her was a bleary-eyed toddler holding a blanket.

I waved my arms. "Get back inside. Get back inside!"

She spied my gun, jerked back with an "Oh shit!" expression, scooped up her kid, and ran inside.

The door slapped shut behind her, and I bent over and sucked air, my nostrils flaring with each breath. Wilco licked my hand and sniffed my leg. "Run more. Run more," he seemed to say. My lungs burned. I coughed and sputtered, spit out a stream of phlegm. Then voices murmured, faint and low, masculine. I squinted down the street. Too dark. One last deep breath and I squeezed my gun grip, lowered my chin, and walked toward the noise. Twenty yards out the scene came into focus. Sean and Katie Doogan. Sean's shotgun was trained on Katie. I motioned to Wilco to stay put as I stepped closer.

"You idiot, Sean. You could've killed someone." I forced a

tone of simple irritation instead of confrontation, but my heart thumped wildly.

"I *am* going to kill someone." He shook his gun at Katie. "This bitch right here."

"I can't let you do that." I needed Katie's confession and needed to keep Sean from killing some innocent bystander. And another fact clawed at my gut: I wanted to kill her myself.

Sean's grip tightened on the gun. "She killed my cousin."

"No!" Katie's eyes glistened in the moonlight. "That's not true. I could never hurt him. You know that. I loved Kevin. We have kids, and—"

"You killed him, and you were just tryin' to kill my aunt."

"No. No. Listen, Sean, you don't understand. I just wanted to see my kids."

"You don't know nothin' about love. What type of mother kills her kids' daddy?"

"I didn't kill him. It was suicide. Even the cops say so."

Sean laughed. "I know my cousin. There's no way Kevin would kill himself."

"But the note—"

"We have writing samples," I said. "He didn't write the note. There's more evidence, too." I needed to get her confession, and would say anything to get it.

Katie kept her gaze on Sean. "Don't be stupid, Sean. She's a cop. She's playing you. They're all playing you."

Sean wavered, but not me. I couldn't shake the image of Doogan lying in the alley, with a gunshot to his temple. And his kids, especially his son, the one who looked like him, forever without a father. I kept my edge, tried to force the truth from her. "He was going to leave you."

Her eyes turned to me, burning with insanity. "You turned my husband against me. Made him hate me."

"I didn't even know he was married."

"Liar! You knew, but you pursued him, anyway. You're pitiful. All burned up the way you are, scarred and ugly. He felt sorry for you. That's all it was. Pity."

"Shut up."

"He told me, you know. He told me about how you were damaged goods. Already used up."

Damaged goods. The rape, the war, the scars . . .

Her mouth twisted into a sneer; she was spiteful, yet with an edge of triumph, like a rabid dog about to fulfill the urge to bite. "Look at yourself. Nothing but a mule, a half-breed. Only half Pavee. And only half woman."

My finger rubbed the trigger. *Keep control, Brynn.*

Her eyes were tiny slits of hatred. "I'm the one he loved. He told me."

I cocked my head, as if amused, kept my voice steady, while my blood boiled. "Yet the whole time we were together, he never once mentioned you. Why would that be, Katie?"

"You're wrong! He loved me. Not you . . ."

"Oh, I don't think so, Katie. I saw him the day he died. He asked me to go away with him. Begged me to join him so he could get away from you. Said you were crazy."

Her lip trembled. Her eyes darting and unsure. She was remembering something . . . and crumbling.

I went on. "But you already knew that, didn't you?" Had he told her he was leaving her? But he hadn't known she was in town until I told him. So what was she recalling now that . . . ? I remembered the noise I had heard in the alley that night. A rat, I'd figured, but no. Now I knew. "You'd followed him. Or maybe me. But you were in the alley that night. You heard our conversation. He thought you were insane. He was going to take your kids. That's why you killed him."

"No . . ."

"He didn't think your kids were safe with you. He told me about the puppy. You killed your boy's puppy because you thought he loved it more than you. That's sick, Katie. What type of mother kills her boy's dog?" I gritted my teeth. "You went after my dog, too, didn't you?"

Her gaze slid to where Wilco obediently sat and awaited my next command.

I continued. "Killing comes easy to you, doesn't it, Katie?"

"Shut up! My husband killed himself. With your grandmother's gun. And the police know it. I made sure of it."

"You called in the tip."

"Yeah. Poor, poor Gran. You love her, don't you?"

Adrenaline surged through my veins. I heard Doogan's pleading . . . saw his dead body in the alley . . . and Gran, poor Gran, shaking in her bed. I couldn't find my voice.

She lifted her head, eyes gloating. "You see, I visited her, you know. And I told her everything, how I knew what she'd done, and how you seduced my husband into coverin' for her killin' Dub Costello. And all the lies you been tellin' to cover for her. And then I told her that my husband hated himself for what he'd done. And how it had wrecked my family. Children without a father now. A father without his children. How all the guilt and the pain had driven him mad. I was so worried for him . . . Yes, I was. That he might do somethin' drastic. And you know what? That stupid old woman just sat there, takin' it. Not a word. Just a retarded look on her face. I should've figured you'd have a retard for a grandmother."

The gun shook in my hand. I walked forward, passed Sean and his shotgun, raised my gun and placed the barrel against her forehead. It danced along her sweat-slicked skin.

She laughed. "You're too weak to do it."

"You're wrong."

"Then go ahead. It's easy." She made a gun with her fingers and held it up to my face. "Boom."

"Just like you did to Doogan."

Her eyes danced with hatred. "Yes. He deserved to die."

Sean's voice came from behind me. "Move out of the way, Brynn."

Tears ran down my cheeks now. "Why'd you have to kill him? Why couldn't you just let him go?"

"I'd never let him go. Never let him live . . . not without me."

And there it was: what I'd needed to hear and all I needed to haul her in. . . . And then what? She'd deny, lawyers would argue, settled law would drag its heels while Doogan rotted and Katie lived. Justice came slow if you abided by the law books I'd sworn to uphold. But the clan's vengeance ran swift and cut at the heart of evil.

On which side did I stand?

Sean's heavy breath was inches from me, filling the air with sour hatred. My nerves burned hot through my skin, and I felt the cold trigger against my finger. . . .

Moments later a gunshot pierced the air.

CHAPTER 43

I hadn't pulled the trigger. Sean had. But I had walked away and let him do it. Now the sound reverberated through my ears, echoed in my skull, and reached every cell in my body.

I'd seen gun wounds, in the military, yes, but more recently as a deputy, and they haunted me . . . one in particular. It was a kid, and he'd . . . The call came over dispatch, and we went, Wilco and I, and we found the mother doubled over in the front yard, the father pacing, tearing at his hair, younger siblings. . . . And Wilco, half crazed with the scent of corrupting blood . . . the scene, raw, merciless, gnawing . . . The blast had shattered the small body, scattered its contents, and left behind nothing but blood and heart-wrenching devastation.

And now Katie's body. How must it look?

Clan justice. Brutal and deadly and vengeful. Right? Wrong? Did it even matter anymore?

One truth remained: I'd allowed this. I'd walked away. The same as if I'd pulled the trigger.

And guilt settled over me like a permanent stain, as ugly and grotesque as the scar on my body.

I needed my grandmother.

I took Wilco back to the trailer and drove to the nursing home. Lights were dimmed; halls deserted; all voices hushed and distant. Jarvis, ever loyal, was slumped in a side chair, book tented on his belly, rising and falling with the soft sounds of his snores.

I woke him, thanked him, and sent him on his way. There was no more need to guard Gran.

I looked down at Gran, a mere bump in the sheets, tiny and as white as cotton. She slept droopy side up, head on the pillow, drool running from the slack side of her mouth down her cheek. I snatched a tissue, crawled under the sheets, and dabbed at her face. She flinched, her eyes popping open, stark and anxious, then fuzzy and soft. She attempted a smile, gave up with a sigh, and instead shifted until we were face-to-face, her hands holding mine, our knees touching, and my forehead resting on hers. I was a kid again, the weirdo, shunned at school, shunned in the clan, scared, and wishing I had a mother, but so grateful, *always* so grateful for Gran.

I snuggled closer and whispered the words on my heart. "You're the only mother I've ever needed."

The next morning, Mo was on my front walkway steps.

"Hey, Mo." I leaned out and glanced over at Doogan's place. It looked empty. Callie Doogan and Sean and the kids had vacated under the cover of night, the Pavee way, silent and quick.

Mo stepped forward. "We need to talk."

"Can it wait? I'm late for work."

"No. Now."

I tried to sidestep her. "Okay. But Wilco and I need to—"

"I want Hughie released." She was in my face now.

"It's not up to me. The DA hasn't dropped the charges." The

news had reported a house fire and two recovered bodies. That was it. I wanted to reassure Mo but couldn't give any details. It wasn't public knowledge yet that they were looking for Georgia Farrell for the murders. "I'll do what I can, Mo."

"I . . . I just want him back home." She let out a shaky sigh.

I wasn't getting to work anytime soon, so I gave up and indicated that she should take a seat on the step. Wilco was a few feet away, his backside hunched. We sat together on the front stoop, not knowing what to say next, watching my dog take a crap. He finished and trotted over for a little attention before dashing off to chase a dragonfly.

"Honestly, Mo, I'm surprised you want him home. I didn't think things were that good between you and Hughie."

She set her jaw. "That was his fault. After the accident he did nothin' but lay around all day, feelin' sorry for himself. Got real mean, too."

"He ever hit you?"

"No. Never. Not like Queenie's husband does her. I don't know why she puts up with that."

Because she's never known differently. Poor Queenie had always been someone's punching bag.

Mo continued, "He can't work no more, you know, can't take care of us like he wants." She lowered her eyes. "Can't take care of me, neither."

I knew what she meant. "I'm sorry, Mo."

"He isn't the man he used to be."

"So, you went looking elsewhere."

"The booze made me do that."

"Oh, come on, Mo. A couple drinks and you cheat on your husband?"

She glared. "I told you. Hughie couldn't take care of me no more. I was lonely. I just wanted to feel like a real woman again. Any woman would feel the same way."

Really? Is that all it takes to feel like a real woman again? Sex? Guess as a "half woman," I wouldn't know. "So, you wanted to sleep with him so you could feel like a woman?"

She folded her arms. "I told you already. I didn't do it."

"But you would have. You only stopped because things went bad."

"*Bad* is an understatement. He wanted it rough and dirty. Like I was some sort of . . ."

"Whore?"

"Yeah. But I ain't."

I raised a brow.

"He got pissed real fast. Mean too." She rubbed at her neck, which was fine now. The bruises had faded away. "If that woman hadn't come by, hard tellin'—"

"Nikki."

"Who?"

"That woman was Nikki. Chance's girlfriend." And a woman who made a living playing rough and dirty.

"He had a girlfriend?" She seemed surprised, betrayed even.

"You have a husband."

Her mouth twisted in anger. "Like you have the right to judge me."

What?

"You been a bit manky yourself, Brynn Callahan. At least that's what I heard."

"Manky?" *Whorin' around.* "Why do you say that?"

"Heard you'd been with a married man."

"I didn't even know he had a wife."

"Maybe you didn't look hard enough. Maybe you got more of your mama in you than you know."

My shoulders tightened. I stood.

She stood. "I'm sorry, Brynn. I didn't mean it."

"Yes you did. I'm heading to work." I looked around for Wilco.

Mo snatched at my arm, wheeled my focus back to her. "Listen, Brynn. I didn't mean it. Really. I'm just so tired. You know how it is."

I shook her off. "Yeah. I know how it is, Mo." I glanced back at Doogan's trailer. Suddenly, I was wearier than I'd been in months.

CHAPTER 44

I finally made it to work. Wilco stretched out next to my desk, eyes watching as people filed into the department.

Parks never came in, so I called her. Her cell went to voice mail. I left a message and filled the rest of the morning with minute tasks: reports, a DNA request on a cold case, a phone interview, and prep for an upcoming trial. At any given time, I'd have a half-dozen open cases on my desk. I was in the middle of a phone call with the crime lab when Pusser called me into his office. I gave Wilco a quick pat and motioned for him to stay put.

Pusser was tipped back in his desk chair, rubbing his midsection. A pained expression on his face.

"You okay, boss? Did you hear something about Asher?"

"Called ICU first thing. The kid's holding his own." He pulled a roll of antacids from his shirt pocket and popped a couple. "Got men out in those damn woods round the clock, plus half the county lookin' for Georgia Farrell. Can't find her nowhere." He sat forward. "And you were late again this morning."

"Mo came over to my place this morning. She's upset."

"Because her husband's still in custody?"

I raised a brow. "Yeah. That would be the reason."

He glared at me. "Can't do much about it. The prosecutor hasn't dropped the charges. The ID on that implant is taking longer than we thought."

"It's got to be Walker."

"We don't have proof of that. And until we do, we can't assume he's the body in that second barrel. And the DA has more than enough probable cause to keep Hughie locked up."

Ridiculous. Pusser had been in that taxidermy shop, had seen Georgia's handiwork firsthand. Georgia was a killer. The only killer in this case. No need for an innocent man to be kept away from his children any longer. The DA's office was stalling. How much did the tension between Jake and me have to do with that?

"You've got bigger problems than Hughie Black. DA's office asked for *your* file."

"What? Oh, come on. Is this about Kevin Doogan?"

Pusser nodded.

I continued, "Doogan didn't kill himself. You know that. That note was a setup. The handwriting samples alone prove that—"

"We've been through this before. Is there anything else I need to know about, Callahan?" He reached into his pocket for his cylinder of toothpicks, his eyes never leaving my face.

"No. Nothing."

"Grabowski's asked to see you."

"Grabowski? I'll give him a call."

"In person. It's forty-five minutes to Greeneville. You can head out now."

"Maybe tomorrow. I've got—"

"Go today." He slid a piece of paper my way. "Here's his address."

* * *

Grabowski's house was a 1970s brown and yellow split-level surrounded by a weed-infused chain-link fence. The yard housed a yappy dog, a little brown thing with a thick neck and a giant pair of balls that wobbled with every bark. Wilco stuck his nose through one of the links for a sniff, found nothing interesting, and turned away. Put out, the dog launched into a barking tirade.

We continued down the walk, the boisterous little mutt following along inside the fence. I'd pictured Grabowski living in a neat condo or maybe a Craftsman with overflowing bookshelves and worn leather furniture, not in this Brady Bunch house. And especially not this stupid little dog. Maybe I had the wrong address.

I raised my hand to knock.

Grabowski's voice floated through the door. "It's open. Come in."

We entered and passed through a nondescript entryway into the living room. Grabowski was there, reclining on an upholstered sofa, legs propped on an ottoman. A walker was parked nearby.

I settled in one of the chairs, flowered pattern, and heavy on blues. Maybe Grabowski's wife did the decorating. Did he even have a wife? "Are you okay with my dog being in here?"

He smiled at Wilco. Wilco didn't notice. He was busy sniffing a doggy bed in the corner of the room. "Sure. Did you meet Earl?"

"Earl?"

"My dog, Earl. Like in Earl Scruggs."

"Who?"

"Never mind. The kitchen's that way. There's iced tea in the fridge. Help yourself."

"I'm good. Thanks. How's the hip?"

"I'm thinking of putting out a hit on my physical therapist."

"That bad, huh?"

He chuckled, then turned somber. "Thanks for driving over, Brynn."

"Pusser insisted."

Grabowski waited for me to say more. I didn't. Throughout the drive over, I'd debated why the insistence on my needing to see Grabowski. No good answers. And no way was I going to open up. I didn't need to volunteer anything. Not to my boss and not to the department's Mr. Analysis, either.

Finally, he pulled a blue file folder from between the sofa cushions. "It's a copy of the ballistic report from the bullet in Kevin Doogan's skull."

My mouth went dry. A long, tense pause followed. Outside the window the late-afternoon sun washed over the neighbor's yard, where two men scraped a fence, white flecks of paint dotting their browned forearms like salt on a pork shank. *Scrape, scrape, scrape* . . . I couldn't tear my eyes away. *Scrape, scrape* . . . Why was I here, and not at the department? "Is this conversation off the record?"

"For now." He handed me the report. "The bullet is a match to the bullet found in Dublin Costello's remains. And there was that tip that came in about the gun and your grandmother."

Cold anxiety shot through my veins. I crossed my arms tight, trying to hold myself together. *I will never turn on Gran. Never. Even if I have to take the rap for this myself.*

He handed me another piece of paper. "And this is a copy of the suicide note."

Dark stains splattered across the handwriting. Doogan's blood. My hands began to tremble; the paper shook. My eyes blurred with tears, and I could barely read the words.

> *Dear Brynn, I can't cover for you anymore.*
> *The guilt is too much. I've lost everything and*
> *can't go on. I'm sorry.*

"This isn't his handwriting or his words. You already know that. They've compared samples of his handwriting. Katie Doogan wrote this. She's jealous and vindictive. If she couldn't have him, no one would." Almost her words exactly. Before she died from that shotgun blast.

Grabowski studied me. "I want to believe you."

"You can believe me. It's true. Get samples of *her* handwriting. Make a comparison."

A slight smile from Grabowski. "Pusser's already on it. He got samples from Katie's family. Preliminary looks good for you. There are several similarities, but an expert will have to make the official determination."

My spirits lifted. "That's good. About time—"

"But it's the gun. That's the sticking point. We can't trace it to Kevin Doogan or his wife. But there's that tip—"

"From a burner phone. So it couldn't be traced. Was the voice male or female?"

"A woman."

"Katie. It had to be. The forged note, the tip, it all points to a frame job."

Quiet again. I knew he was running the facts through his head. It could go either way. Frame or cover-up? Truth was, a bit of both. Katie was framing me for Doogan's death. And I was covering up Gran's part in Dublin Costello's death.

"I know how it looks, Grabowski, but you have to believe me."

He leaned forward. His voice was eerily calm when he said, "You were still in contact with Doogan this whole time."

"I . . . We were friends." I felt my gut clench, and I wrapped my arms around myself. *So complicated. Why is it so damned complicated?* "My whole life no one . . . no man ever really accepted me. Not my grandfather, not anyone, maybe not even Doogan. I mean, he lied to me. He had a wife and kids, but he was my friend." A liar, yes. A cheat, yes. But also a friend. He was there for me and my grandmother when we needed him most. He risked everything to help us, to protect Gran, and I had never really understood why. But maybe it was simple: friendship and the type of love that flowed from friendship. "He accepted me just as I am."

"And what are you, Brynn?"

What am I? The question and answers I'd heard my whole life passed through my head—half-breed, loser, weirdo, gypsy whore, scarred, and only half a woman—but the one that stuck with me was the one that was the most accurate. "Damaged. I'm damaged."

Grabowski sat back and closed his eyes, said nothing for a while. Then just one simple statement. "I think I understand."

I quietly sobbed, the sound of my sniffling filling the room. Grabowski pulled a tissue from the box on his coffee table and passed it to me. I blew and swiped and cleared my throat. "Why am I here, Grabowski? Pusser could have asked me these things himself, at the department, and on the record."

"Because regardless of what you think, there is a man who cares about you. Frank." He handed me a fresh tissue. "And I care about you, too, Brynn."

CHAPTER 45

I left Grabowski's; stopped off at the department just long enough to change vehicles and get out of my uniform, pull on the only jeans and crumpled T-shirt in my locker; and ended up ten minutes late for my sobriety meeting. Wilco and I slinked inside—I'd forgotten Wilco's lead—and I took the only empty chair, the one next to Colm. He picked up his Bible to make room for me and smiled. I squirmed into the chair, tucked away a strand of unruly hair. I felt wrung out and likely looked it. My talk with Grabowski had taken its toll. Now I had the additional burden of knowing he and Pusser wanted to be on my side. Theoretically, a good thing, but for the moment it just felt like two more people I was letting down.

Colm shifted a little, glanced at my hands, or was it my lap? There was a stain on my jeans, red—sauce or blood?—and I thought of Katie and the blast of the shotgun. I'd let that happen. I rubbed at the stain on my pants leg, but it remained. Rubbed some more, and . . . and someone laughed.

My head popped up. More people laughed, and Wilco let out a shallow little howl, happy and playful as he bounced from person to person, sniffing feet and wagging his tail. Even Mrs. Chairperson cracked a smile.

Wilco, Mr. Social.

And then Colm laughed, too, his gaze sliding away from the stain—barbecue sauce, I'd decided, from my pulled pork sandwich a few days ago—to my dog, then back to me, fully on me, open and accepting and not judging. One more man in my life who believed in me. One more to let down. I shook my head. *Don't go down that road again, Brynn.*

I tuned in to the meeting.

Ashley was talking about how dating was so hard without wine. *Whine, whine, whine . . .* It was difficult being Ashley. To my left, crazy-eyed Mitch nodded sympathetically; he'd be willing to make everything better for Ashley. You bet, he would. And, speaking of that, there was Jake, sitting across the circle from me. I glared his way. *When we get done here, buddy, I'm going to have a word or two with you.* No way would I let him destroy my career, or Gran's life, with his toxic spite.

He felt my stare, averted his eyes, looking everywhere but at me. *I'm not looking at you, not, not, not. . . .*

Then all eyes looked at me. No, not *at* me. Behind me.

"Nikki!" I stood.

Colm stood, too. "Nikki. Welcome. Come in. We're glad—"

She looked at me, fear flickering across her face, and I nodded, with a tight smile. I mouthed, "It's okay," praying she'd stay. Colm had apparently gotten through to her, and she needed to be here, and I needed to talk with her. For a second, I thought I had her. Then her gaze darted away from me to the others, and she bolted. I stood rooted in surprise. *Damn!*

The upstairs door slammed shut, and the noise jolted me into action. I went after her, bounding up the steps with someone behind me. I glanced back. Jake. A few more steps and we burst through the door, stopped, and . . . nothing. She was gone. I scanned the alley and the back of the rectory, then jogged around the corner of the church. No one was in the parking lot. *Where is she?*

Jake caught up to me. "Was that the prostitute?"

"Her name is Nikki."

He raked his hand through his hair. "Been trying to pin her down. I've got questions for her."

"Yeah, so do I. Last time I chased her was in a parking lot, too. Guess it spooked her to see me again. I wish she would have stayed."

"Like a meeting or two will save her. She's a meth head, Brynn, probably a gram a day. She's in too deep. And it's not just the meth that she's addicted to. It's sex, control and power, danger, and the thrill she gets every time she gets away with it all. She's hopeless."

"It takes one to know one," I wanted to say, but instead, I spouted our addiction group's party line. "No one is hopeless."

He tipped his head back and laughed. "You and that priest in there. Hope and faith will save the world." His mouth twisted into a thin line. "Well, good for you."

"What's your problem, Jake?" He was condemning Nikki without an ounce of finger-snapping caring. Were his own demons eating at his gut? Or was it something else . . . ?

He walked toward his car.

"Hey. We need to talk about this investigation you're conducting of me." I trotted after him.

"Not now. I've got stuff to do."

"Bullshit. I need to—"

The back door of St. Brigid's opened, and folks filed out. Toby first, cig dangling from his lips, cupping his hands and flicking his lighter. Aw . . . the first drag. Then Ashley, Mitch, Josh, and Lily. Lily shot me a little wave. *Wave right back at you, Lily.* Juan and a couple more people, then Colm, Wilco at his side.

"Brynn, did you catch up to Nikki?" Colm asked.

Wilco rubbed against my leg, happy to find me again. A car beeped. I spun to see Jake getting into his Mercedes. "Crap."

"What's that?"

I turned back to Colm. "No. I didn't catch Nikki. She's gone."

His face fell. "Too bad. I thought maybe she'd . . . Well, let's just say I was hopeful."

Of course he was. *Hopeful that meth-crazed Nikki will live through another day. Hopeful that I'd stay on the straight path. Hopeful, hopeful.*

"I'm glad you're still hopeful," I said, my voice edged with the sarcasm that I hadn't meant to express. I got caught up for a second in his dark gaze as concern crossed his face. Not the worry of an ex-lover. The look of a priest worried about just one more wayward sheep: me.

CHAPTER 46

Jake had blown me off. I was ticked. And I knew where he lived. But as soon as I got my dog and myself in the car, my cell rang.

It was Parks. "I need to talk to you about something important. Where are you?"

I grinned, then shook my head. I was right. She was pregnant, no doubt. All the signs had been there. Good news—great news, actually—but now wasn't the time. I put the phone on speaker and pulled out of St. Brigid's lot. "I'm tracking down Jake Sheehan. I've got some questions for him. Heading to his place now."

"Jake's house. Why? Wait, okay. It's really important that we—"

I careened around the corner, took it too wide, and over-corrected. My phone slid to the floor. Wilco slid, too, bumped against the passenger door. He let out a yelp.

"Sorry, boy."

"What?" Parks's voice floated up from somewhere on the floorboard.

"Hold on!" At the corner, I pulled over, dove for my phone,

and got it to my ear. "I want to hear all about it, but can't talk now, Parks. Okay? I'll call you back."

I clicked off, and the phone rang again immediately. I let it go and continued to Jake's place. His Mercedes was in the carport. I parked behind it, cracked my windows, and got out, ignoring my dog's whiny pleas to be let out of the car.

I went to the side door, raised my hand, and stopped. Noises, dull banging, scraping, and . . . Jake yelling. *Something's not right.* I turned the knob and cracked the door open, peered into his kitchen. Nothing but an overflowing garbage can and messy counters. I pushed the door all the way open and stepped through.

Jake was on the floor. Motionless, faceup.

"Jake?"

My hand flew to my holster. *Crap! I'm in street clothes.* Movement behind me. I turned. A woman's face, dark and angry, and the blade of a knife. I jumped, my back arched, and hit the wall. I slid to the floor, rolled over, got halfway up, and stumbled toward the door. But she caught my arm and twisted. I squirmed, broke loose, and jumped back again as a blade flashed in front of my face. I raised my arm; a hot slash tore open my bicep. I screamed and backhanded her, connected with her jaw. She stumbled back and sank to the floor.

I started for the door, but she raised her head, eyes blazing. She jerked back up, then forward again, the blade slicing the air before me, backing me up to the wall. . . . I turned my shoulder, threw my weight, and rammed her. *Ping.* The knife had hit the floor. I bent, but fingers clamped around my face like claws, gouged my cheeks, and pushed me back until I was flattened against the wall. I squeezed my eyes shut and pushed back, but her fingernails dug along my cheeks, moving toward my eyes, and screaming, screaming, me screaming, the pitch higher and thinner. *She's scratching my damn eyeballs out. Aaah.* Pain, pain . . . I squirmed, got free, turned away, and . . .

Thud. Hot, searing pain shot through my head and neck, my knees buckled, and . . . blackness.

"Brynn." Words hissed through the darkness of my mind. "Brynn. Get up. I've got to get you out of here."

I stirred and blinked hard against my swollen eyelids. *Parks is here. Parks!* But then she was gone, and I heard more scuffling noises, something moving, voices, distant and blurry. My cell was gone. I groped my way along the floor. *Where's Parks? Where's the knife?* Blinking, blinking. A little light now. Less blurry, like looking at the room through oil-smeared glass. I blinked again and heard a woman's moan. *Georgia? Parks?* It had come from the left and below me, as if under the floor.

Then Georgia's voice said, "You made this easy on me, Nan."

I crawled to the right, toward Jake, felt for a pulse. No pulse. I ran my hands down his chest, wet and sticky with blood, to his belly, his waistband, his jeans pocket, and it was there. His cell.

My head pounded. My vision flickered like strobe lights, numbers in and out, in and . . . I dialed nine, one . . . missed and missed again and hit on his last contact. A male voice answered.

"I need help! Jake Sheehan's house in McCreary. Call nine-one-one. There's a woman. She's going to kill—"

A squeal pierced the air, like that of a baby rabbit clenched by a coyote. Parks!

I jolted upward, dropped the phone, and turned toward the noise, fumbled my way along the wall. Another squeal and more noise. I moved toward the sound, found the basement door. *Tiptoe, tiptoe . . .*

Georgia's voice. "Do you ever think about my boy when you look at those precious children of yours? Do you? Do you ever think what it would be like to have one of 'em dead?"

I reached the bottom of the steps, my eyes straining, my vision clearing a little, and there was Parks, bound and gagged, on the floor. My vision blurred, in and out, a field of dancing black dots, and Georgia became a mere outline, a scrappy thing, I could tell, maybe a hundred pounds. Wiry and strong, accustomed to hauling dead horses and critters. And bodies.

Georgia leaned over, a long gray braid dangling and sinewy arms stretched forward. A hand spread the lids of one of Parks's eyes wide open; the other hand held a knife, the blade poised above her eyeball.

I lurched forward. "No! Drop the knife, Georgia. Drop it!"

Her boots scuffled as she jolted back; her breathing came sharp and shallow, nervous. Labored. She had nothing to lose now. I needed to buy time.

I took another step forward, my hands up where she could see them. "I get it, Georgia. Walker and Bannock, they killed your boy, didn't they? I get the hate you feel. But let Parks go. She's not—"

"You don't get nothin'," she spat, waving the blade in front of Parks. "She helped 'em. She was right there with 'em."

Parks? Things started coming to me: how she had been conveniently absent during interviews, and her sickness. I'd thought it was . . . My gaze moved to Parks. Her eyes bulged under Georgia's blade, then rolled to me, pleaded with me. *Parks?* I couldn't believe it. Georgia was insane, but something in Parks's eyes told me there was a truth to her words, as well.

"You listenin' to me?" Georgia shrieked. "They kilt my boy! Left him on the tracks. Didn't even leave me enough to bury."

"That was a long time ago, Georgia."

"Not to a mama's heart."

"I suppose not."

Sirens wailed in the distance.

I softened my voice. "How did you know what they did? And why did you come after Jake Sheehan?"

"That ain't important."

"Jake Sheehan was an attorney. He was a—"

"Lying SOB is all he was. Nothin' more."

Was Jake somehow involved in Zeke's death, too? The way he'd played me for information, and other things, coincidences, which now I recognized as manipulation. I swiped my swollen eyes, shook my head, tried to focus, saw her bend down and pick something up.

"Let me finish this, Georgia. I'll make sure Parks is—"

"You damned cops don't give a squat 'bout us folks. You's as bad as 'em all."

I strained to make out her face. Couldn't.

The sirens were near.

"It's over, Georgia." I inched forward.

She sneered. "But I ain't done yet."

"Georgia, don't. Don't do it."

She charged, knocked me back to the floor, and I hit hard, was stunned for a second, then heard her cry out a few feet away, at Parks. "For you, Zeke. For you—"

Parks's gagged scream pierced the air.

"Nooo!" I rolled, reached out.

"Stop! Police. Sto—" *Crack. Crack, crack, crack . . .*

Georgia jerked and twisted with each shot fired from Harris's gun. Then fell forward, bloody and silent.

It was over.

CHAPTER 47

The stupid ER doctor wouldn't give me anything for the pain. Over twenty stitches ran along the underside of my arm, a patch-up effort from the three inches of flesh Georgia had slashed out of my bicep. It hurt like hell, and the doc had given me nothing. Over-the-counter would take care of it, he'd said.

Whiskey comes over the counter. Thank you. Doctor's orders.

Buying the bottle had been a bad choice, but Parks's screams, so agonizing and ethereal, that even now they wormed through my mind . . . A woman I had worked with, shared so much with, yet apparently had never really understood. She had held a secret that could shatter her life, destroy everything, and I had never known. Had she ever suspected I had such secrets, too? We wrap ourselves in the fear of exposure of our own sins and failures, and yet we blind ourselves to those same gnawing burdens on others. And when they surface, we suddenly know: we are all victims of our past and vulnerable in our present. Parks's screams would last a lifetime in my mind.

What I could do was numb it all. I wanted to forget what I had seen. I wanted to wipe it out of my mind. Drink myself and the memories and all the pain into oblivion, like I'd done so many times before. But each time I raised the bottle to my lips, Wilco nudged me with his nose, whimpering and whining, and gave me that look. He was worse than Meg.

But it was enough to make me stop before I even started. Instead, I smoked a couple limp cigs that I had found hidden in Gramps's dresser drawer. Nasty things, but enough to calm my nerves. And I sat up until the sun rose in a bright orange morning sky, and tried to piece together the crime. Parks, Jake, Chance Walker, and Reed Bannock. How did they fit with Zeke Farrell and what had happened between them that ended with Zeke's death? Jake had been working as a deputy DA at the time, and Georgia said that he had somehow been involved. Others must have been involved. Johnson or his partner at the time? And how did Georgia know who had killed her son? And why wait until seventeen years later to avenge Zeke's death?

I didn't come up with any answers. And it'd be a while before I got any. Both Jake and Georgia were dead, and Parks was hospitalized, and may or may not recover. The knife had penetrated her frontal lobe. The doctors were waiting for the swelling to recede before they could estimate brain functioning. So, four people murdered and maybe another permanently altered, not to mention the fallout for Parks's family and no real answers.

"I need answers," I said to my dog. He got up and walked to his food bowl and turned to look. Obviously, food was the only answer Wilco cared about!

"Good morn—" Meg began, then stopped and stared. "What happened to you?" She ran her fingers along my shoulder and gently turned my arm over and let out a small gasp. "Brynn. Who did this to you?"

"A woman named Georgia Farrell."

"A woman? Why?"

I stared at Meg, but I didn't speak. Didn't even know where to start.

She stared back and didn't speak, either.

An awkward moment passed between us; then she took a seat and placed a gentle hand on my shoulders, and we sat at the table silently, Meg just letting me know she was there for me. Family. I had so little of it left, but Meg was there for me, and I knew she always would be. If I let her in.

I took a deep breath and tried to explain what had happened the night before. She listened with round eyes, nodded as if she understood—not that anyone could or would—then said she needed to make coffee. Too much to take in without caffeine. After it brewed, we added milk and sugar and carried our mugs to the front room. Meg wanted to see if the story had made the news. They wouldn't have the particulars yet, so it would likely be just a shocker headline, but at least we'd see what had been released so far.

"Where's the remote?" she asked.

I slid into a chair. "I don't know. You had it last."

"Not me. I worked the closing shift last night. And the night before. Didn't have time to watch any TV before I left for work." She kept looking, under the junk on the coffee table, beneath the sofa cushions. "Did Wilco get ahold of it?"

"No. What would he do with a remote?" I got out of the chair and got down on all fours and looked under furniture. The carpet felt greasy against my palms and smelled like dust and dirty feet. "I'm not seeing it." *Damn it. Where's that remote?* I sat up, wiped my hands against my pants—ick, sticky and gross—and I remembered. Nina and her sticky fingers. Just a couple days ago, she had been here, and her hands had roamed over the stuff on my coffee table. She hadn't been able to resist taking it. As if the remote to our TV had any value to her at all. Like it mattered. She took anything within their grasp, useful or useless, so long as it was shiny or pretty . . . or belonged to someone else.

All these years that I'd known, and she'd known that I'd known, yet she could never stop her impulses. Maybe she didn't want to stop. An addiction to stealing. I thought of the past couple weeks, the Vicodin, the whiskey . . . Who was I to judge? *I just want my TV remote returned.* "I think I know where our remote is. Be right back."

I walked fast, heels pounding the pavement, as I passed neighbors' trailers. Mrs. Black's curtains parted; old man Nevan stood outside his door and blew smoke from a hand-rolled cigarette. The next street down, I heard the Murphys' new baby crying, and Mrs. Gorman was on her front step, drinking coffee. And then Nina's street.

Most Pavees lived in trailers or mobile homes, manufactured homes, some called them, but Nina lived in a converted food truck. She'd gotten it for a steal—I shook my head at the irony of the idiom—a couple summers back, when some carny passing through got busted for assault and battery and needed quick bail money. Nina had made out. Tiny but efficient, with the original stainless-steel kitchen, and fitted with a fold-down bed and a camper-sized bathroom, the food truck had everything she needed. But some Bone Gap folks looked down on it, which was why her place was tucked out of the way on a secluded lot. Out of sight, out of mind.

She opened the door and stared at me through mascara-smudged eyes. "Hey, Brynn. What's up? It's early still, and I'm . . . You look horrible."

"Yeah? Well, thanks. I want my remote back."

"Your remote?"

"My television remote. You lifted it the other night, when you and the other girls were at my place."

"Did not."

"Let me in, Nina."

"Really, Brynn? This is stupid. Why would I have your remote?"

"Because you're a thief."

I stepped up and pushed past her. The air smelled like sleep and bad breath and hair spray. "Where's the stuff you've stolen?" I knew she kept her stolen treasures in a hidden stash.

I started with her kitchen cupboards, while she stood by, whining. "You can't do this. *Stop*."

I ignored her and checked the rest of the cupboards, found nothing except several bottles of gin and some cans of soup. I took three steps and reached for the stowaway above her bed.

She slapped my hand away.

I must be getting closer.

"You have no right—"

"Like you have the right to steal people's things. Where's my remote? And what about Queenie's sunglasses? She lost those last week. Did you take those?" I opened a stowaway compartment: Just rolls of paper towels, toilet tissue, and cleaning supplies.

"You know I don't want to be this way. It's an illness," she said. "Mama always said it was somethin' that went wrong in my brain when I was a baby. I can't help it. None of the stuff I take is expensive. It's just crap."

"Yeah, but it's someone else's crap, not yours." I turned the latch on another stowaway compartment, and a bunch of stuff tumbled out: a scarf, key chain, lipstick tube, several nail polishes, a pair of sunglasses, a small bag, and . . . my remote. "You *do* have it."

"Oh. Sorry. You can have that back."

What the hell? "It's mine, Nina. And you shouldn't have taken it in the first place." I ran my hand through the pile, held up one indictment after another. "Queenie's glasses. You took them at the bar that night, didn't you?"

"Yeah. Maybe."

"And Mo's scarf. Bet she's been looking for this."

She crossed her arms. "Usually I don't take things from friends. Just stores. And y'all know they rob us, anyway. The way they mark things so high. They're stealing from us to start with."

"That doesn't make it okay."

"I'm careful. Most of the time no one even notices something's missing."

"Do you hear yourself, Nina?" I pointed to the pile. "This is sick."

"Well, if I'm sick, you are, too. You've known about it since we were kids. You're just mad now because I took something of yours." Her eyes grew wide. "You ain't goin' to arrest me, are you?"

"Who does the rest of this stuff belong to? Whose bag is this?" I unzipped a small flowered bag: lip balm, lotion, a couple wadded bills, and a work badge. "Where'd you get this?"

"Some lady's purse at the bar."

I flipped the badge over. MCCREARY COUNTY NURSING HOME. SADIE JONES. I looked closer at the photo. It was Gran's aide, Sadie. "You got this at the bar?"

"Yeah."

"When?"

"At Dee's hen party."

Maybe Sadie had been out with a few of the staff from the nursing home for a little fun. Pretty nervy of Nina to steal in the middle of a different group. Nina had never seemed the nervy type. At least not till she had swiped my remote.

"Was she alone in the restroom or something, and you grabbed it from her stall?"

"No. That's gross!"

"Really? Like stealing isn't gross?"

Nina rolled her eyes. "She was sitting by herself a few tables back from ours."

"And you just walked up and took this?"

A little glint flitted in her eyes, like a shiver of a thrill, an addict's rush as she recalled a fix. "She had no idea. She was caught up in the entertainment, like Mo."

"What do you mean?"

"She couldn't take her eyes off the guy. Walker, the stripper."

"Yeah, while your eyes were on every loose object in sight." I snatched up the stolen loot and shoved it in an embroidered carry bag—no doubt another of Nina's "finds"—and headed to the door.

"Brynn?"

I just shook my head. *What can I do? Tell her not to do it again or that she needs help? She's not ready to listen to all that.* "I've got to go."

I stormed off, now in possession of a bag of stolen goods myself. I sighed and took the next corner. Mo and Hughie's repurposed school bus was parked not far from Nina's food-truck conversion in the cast-off section of our little unsettled settlement.

Mo was just stepping out of their shanty of a latrine with one of the twins when I called out, "Hey!" Mo looked up, anticipation in her eyes, and I quickly held up a hand. "No, Hughie isn't out yet, but he will be. Have you seen the news?"

"No. Kids got the cartoons on, but I'll go—"

"Wait. Listen, I just wanted to return this." I told her about Nina. I was done carrying the secret of Nina's addiction around with me. I had enough secrets around my own neck. But Mo simply nodded, not at all surprised, as if she had known about Nina's problem all along.

I sighed, opened the bag, and pulled out Mo's scarf, but the lanyard on the badge was tangled with it. As Mo and I separated them, she suddenly stopped, held the badge up close.

"That's her! So you found her," she said.

"Huh?"

"This is the blond woman who came up to the truck when Walker let go of me and I ran off. I told you about her. Remember?"

"You said you didn't get a good look at her."

Mo shrugged. "Well, good enough to know this is her. So, you found her? And you know my Hughie wasn't the one lurking around the truck. It was her."

I took the badge, and my mind flipped gears, putting the pieces together. I'd assumed it was Nikki in that lot, lurking about, checking up on her boyfriend. But it was Sadie Jones. She was the last person to see Walker alive. And she'd been at the bar alone? Guys, sure. Guys sat alone in strip joints. But women? They went in packs, but not Sadie. According to Nina, Sadie had sat alone, concentrating on Walker. Then Mo had seen her walking around his car in the parking lot? I looked again at the picture, at her sunbaked skin, shallow cheeks, tight lines around close-set eyes. The same small frame and facial features as Georgia Farrell, just younger. Georgia's daughter? We'd figured Georgia had been hiding somewhere, but we had no record of family for her.

Had Sadie hidden her mom? Or even been a part of this revenge scheme? I thought of the horse head we'd found in the woods and how we'd figured it would take a couple people to haul both Bannock and the head out of there. But when I found Georgia alone, going after Jake, I'd thought it was over, but . . .

I phoned Pusser. I knew by heart now the schedule of the aides working with Gran, and it wasn't Sadie's shift right now. She would be home. Pusser was on it, would find an address for her and would send a unit out. I hung up, relieved. I'd head in later and take a crack at interviewing her, but I'd make another stop first.

I got my dog and my car, gave Meg the television remote, told her that I had to go, and that I'd fill her in later. Twenty minutes later I pulled up to the nursing home. I walked down the old people–perfumed corridor, stopped outside Gran's door, and pushed through it quietly. Gran was in her chair.

My breath caught. Sadie squatted in front of her, a spoon in hand.

Gran's mouth worked overtime, like that of a cow chewing its cud. A line of brown puree dripped from her lips and dribbled down her chin, but Sadie wasn't paying attention. Her gaze was riveted on the television screen. "A fatal altercation occurred late last night in a downtown residence. Local police departments are still on the scene at the victim's home."

Sadie's face paled.

"Hey, Sadie."

She looked up. Her eyes glazed over with shock.

I took a few steps closer. "How's my grandmother doing?" *Keep it light. Simple.*

Her expression hardened. She got up and stood behind Gran.

Nice and easy, Brynn. Keep calm. I worked my way closer, stopped about five feet away. "I just came by to see Gran. I can feed her, if you'd like."

Gran's head sagged to the side, but her focus was on me, her eyes warm and calm and loving. Just as always.

Sadie glanced back to the television reporter, who said, "Police have yet to release a full statement but have indicated that this crime is related to recent murders in the area."

"That's my mama they're talkin' about, isn't it?" She shot me a look. "You comin' for me now, is that it?"

"Zeke was your brother. I'm sorry, Sadie. It must have been awful what happened back then." I started to take a step.

"Get back, ya hear? I don't trust nothin' you say. Where were you cops all those years ago, when they killed my brother? Y'all covered for one of your own, you did. I mean, how's it goin' to look if the big attorney in town got a young girl knocked up? And then she turns round and helps kill a kid, huh?"

Young girl? Did she mean Parks? Jake?

She continued. "Used his job to help them kids cover it all, just to save his own hide. Bunch of crooked cops, that's what you are."

So there it was: Jake stood to lose a lot, too much. He'd fathered a child with an underage girl. Parks. Maybe she had threatened him if he didn't help. Or maybe he couldn't risk his career. Whatever the reason, Jake had helped three teenagers bury the truth along with the mutilated body of a throwaway boy.

"We'll open an investigation. Find out what happened to your brother."

"No need. I already know. Some dopehead came by here and told me. All she wanted was a little cash in exchange for giving me information 'bout Zeke's death."

Nikki.

She went on. "Her meth-head boyfriend got high one night and told her how it went down back then. It was 'pposed to be a prank." Her eyes wandered now, as if she was envisioning the scene that had destroyed so many lives. "Drink some booze. Have a little fun with the stupid kid. They didn't expect Zeke to fight back. But when he did, they ganged up on him. Bannock, Walker, and that cop friend of yours, Nan Parks. The boys took turns kickin' him, while the girl stood by and let it happen. He didn't get up from that fight . . ."

And then they put him on the tracks to cover their crime. "I'm sorry, Sadie. So, you told your mother, and she—"

Her eyes snapped to me, hatred burning deep. "She'd just wanted the truth all them years. So I told her. Yes, I told her, and then Mama knew what to do. Mama always knew what to do. See, she brought us up on her own, she did, taught us to live right. Zeke needed special care, you see, and nobody cared. So, she taught us good at home."

"I'm sure she did her best—"

"Hear no evil, speak no evil, see no evil." Sadie recited the words like a litany, something she'd heard and said a thousand times while she, along with her younger brother, learned how to "live right" at the hem of their mother. A mother who, in the end, wanted justice for her child, the boy who'd been targeted and beaten and mercilessly killed.

In the distance I heard a siren. "How did you find them?"

Again, Sadie's eyes wandered as she recalled what had happened. "I waved a few bills at Chance Walker, and he drove to my place, no problem. That one was easy. Bannock heard what we did, and he knew we'd be comin' for him. Ran, he did, the bastard. But we got him."

"And Jake?"

Sadie shook her head. "I told Mama it was all over the news, and just a matter of time before they'd come for us, Jake knowin' and bein' in the law and all. Shoulda done him first. Mama got scared, said she didn't care if they got her, but she didn't want to lose her daughter, too. Torched everything, tryin' to destroy any record of me. I been tryin' to talk sense into her. Get our stuff together and leave town. But, no, she wouldn't leave it alone. 'See no evil. See no evil,' she kept sayin'. I thought she'd gone to bed last night, when they called me in for a double shift."

Sadie looked up at me, her hands clasping the back of Gran's chair, hope and fear at war in her face. "Is my mother . . . ? Is she . . . ?"

"I'm so sorry, Sadie, but—"

Heavy footsteps sounded in the hallway, and a handful of cops burst through the door.

Sadie panicked. Her hands jerked forward, and she put one on Gran's chin, the other on her head. The same pose a hunter might take to snap the neck of a wounded animal, fast and lethal. "Don't you come any closer."

I held up my hand, motioned to the guys to stay put. Then to Sadie, "I understand, Sadie. Let me help you."

One of the guys broke from the group and moved out at an angle. Positioning himself. The cop's gun was locked on target. He gave me a nod.

A slight shake of my head. *No. No. No.* If he shot, he could hit Gran.

Sadie's nostrils flared, in and out, and her grip on Gran's head tightened. Her voice hissed, "Help me? I ain't got nobody left, don't you see? You want to understand how that feels? See what it's like to have nobody . . ." She started twisting.

"Nooo!"

Bang.

Thud.

And a second thud.

Gran . . . "Gran!"

She was on the floor, limp, eyes closed, her breath coming in shallow rasps. *Shot?* "Gran? Gran? Someone help!"

CHAPTER 48

We kept the curtains drawn, Meg and me, because we couldn't bear to let light into Gran's room. Gran was dying, and our world would forever be darker.

So, we gathered there in the gloom, all her loved ones: Meg on one side, Wilco and I on the other. At the foot of the bed, Aunt Tinney, with tight lips and moist cheeks; and Gran's brothers, Jarvis and Paddy, lingering in the corner, stoic but pale. A close-knit family, we were. *All Pavees are. God and family, that's what it all comes to in the end.*

Wilco paced along the side of Gran's bed, pausing here and there for a deep sniff and wrinkling his eyes my way. He knew. He sensed Gran's death, and he wanted me to stop it. But there was no stopping this. The fall had caused a bleed in Gran's brain, and despite all efforts, the doctors had said there was no hope. It was her time.

Colm used the oil. Prayers, English and Shelta mixed, were muttered through the room.

And then the doctor looked to me. It wouldn't be much longer.

I squeezed my eyes against the sorrow devouring my heart and nodded.

The nurses stepped back allowing the family to draw closer. Gran rested motionless against her pillow, arms at her sides and sheets carefully positioned around her body, like a child's doll tucked in for the night. Colm sat next to her and spoke in a low, soothing voice as he said the final prayers. He finished, leaned forward, gently cradled Gran's face in his palm, and tilted her chin upward, and time stood still as he slipped a tiny white sliver through her slack lips.

A quiet peace settled over the room.

Except for Gran's breathing, shallow and labored, her chest rising and falling in uneven spurts.

She was slipping away.

Meg's tears fell against Gran's face as she kissed her cheek and whispered something in her ear.

Then my turn. I took Gran's hand in mine, traced the criss-crossed road map of blue veins under her thin skin, and rested my face against hers, felt Meg's tears, and closed my eyes against the flood of a thousand memories: warm summer days, laughter, the swish of a swing, rose water and soap, the ever blue of Gran's eyes, and her sweet voice calling, *"Me lackeen, me lackeen . . ."* my girl, my girl.

Her chest rose. And fell for the last time. A small exhale and then . . . stillness.

Sobs broke through the room, and Wilco paced and whined and whimpered and pawed at Gran's sheets and paced again, his nose twitching, his head thrashing back and forth, pacing, pacing, pacing. . . . Then he stopped. His tail flattened, straight and parallel to the floor, with a hitch at the end.

He turned his gaze to me, and I saw my own pain reflected in his eyes.

He'd hit on scent. Gran's scent.

Agony gurgled up from my throat and burst from my lips in a loud wail. Wilco came to me, whimpered, and rubbed his nose against my leg, then tipped back his own head and let out a doleful howl.

And our mournful cries mixed together and floated to the clouds.

Acknowledgments

First of all, thank you to my literary agent, Jessica Faust, a fearless champion of authors and their stories. Without your amazing agenting, this series would not have happened.

Michaela Hamilton, my editor, is not only brilliant but also patient and encouraging. I've learned a lot from you, Michaela. Thank you. My sincere gratitude to the entire Kensington Publishing team. Thanks for all you do.

The following people contributed their expertise to this book: Sandra Haven, freelance editor and writing mentor; Leah Snyder, Indiana K9 Search & Recovery; Cheryl Shore, APRN; Amanda Bourg, PhD, psychologist; Sergeant Leanna Miller-Ferguson, USMC disabled veteran; Kathy Chiodo Holbert, owner of Chiodo Kennels and former civilian HRD canine handler, Iraq and Afghanistan; and Staff Sergeant Vern Smart, US Army veteran and firearms expert.

A special thank-you to the staff of Loving Paws Pet Clinic for helping me get the facts right. Wilco thanks you, too.

And last but not least, big hugs to my husband and our children for their love and support. I couldn't be more blessed.

SHATTERED JUSTICE

Susan Furlong

ABOUT THIS GUIDE

The suggested questions are included to enhance your group's
reading of Susan Furlong's *Shattered Justice*!

DISCUSSION QUESTIONS

1. Brynn struggles to avoid drinking during the hen party at the bar with her friends. Meg understands Brynn's addiction problem. Do the others understand but just don't care as they offer her drinks? Why would they do this? What would you do if a member of your circle had a drinking problem and a social event included alcohol?

2. Statistics show that spousal abuse is more prevalent in some cultures than in others. What perpetuates this abuse? Should Brynn have done more to help her friends with this problem? What approach could she take that might meet with the most success? What societal influences lead people to ignoring such issues?

3. In *Shattered Justice*, Brynn needs to work closely with other deputies in the department. How does the combative relationship she has with Harris influence her performance? Have you ever dealt with a difficult coworker who has impacted your work? How did you resolve this conflict?

4. Brynn has a comfortable working relationship with Deputy Nan Parks. Has this caused Brynn to overlook important issues? Have you ever been shocked by the truth about someone you had befriended? How has that revelation changed the way you react to others?

5. Mo Black had been with Chance Walker the night he was murdered, and Mo's husband's violent temper points directly at Hughie as the murderer. Brynn is not convinced. Is her doubt based more on the facts or on her sympathy for her fellow Travellers? Have you judged

someone in your life based on your sympathy—or bias—only to discover your judgment was wrong? If so, how did you handle it?

6. Brynn speaks to Wilco often, even though she knows he is deaf. Why do you think she does that? Does this serve a purpose for Brynn herself? Or for others around them?

7. Wilco helps Brynn deal with her depression. Many pet owners agree that pets can sense their owner's mood and act as a comfort or encouragement. How do you think pets sense those moods? In what ways are animals more sensitive to a person than other people might be? What can people learn by witnessing this awareness in animals?

8. The maxim "See no evil, hear no evil, speak no evil" comes from seventeenth-century Japan, yet it was handed down as "good teaching" by an Irish Traveller family. However, it resulted in murder. Is there a saying that has guided you or your family? What is it? How might that maxim result in negative actions?

9. Brynn thinks about *haunted warriors and untold truths* as she recounts horrific deeds done in the time of war that were conveniently buried with the participants. What would be justifications for hiding truths in time of war? In what ways would revealing the truths be healing or more devastating?

10. While trying to work on this case, Deputy Parks seems distracted by her daughter's troubles. Brynn is distracted by her fears for Gran. Discuss how your job has been impacted by family issues. Have you found a way to balance job and family responsibilities without jeopardizing

either one? How much leeway would you give to an employee with personal problems that affect his or her work?

11. For years Brynn has known that Nina is a kleptomaniac, and yet she has not revealed this to their other friends. Why do you think she does that? How could Brynn handle this situation in a different way, one that would benefit Nina? If she reveals the truth to their friends, how would that influence their relationship with Nina and with Brynn?

12. Justice is shattered in this book because no justice was ever given to Zeke's family years ago. Discuss if there is a time element to justice—after how many years would/ should a crime be forgiven? Have you done wrong things in your past that still haunt you? At what point might you forgive yourself?

13. The Pavees are fiercely loyal to clan members and mete out their own forms of justice to offenders. Do you think this can help prevent crimes within their clan? Or are these acts of "justice" crimes in and of themselves? Is your view of justice always "by the book," and if not, how do you justify your view?

14. Princess, the stuffed remains of a long-dead cat, is the object of Mrs. Handie's affection, and she treats the taxidermic cat as if it is alive. Discuss whether this is a comfort to Mrs. Handie or a hindrance to moving on. Have you known people who have what you consider an unnatural attachment to a pet or a person or an object? In what way has it helped or hindered their life?

15. In their careers, Brynn and Wilco deal with death, which requires an ability to be detached. But when death comes to one of their loved ones, it hits them as hard as it does most people. How far removed does someone need to be from your circle of family or acquaintances before you can feel detached from his or her pain or death? Discuss how this "distance" issue influences our worldview. Can you cite recent examples from the media of the concept of distancing from involvement?

16. Kevin Doogan's cousin, Sean, says to Brynn, "Kevin told me about you. That's why I recogni—" and breaks off his words, realizing he recognizes her from her scars. How do you handle meeting people with scars or an obvious disfigurement of some sort? Do you mention that person's disfigurement to others when you are describing him or her? Discuss whether this is a natural reaction and whether it is helpful or hurtful.

17. Brynn isn't the only character suffering from PTSD. Roger Meyer, the train conductor, says he is still haunted by the memory of Zeke on the tracks. Georgia Farrell also suffered from the death of her son and the lack of justice. As a society, do you think we give more attention to traumas suffered by civilians or by our veterans? Why? What are some of the ways to recognize if someone is hiding a trauma or PTSD? What is the best way to help that person?

18. Pusser comments, "Trauma does weird things to memory," making the point that witness testimony can be unreliable. Have you witnessed an incident with someone else and afterward remembered it differently than he or she did? Discuss how faulty memory of a trauma can hurt and benefit us individually and in our court system.

19. Brynn has issues with abandonment, and she finds it hard to let Meg into her life. What reason does she give herself to justify not telling Meg everything? What fears do you think really motivate this behavior? Discuss the importance of having someone to talk to in depth. Have you found people in your life whom you can trust at that level, and if not, why? If you do have someone whom you trust at that level, what challenges has this created in your relationship?

20. FBI agent Grabowski specializes in criminal profiling. When he talks to Brynn, she knows he is analyzing her, as well. How does his analysis help and hurt Brynn? Discuss how you react when you sense someone is analyzing you. How does it influence your actions and your relationship?

21. A shift occurs in Brynn's relationship with Pusser and Grabowski in this book. Are their feelings for her based on their desire to help a coworker, or does each of them have personal reasons for wanting to help her? What do you think those reasons might be? Brynn still doesn't open up fully to them. Think of people who wanted to help you in the past, yet you found it uncomfortable—or threatening—to open up to them. How did you handle that?

22. A long-festering trauma leads to the deaths of several people in *Shattered Justice*. Do you think people can overcome trauma even if justice is never served? If so, how? Have you been hurt by an injustice that will never be resolved? Discuss how this could influence the rest of your life—and how you might resolve it.